THREE DOWN

THREE
DOWN

RICHARD PHILLIPS

The Book Guild Ltd

First published in Great Britain in 2024 by
The Book Guild Ltd
Unit E2 Airfield Business Park,
Harrison Road, Market Harborough,
Leicestershire. LE16 7UL
Tel: 0116 2792299
www.bookguild.co.uk
Email: info@bookguild.co.uk
X: @bookguild

This work is entirely fictitious and bears no resemblance to any persons living or dead.

Typeset in 11pt Minion Pro

Printed on FSC accredited paper
Printed and bound in Great Britain by 4edge Limite

ISBN 978 1835741 009

British Library Cataloguing in Publication Data.
A catalogue record for this book is available from the British Library.

To my huge and delightful family.

Whether we fall by ambition, blood or lust,
Like diamonds we are cut with our own dust.

John Webster

CHAPTER 1

Jack's mobile lit up and vibrated against his glass of negroni.

'Hello.'

'Jack, I've been trying to reach you all day. Has your phone been off?'

'Yes, sorry – I'm on holiday, remember? What's up?'

Jack's secretary, Samantha, normally so calm, was agitated. 'I don't know how to put this gently, but some bailiffs turned up last night as I was leaving. They slapped tickets on everything and took some files. They told me to leave and locked the place up. They would only let me take my own personal stuff. Anything they thought was yours they took. I'm so sorry... Jack? Jack?'

Jack switched off his mobile and threw it into the sea. The Amalfi coastline shimmered in the warm night air. The faint sound of music and laughter from nearby bars mingled with the gentle lapping of water against the hull of the yacht. Jack started the engine and pressed the button on the windlass to raise the anchor. The motor hummed powerfully as the anchor warp disappeared smoothly into the bow of the boat. As the anchor broke the surface of the deep blue water, it glistened in the moonlight.

Jack set the autohelm to 270 degrees and the boat speed to five knots. He knew that it would not hit land until the next day. The 53-foot Oyster slid gently away from the shore, coaxing its only passenger into the Mediterranean night. Jack stood motionless on the edge of the stern until the lights of Amalfi had disappeared from view. Then, without taking a breath, he allowed his legs to crumple beneath him and collapsed into the sea.

CHAPTER 2

1984
Five years earlier

"Africa" was far distant yet Toto's tuneful evocation seemed ever present.

Jack closed the door of the restaurant as much to mask the incessant and over-played sound of the decade's favourite pop song as to be able to focus on next steps. What could possibly go wrong?

A year earlier, Arthur's had opened to queues down the street. The genteel honey-coloured Regency terraces of Bath had not been prepared for such vulgar success. The local magistrates had not quite understood what Jack had in mind when they approved his liquor licence.

The chef was mad. And French. Jack had suspected this might be a hopeless mixture, but he took the risk. After all, being in his late twenties, risks were something he was happy with. Pizza dough and half-cooked crêpes volleyed out of the upstairs kitchen window through the gentle spring air and onto the pavement below, sometimes landing on an innocent passer-by; exotic French expletives followed the debris. Small crowds would assemble to witness the spectacle. But this was part of the attraction.

And so were the pretty staff and the loud rock music. And the cocktails. Bath had not come across a Slow Comfortable Screw before, let alone one Against the Wall, but its inhabitants who had ventured up to London had some experience, and wanted more locally. The bar dispensing such exotic escapism was, fortunately, underground, shielded from the gaze of the more easily offended. Large-breasted girls with unfashionably short skirts shook stainless-steel cocktail shakers in front of their admiring male customers so that their low-cut tops barely restrained what shook inside them. In the early eighties, asking a voluptuous girl for a Slow Comfortable Screw Against the Wall was still somehow novel and amusing. And Jack knew there was money in it.

Jack's recruitment technique was also novel. It was not included in the syllabus of his recently completed MBA from Cranfield. Nor did it form part of his experience during his few years in industry. Indeed, a yearning for relative glamour was one of the reasons that he had left. And the chance to make some money for himself.

The restaurant was to be staffed by the most attractive girls Jack could find in the town. Making this explicit in advertisements at that time was already arguably illegal. So Jack had to use other methods. "Route One", he called it. "Route One" involved directly approaching suitable candidates in the street and asking them if they wanted a job. Sometimes Jack was ignored. Sometimes Jack's advance was politely declined. Sometimes Jack was slapped (although he thought that those who did that were the most likely candidates), but, more often than his sceptical friends had anticipated, the technique worked. He did have an advantage. He was tall with tousled blond hair, an athletic torso, blue eyes and a firm square jaw. He had been told by his mother, in a moment lubricated by gin and tonic, that one of her friends had compared him favourably to a Greek god. 'But don't let that go to your head,' she had said.

On one occasion the target of Jack's approach, who looked about eighteen, was accompanied by an older but more attractive woman. The younger girl's face lit up at Jack's invitation to an interview, but before she could reply, the older woman purred: 'Can I come too?' Naturally blonde and blue-eyed, like Jack, she wore tight white jeans over long legs above trim ankles.

Early forties, works out regularly, cute smile, no wedding ring, probably divorced, thought Jack. 'Sure,' he replied, swiftly suppressing an adolescent fantasy.

The restaurant buzzed with excitement and rocked too loudly for the more sedate inhabitants of Bath. Laughter spilled out onto the street nightly as the young male professionals of the town poured champagne down the necks of their targets and money into Jack's coffers. Life, for Jack, was good.

Life had been less good for his old prep-school friend George Thomas, whom Jack was pleased to now call by his Christian name, George, rather than by the public-school label of his surname. George's early stint in the City had ended prematurely when he failed to meet his revenue targets in two successive quarters. The bottom twenty per cent as measured by performance were made redundant each half-year, and George was one of those.

'I told you the City wasn't for you,' Jack had reminded George. 'Why don't you come and work with me for a bit whilst you sort out your next move? You could run the bar and help me manage the place. I could do with some intelligent help – but never mind, you'll do!' he added. 'And we could have some fun. You'll like the staff. All women. Handpicked by me. I've just met a mother and daughter, Sian and Mona – the stuff your dreams are made of. I don't care whether they have worked in a restaurant before, they will pull in the punters.'

There had only been a slight pause on the other end of the phone before George replied. 'OK. Great. Thanks. I'll get the train down from town on Saturday. Can I stay with you until I find my own place?'

'Sure. See you at the weekend.'

Now Jack cut through the Parade Gardens where the sun had brought out the first lovers of the year to lounge on the grass, freshly mown. The smell made him smile and reminded him of his childhood. The sound of the lawnmower in the garden at home, punctuated by his father, David's, swearing as it stopped and refused to restart. Jack remembered his suspicion that his father had a crush on the Swiss au pair girl who looked after him and his brothers when they were young. Certainly, whenever she arrived to give David a cup of tea her presence altered his mood. He was a strikingly handsome man, with an attractive, slightly hairy torso, and as he stood there beside the offending machine, stripped to the waist, there was laughter between them that seemed to be of an unnecessary kind… Jack was brought firmly back to the present by a dog who, wet from the fountain, shook himself so close to him that his trousers were showered with water. He looked up and noticed the owner was a woman in her thirties with a soft warm smile.

'I don't suppose you want a job, do you?' Jack asked.

'Well, I'm not looking for one. Or do you mean drying your trousers?' she replied with a laugh.

'No, that's OK,' said Jack as he turned away with a grin.

The next day he arrived at Arthur's before lunch, having spent the morning with his accountant reminding himself of the principles of stocktaking. He knew he would find the process and its regularity tedious but had been advised that it was essential, because giving away drinks and stealing cash and bottles was common in the trade. This was a way to spot if it was happening. Jack was pleased to notice that a familiar large yellow Rolls-Royce was parked outside the restaurant.

Brilliant, he thought. *Jonas and, with luck, his wife. And we have just taken delivery of more champagne.*

Sure enough, two regular customers, Jonas and Rachel, were sitting at the large round table at the back of the restaurant, already three bottles of champagne to the good, with two of their female acolytes in attendance. Jonas was wearing his familiar brown leather trousers, baggy white shirt, long tied-back hair and a Permatan. Rachel was also clad in leather trousers, impossibly tight, and a white plunging blouse that hardly attempted to hide her implanted braless breasts.

'Jack, how lovely to see you. Do draw up a chair and join us for some shampoo,' crowed Jonas.

'Jack, baby, how do you like my new tits?' shrieked Rachel, drooping her arms around him so he could not fail to notice them.

God, how ghastly you both are, thought Jack, *even though you're just great for business.* But he said, disingenuously, 'Good to see you both too. I didn't think you could improve your figure at all, Rachel, but I see I was wrong. Can't join you, I'm afraid, but I will send you over another bottle, on me.'

'Good man, and could we have four rare steaks? I see you have a couple of lovely new waitresses. I'd like them to join us, please,' said Jonas.

Jack knew why Jonas asked for new ones. He or his wife had already tried most of the others. The restaurant wasn't otherwise busy and so he sent Sandy and Steph to join them.

By the end of a long lunch, they had drunk almost a case of champagne. Sandy had had most of it. She, Steph, Jonas and Rachel's two other female guests all crammed themselves, giggling, into the yellow Rolls-Royce. Jonas squeezed himself into the driving seat, next to Rachel and Sandy, who was on Rachel's lap. She caressed Sandy's thighs. Jonas was sober. He needed to be. Even though the procurement of drunken young girls was mainly for the benefit of his wife, when back at the house he might be invited to join in, as it were.

'Bloody hell, Jack,' yelled Sandy the next morning. 'You didn't warn me that Rachel was a lezzy.'

'I thought you'd find out soon enough. How did Steph get on?'

'Well, from what I could see, she seemed to enjoy herself, and so did both Jonas and Rachel, and at the same time.'

Situation normal, thought Jack. *Still, good for business.*

*

'There is another site I'm after, in Bristol,' Jack told George between hurried slurps of strong coffee. 'My first offer was turned down so I'm going to go and see the bank to persuade them to back me for more. Then I'll return to the vendor with my revised offer.'

'But you haven't any money, Jack. You spend most of it on women and booze, and you waste the rest.'

'That's why I'm going to the bank. That's what banks are for.'

'Jack, a bank will only lend you an umbrella when it is sunny and you don't need one. And don't bother going to a merchant bank, because they'll only lend you one in the same circumstances and it isn't even theirs to lend you.'

'Yes, I've heard that one. Just wait and see, smart arse.'

George was academic. Clever at school. Always able to quote from the Classics at the appropriate moment. He was as tall as Jack, but not as striking, with glasses and long straggly hair. He gave the impression of being a young Oxford don who would surely become a professor in time, covered in dust and sharing sherry with the more intellectual of his students. Indeed, he had considered becoming an academic, staying at university for ever. But he'd been lured by the money on offer to bright minds in the City. He knew Jack well, having met him when they were eight years old. He knew Jack's weaknesses. And the contradictions in his personality.

*

'Mr Jones will see you now,' said the manager's secretary with a cool and sceptical expression on her face. Jack tried one of his winning smiles and noticed a slight melting of her stern, tweedy expression.

Mr Jones was as ordinary as his name suggested. He wore a slightly shabby grey pinstriped suit, the provincial bank manager's uniform, with trousers that had developed a shine on the knee. His greying black hair was greased and combed into position so as to fail to cover his balding head. A few specks of dandruff nestled on his collar. His glasses were slightly smeared and his teeth were yellowing from the tobacco that smouldered in the pipe on his desk.

'Nice to see you again, Mr Mayhew. Mind if I smoke?' he said, picking up his pipe and jabbing it eagerly into his mouth and lighting up without waiting for a reply.

'Er, no, of course not. Nice to see you again too.'

After a couple of languid puffs, while he gazed at a small pile of papers in front of him, Mr Jones launched into his familiar script.

'Well, I have looked at the accounts for last year, which seem satisfactory, and your proposal for your second restaurant. I have some reservations – excuse the pun! – despite the obvious success of your first venture.'

'Oh,' said Jack having heard these lines before.

'Whilst your cashflow forecasts have some credibility, based on your experience, you seem to me to be proposing to pay a lot for the lease of this second place. In a sense that is your business not mine, but I am bound to say that when it comes to looking at the bank's security for your suggested borrowing, it looks a little thin.'

Mr Jones took a large drag on his pipe, leaned back triumphantly in his high-backed chair and studied Jack through the pipe smoke, waiting for his reply. Jack had not yet told Mr Jones of the higher price he intended to agree with Miss Gosling, the vendor, and so shuffled his feet, took a sip of the coffee he had been given and pretended to see something out of the window whilst he grappled for a convincing reply.

'Well, I'm sure the lease of Arthur's will have increased in value since we took it on so that should cover it, even though I will have to increase my offer to nearer £20,000 to secure the premises. There are others after it at that price so it must be worth that.' Jack had taken some wild guesses.

Mr Jones gave a slightly condescending chuckle. 'If I had based my lending decisions on that type of argument I wouldn't be where I am now,' he said, evidently pleased with his progress to manager of a small provincial branch. 'Any increased value there may be, can evaporate overnight and I don't immediately see where you will find the additional security we require. We already have your personal guarantee, but, with respect, if we have to enforce our security, I don't think you have the means to cover it, unless…' He paused and Jack cocked his head on one side, hoping to hear a suggestion that would bail him out.

'Unless you would be prepared to reduce your loan request by £4,500 – that is, to the level on these papers in front of me and so before you increase your offer. And we would ask you to put your flat in Bath on the market and remit the proceeds to us when it has sold. That way we would be more secure.'

Shit, thought Jack. He had no idea where he would get the additional money he thought he might need.

'OK,' he said, 'I will provide the additional money myself, but do I really have to sell my flat? Surely the security of that is enough?'

'I'm afraid so. Even though we have the flat as security, the bank would be reluctant to foreclose on it. We don't want a reputation for throwing people out of their homes.'

So you throw them out in advance, thought Jack. 'All right, I will put it on the market,' he said, thinking to himself that it might just be that he could conveniently contrive not to sell it.

'Splendid, dear chap,' said Mr Jones, standing and relighting his pipe. 'I hear that some people in Government think that smoking in public places – including one's own office, heaven forbid – should be banned! Whatever next? They will be telling us that we can't chase foxes soon!' He thrust out his hand as he walked towards the office door and added, 'I'll get my secretary to type up the loan agreement and get it to you in the next couple of weeks.'

Take your time, thought Jack as he shook Mr Jones's hand and gave him his winning smile.

As he left the bank Jack punched the air before his elation was curbed by the cold truth that he had no idea how he would raise the additional money.

Arthur's was almost full. The music, a little too loud, increased the sound of laughter and cocktail-fuelled conversation.

'Hi, Jack,' said several female voices as he strode purposefully over to the bar.

'Jack, what can I get you?' asked Vicky, who was mixing a Harvey Wallbanger, the bar's top seller.

Jack whispered in her ear.

'Well, I have already agreed to go out with George after work but seeing as it is you – OK!'

Jack whispered in her ear again.

'OK, thanks. If I can finish work early that's even better. I'll see you outside in half an hour.'

Jack winked at her and then moved over to the other end of the bar, where Desmond and another man were standing drinking Michelob from bottles.

'Let me buy you another of those, Desmond, and then you can tell me about those expensive loans that you can fix,' said Jack quietly.

'Hey, are you serious? You must be desperate.'

'Yes, and I am. Well, not exactly desperate, but there is a deal I want to do that is too good to miss.'

'I believe you,' said Desmond doubtfully. 'I'll get the forms round to you in the morning.'

*

George slammed the door of the flat as he returned, to let Jack know he was back and to put Vicky off her stroke.

But all George heard was some giggling and so switched on the television to mask the evidence of Vicky's duplicity.

She sneaked out later, whilst George was in the bathroom, probably to save herself the embarrassment of bumping into him.

'That was a shifty thing to do. More evidence you don't play golf,' said George.

'All's fair, etc., according to Shakespeare.'

'John Lyle, actually,' said George.

'What do you mean?'

'It wasn't Shakespeare. It was John Lyle.'

Jack rolled his eyes.

George was going through a promiscuous phase as well as Jack. He persuaded himself that this was a reaction to a troubled time in the City, where neither his job nor his sex life had gone according to plan. Most of his friends seemed to score better on both fronts. But he was surprised at Jack's change in behaviour. *This isn't you*, he thought. When a young man in his late teens at school and then at Oxford, Jack had treated women with respect and sensitivity, unlike earlier generations of men. Although outwardly his friends scoffed at Jack's New Man stance, inwardly it was something that many of them admired. He had led the way as a social revolutionary at school too, civilising the relationship between the boys. Not even the threat of disease appeared to moderate his promiscuity. 'Intercourse never did any good, and it's lucky if it does no harm,' George had said, quoting Epicurus. The vestiges of school rivalry meant that he was pleased that his knowledge of the Classics was more complete than Jack's. But his words seemed to fall on deaf ears. In a drunken moment, and if by way of excuse, Jack had confided in George that he was terrified of rejection, particularly by women. When George said that this was because he had been dumped at boarding school when he was eight and so just wanted to be mothered, Jack propelled most of his remaining beer over George's head.

'Well, after that,' said George with a laugh, 'I don't see why I should do you any favours, but I may have found you someone who could be suitable to take over as manager for Arthur's when, or should I say if, you leave to set up the next place,' said George. 'He came in the other day and introduced himself. His name is Steven Gregson. He's been in the business before but his place burned down and he lost all his money. He was a showjumper and rode for England a few times, he says. You may want to check him out, though, because while he appears charming, I'm not entirely sure that all his story is plausible.'

'Why so?'

'I don't know. Just something made me uneasy. Still. Might be my suspicious nature. He may be great. He's quite well known locally, certainly knows the business, and, well, it appears you may need someone quite soon. I'm not your man, as you know. I plan to get back to the City before too long. Here's Steven's number. Steve to his friends.'

'Hey, thanks for the introduction. I appreciate that. I'll give him a ring.'

In bed that night, what George had said about his relationships with women and his separation from his mother played on his mind. As he slept, his first days at boarding school dominated his dreams.

*

Jack was proud of his new school uniform when he first put it on at home. His mother had complained it was silly that Gorringe's in London was the only place where it could be bought, even though it was that type of school. But now, the smell of the new jacket and the roughness of the Aertex shirt on Jack's sensitive eight-year-old skin was discomforting.

'My advice is to make your goodbyes quick, Mrs Mayhew,' Mr Banborough, the headmaster, quietly counselled his mother.

As his parents' old blue Hillman disappeared slowly down the long drive of his new school the corners of Jack's mouth curled. Tears fell down both cheeks. And then, standing alone at the top of the drive, with the evening sun playing happily through the chestnut trees, deep sobs heaved through his little chest. He tried to catch a final glimpse of the car at the bottom of the drive, but it was gone. His glasses were smeared with tears and, no longer able to see clearly, he sat weeping on the ground.

'Sir, I think that new bug is blubbing,' said Osbourne, whose parents had dropped him off a day early.

'Go and fetch Matron, will you?' replied the headmaster, puffing determinedly on his pipe.

Jack had curled up in a ball on the ground. He remembered his mother telling him, 'We'll see you in three weeks, darling. Only three weeks. Have fun.' She gave him a gentle kiss and a hug. Jack hadn't noticed that her eyes were red as his father steered her towards the door. 'See you soon, darling.'

He didn't know his father had added, "Don't let Jack see you crying," when they were out of earshot.

Jack heard slow footsteps coming towards him. These steps were accompanied by two small thuds on the gravel, a creak and heavy breathing.

'Mayhew, come with me, will you?' a voice said.

Jack looked up. What he saw startled and rather frightened him. Matron seemed terribly old, had dirty glasses and strange metal rods on the lower part of both legs. She was holding two large sticks which had pads on the top which seemed to be supporting her. Her hands were gnarled, her fingernails yellow, bowed and crooked. The crutches, for that is what they were, creaked as she moved slightly on the gravel. As a polio victim from the recent outbreak in 1957, Matron was lucky to be alive, let alone walk. But survived she had and with the aid of the callipers on her legs and two large crutches, she could walk, albeit slowly. Jack was too frightened to move.

'Mayhew, I can't reach down and pick you up and so you will have to stand of your own accord.'

Jack stood, looked up at the terrifying figure of Matron and started to sob again.

'Now follow me to your dormitory, and I will help you unpack.'

Jack couldn't remember where his dormitory was, but he slowly followed Matron up the stairs. Creak, creak went the crutches. As they approached Jack's dormitory, two boys his age ran laughing up the corridor towards them.

'No running in the corridors, you boys. The headmaster has already told you. You won't be beaten on your first day here, but if I have to tell you again tomorrow, you will be. This is a place where you must do as you are told.'

The boys stopped running and looked at Matron a little sheepishly. They then looked at Jack and laughed again, walking briskly away, heads together conspiratorially and saying something about a teddy. One of the boys was the first one he had seen at the school. He had been lying on his tummy on the carpet in the headmaster's drawing room, seeming perfectly at home and happily reading what Jack was later told was a "war mag". There were many of these in the 1960s, all of which seemed to Jack to portray English soldiers as heroic and German or Japanese fighters as evil. Matron pushed open the dormitory door with one of her crutches.

'Now where is your case?' She spoke in a clipped, rather masculine and military voice. Not sergeant major but more public school and Sandhurst captain.

'I don't know,' said Jack, who had now stopped crying. 'Mummy said she would put it on my bed, but I don't know which one is mine.'

A line of beds with heavy black steel frames stretched out in front of him, on both sides of the room. He counted six on either side. All the beds seemed to have Scottish-looking blankets on them except one: Jack's. His mother had bought him a bright, "cheerful" blanket. The blanket did not make him feel cheerful; it made him more miserable. It reminded him of his mother, whom he wanted by his side, and of course he did not want to be different. He wanted to blend in. In fact, he wanted to be invisible.

On top of the blanket on Jack's bed was his teddy.

'I don't think Jack should take his teddy,' Jack had

overheard his father saying to his mother. 'He'll be teased.'

'Nonsense,' said his mother. 'It will comfort him on his first few nights at school, when he is missing home.'

'Now unpack your things from your overnight case and we will unpack your trunk tomorrow,' said Matron.

New striped pyjamas with a cord to hold them up, some smart red leather slippers with hard soles, a children's book of crosswords, and something called a sponge bag. There was no sponge inside it, just a new toothbrush, a new tube of toothpaste, a flannel and a nail brush. Jack had never used one of those and didn't think he ever would.

'When you have finished unpacking, come down to the new boys' dining room for supper, which today is at six. Have you got a watch?'

'No,' said Jack, so quietly that Matron could not hear him.

'What?'

'No,' he said again, this time shaking his head.

'Well, you are supposed to have one. It is clearly marked on your clothes list. How are you supposed to tell the time if you don't have a watch? If you can't tell the time, you will be late for everything and then you will have an unpleasant visit to the headmaster's study. Do you know what that means?'

Jack shook his head again, looking at the floor.

'It means, Mayhew, that you will be beaten with a stick. You don't want that to happen, do you?'

Another shake of the head.

'So when you write to your parents on Sunday, you

had better tell them. The gong will go for supper at six so make sure you are there.'

Matron creaked out of the dormitory and left Jack alone again. He sat on his bed, took his teddy in his arms and sobbed. He remained on his bed, curled up in a ball and pulling threads out of his cheerful blanket until the sound of the gong told him it was time to join the other new boys for supper. He wasn't hungry. He heard some boys laughing while they ran towards the dining room. Why were they laughing? Surely, they felt sad too?

Jack stood at the entrance to the small oak-panelled dining room. There were some old but elegant brass lights fitted to the walls and a very large and faded rug on the oak floor. The floor smelled of polish and some of the boys skidded on it deliberately before they hit the rug, crumpling it up and attracting a rebuke from one of the masters on duty. Some of the other boys were wiping tears away from their faces and being gently encouraged to sit on one of the long wooden benches in front of the even longer dining table. They weren't talking and nobody was talking to them. Jack stood motionless.

A lady, who to Jack seemed very pretty, came towards him and introduced herself as Miss Watson. She put her arm around his shoulder. 'Come with me, Mayhew, and let's see if we can find you a seat and someone nice to talk to.' How did she know his surname? Why didn't she call him Jack? Why was she wearing a white coat, as if she were a nurse? Her uniform looked very clean and Jack could detect the faint smell of sweet perfume.

'Mayhew, this is Thomas. Shuffle up, Thomas, and let Mayhew sit on the bench next to you. Now I will give you some beans on toast and then you can have an apple.'

Why is Thomas called by his Christian name and I'm not? thought Jack.

Jack had never seen baked beans before and anyway was not at all hungry. The plate of beans sat in front of him for what seemed to Jack a very long time. His legs below his little grey woollen shorts stuck to the surface of the bench. The beans went cold.

'Don't you want your beans, Mayhew?' said Miss Watson, who was standing behind him. Jack shook his head.

'Well, you don't have to eat them today but from tomorrow you will have to eat everything on your plate. Now off you go upstairs and get ready for bed. The headmaster is going to read you a story tonight.'

Jack made his way upstairs to his dormitory, following some other boys who had pushed past him. The ones pushing were running and chatting to each other happily as they went. Others, like Jack, didn't speak. Jack's grandmother had described him to his mother as very shy, just as she had warned Jack that he might find it odd that everyone was called by their surname.

Jack fell over trying to get his socks off and Miss Watson, who he had gathered was the under-matron, helped him into his new pyjamas and to tie the cord. He started to cry again. Jack's mother usually helped him get ready for bed and he wished that she was with him now. Two of the other boys were also crying. Miss Watson gently told Jack to go to the bathroom and wash. Jack didn't think he was dirty and had already washed, on his mother's instructions, before he left home with his parents that afternoon. Home seemed far away.

Once in bed, the dip in the horsehair mattress enveloped him. Jack gripped his teddy as the headmaster shuffled into the dormitory. He sat on the end of Thomas's bed and started to read aloud. Jack didn't know what the book was and didn't really listen to what was being read. He curled up in a ball underneath his unfamiliar clean sheets and cheerful blanket and, along with some other boys, cried himself to sleep.

*

Jack awoke from his dream. He wondered why he felt lonely and insecure and craved the comfort of female company. He noticed that this craving was not exclusively extended to those who might be considered classically attractive. There was beauty to be found in most women, he thought. Indeed, he had learned that those not blessed with colour-supplement looks could be more affectionate, more appreciative, more understanding. His staff were almost universally warm towards him. He did not feel, or he would not admit, that this might be affected by their desire for job security. Nonetheless, he set off for the restaurant with the barely subliminal thought that this was a place of safety, and where his needs might be satisfied.

As Jack drove to Arthur's, he was preoccupied by the immediate issues that faced him. Would he manage to assemble enough money to complete the purchase of the new restaurant? Would Steve turn out to be a suitable manager? A great deal was at stake as Jack was stretching the financial resources of the business to the limit, and perhaps beyond. The cash flow of Arthur's would be needed to support the new venture and any deterioration in it would lead to both establishments being squeezed. So Steve had to be right.

An old lady hunched over what looked like a scarf at the side of the road caught Jack's attention. As she struggled to retrieve it, he noticed that the object was not a scarf, but a cat. Jack pulled over and as he approached the woman, he noticed that she was crying. The cat looked to be in pain.

'Someone ran over Patricia,' she said between sobs, 'and they didn't stop.'

'There is a vet not far from here,' said Jack without hesitation. 'Let me take you both there.'

'Oh no, that's very kind, but I couldn't trouble you.'

'Come on, I'll help you into the car. It's a bit small and low, I'm afraid. You hold Patricia on your lap. I'm Jack. Could I ask your name?'

'Johnson. Mrs Johnson. But please call me Edith.'

Jack waited for Edith to emerge from the vet after he had seen the cat. Whether the cat lived or died, he did not feel he could leave Edith on her own, despite needing to be at the restaurant. But Edith refused Jack's offer to take her and the cat home.

'My friend will pick me up. You saved Patricia's life. And what a kind man you are. Here, please take this,' she said, offering Jack some money.

'No, I couldn't possibly. Thank you. I'm just pleased to have been able to help. And that Patricia is OK. I must go now. Goodbye, Edith.'

Distracted by thoughts of the injured cat and Edith's

distress, Jack crossed the main road in his car outside Arthur's as the traffic lights changed to red.

'Shit,' he muttered as he noticed a camera pointing at the road underneath the lights and remembered too late that his licence already sported nine points.

When he arrived at the office, the scent of rather too much of a familiar perfume filled his senses. Fiona was at her desk. She gave him a shy smile and said, 'When are you going to take me out, Jack? Like the others, as you promised? You seem to have been ignoring me.'

'Sorry, Fiona. I've been busy. How about a coffee?'

Fiona blushed. She did Jack's books and the wages. She wore glasses, had short dark hair, lived with two dogs, a goldfish and a cat and reminded Jack of a librarian.

Returning with the coffee, Jack noticed that Fiona had sprayed a little more perfume on herself. Not his choice of scent, but the signal was obvious. She smiled up at him through crooked glasses. After an exciting chat about the effect of his National Insurance bill on cash flow and the health of Fiona's cat, who was incontinent, Jack could bear it no longer.

'Look, why don't we continue this over lunch later at La Reserve?'

'Oh, I couldn't possibly. I have to go back to my flat to check on my pussy, who is ill, as I told you.'

Jack had to turn away to avoid Fiona detecting his giggle. He was in his twenties, and so these innuendoes were still hilarious to him. 'How about dinner then?'

'What, tonight?'

'Yes, I'd really like that and to spend some time with you,' said Jack.

'Oh, OK.'

'Right. I'll pick you up at 8 p.m.'

At 8.15 p.m. – better not seem too keen, thought Jack – he parked his shiny black convertible MGB outside Fiona's modest terrace house where her flat was on the first floor. Jack strode up to the front door and rang the bell. The door immediately opened as if Fiona had been standing waiting. Wearing a somewhat matronly but neat yellow dress and flat shoes, she gave Jack a broad smile. The corners of her eyes crinkled behind her horn-rimmed glasses. He recognised the perfume from earlier in the day.

While Jack held open the car door for her, Fiona got in awkwardly, head first and then sitting and swinging her legs in afterwards. Not used to a sports car, thought Jack, and certainly didn't attend Lucie Clayton's, where instruction on how to enter a sports car wearing a skirt was part of the curriculum. At the restaurant Jack ordered white wine as Fiona had asked but, to Jack's dismay, she made one glass last all evening. *This is going to be hard*, he thought. Nonetheless, Jack turned on as much charm as he could muster, allowing Fiona to do all the talking and showering her with compliments and the occasional suggestive remark, at which Fiona blushed. He tried to touch her hand between courses, but it was swiftly withdrawn.

In the car on the way back to Fiona's flat, however, she let him rest his hand on her leg, although she wriggled away when he moved it up her thigh. One more throw of the dice, thought Jack, as they stood at Fiona's front door, light rain forcing the pace.

'Well, bye, then. Thanks for a lovely evening. I'll see

you tomorrow,' she said, smiling nervously up at Jack, perhaps wondering whether he was going to kiss her goodnight.

'Aren't you going to ask me up for a coffee?' asked Jack, trying not to sound too desperate.

'Gosh, no. Not on our first date.'

'That's a pity,' said Jack, putting on his ironic disappointed face. *First and last probably*, he thought. To his surprise, Fiona stood on her tiptoes and gave him a peck on the cheek, before blushing again and disappearing through the door.

'Damn, damn, damn,' said Jack out loud as he drove too fast through Bath on his way back to the flat. One of his Dire Straits tapes was on his cassette player. 'How appropriate,' muttered Jack. As he arrived at the flat, Steph emerged through the front door; George was waving her off.

'Bloody hell,' cursed Jack.

'Oh hi. How did you get on?' asked George.

'Don't ask. You?'

'Fine, thanks.'

'If that's the case, why didn't Steph stay?'

'That might have been a bit awkward, as Laura is about to arrive.'

Great, thought Jack, trying not to lose his sense of humour and disappearing into his room.

He had no idea what time, but he was later awoken from his slumber by the usually agreeable sound of female orgasm coming from George's bedroom.

'Thanks, mate,' muttered Jack, falling back to sleep. 'No need to rub it in.'

The next day, Jack bounded out of the flat and headed to Arthur's early. He noticed the front door was already unlocked, even though no staff were due in for fifteen minutes. He went upstairs to the office. As he opened the door, Fiona grabbed him by the shirt, pushed him backwards against the wall, pulled his head down to hers and eagerly kissed him on the lips. Seeming out of breath, she stopped for a second or two, took off her glasses, threw them to the floor and continued to kiss Jack with considerable passion. She moved her right hand down to his flies, undid them determinedly and worked her hand behind Jack's pants. Still shocked, Jack gasped as Fiona fell to her knees, taking Jack in her mouth with an expertise that surprised him. Holding the back of Fiona's head, Jack noticed the traffic building up outside the restaurant, and a familiar car trying to find a place to park.

'Someone will be here soon,' hissed Jack; at which Fiona stood, turned around, leaned forwards over the desk and pulled off her knickers, standing on her glasses as she did so. Her skirt was up around her waist, her pale bottom thrust towards Jack. As he placed his hands on each of her buttocks and Fiona grasped the desk with both hands, Jack slid into her. After a muted whimper Fiona started to moan, quietly at first and then more loudly. As she came, she gasped loudly and Jack heard the door of the restaurant open.

Blimey, thought Jack as he pulled up his trousers and tucked in his shirt.

'Thank you, Jack,' panted Fiona, still out of breath, flushed and feeling on the floor for her glasses.

Jack smiled, passed her glasses to her and gently

squeezed her arm. He left the office and closed the door behind him to allow Fiona to compose herself before any other member of his staff saw her.

*

Jack picked up the phone and dialled the number that George had given him for Steven Gregson. A confident voice answered.

'Jack, I have been expecting your call. I can make early evening today. Shall we say 7 p.m. at Arthur's? I'll buy you your most expensive cocktail,' said the voice.

Cheeky bugger, thought Jack, although he said, 'Yes, that would be good. I look forward to meeting you.'

Raised voices from the kitchen made Jack investigate. François, the chef, was in a French mood, waving his hands at Sian as he spoke.

'François, those ladies have complained that their tea was cold. You filled the teapot with cold water,' she said.

'Well, I suggest you go and tell them, "Mesdames, if you wanted hot water in your tea, you should have said so…".'

Sian raised her eyes to the ceiling, glanced at Jack and filled a new pot herself.

'If there was a French Basil Fawlty, I swear he would be it,' she muttered as she pushed somewhat sulkily past Jack.

*

Jack made a detour past Arthur's the following day, before setting off to Bristol to see the lady who was selling the lease of his next enterprise. The kitchen window was open, but no pizza dough was evident on the pavement or attempting orbit. It was a sunny morning and warm enough to drop the hood on the MGB. But François had the radio on in the kitchen from which could be heard the whining refrain of "I Won't Let You Down". Jack wound up the windows to muffle the sound and decided not to remove the hood until he was out of range of what had become his least favourite pop song of the year. He turned on Dire Straits, hoped it was not an omen and drove off towards Bristol.

At a lay-by three miles further on, Jack pulled over and released the levers that allowed him to push down the roof. As he drove away again, accelerating as fast as he could into the morning sunshine, Mark Knopfler sang, "The Tunnel of Love". Loud. Jack grinned, gripped the steering wheel and took the next bend as fast as he could, until the rubber of the rear tyres screeched in protest. Life was good.

Jason's wine bar was in St George's Street where Jack had agreed to meet Miss Gosling, the proprietor who wished to sell. The bar only opened in the evenings and so they could meet discreetly on the premises. Determined not to be late, Jack arrived soon after eleven for his meeting at eleven thirty and parked his car at the end of the road. As he did so, he noticed a tall dark man about the same age as himself leaving the premises and shaking hands with Miss Gosling. Jack thought the man looked familiar, almost like a character from a dream. Something made him uneasy. Although the man, who was about Jack's age, had a face that initially looked harmless enough, he had a manner which made Jack feel uncomfortable. His demeanour reminded Jack of one of George's quotes, in that it seemed to stain the air around him as if he were somehow toxic.

Jack crossed the road and watched Miss Gosling's visitor walk towards a shiny black 3-series BMW parked down the street. He got in and drove away, but not before Jack made note of the number plate, which was unmissable. OSB 5.

Flash bastard, thought Jack without being able to put his finger on why he felt the need to insult the man, other than the fact that he had a distaste for personalised number plates. His mother had thought them dreadfully nouveau riche and he had to admit that this had probably influenced his own opinion.

Jack walked around the block to kill time before his meeting and arrived back at the door of Jason's just before eleven thirty. Miss Gosling was waiting for him. She was a wiry middle-aged woman with glasses, a long grey-looking pullover and scuffed sandals. There was something in her manner and appearance that made Jack realise why she had not managed to make a success of her wine bar. Aside from that, the place looked run-down.

'Hello, Mr Mayhew. How nice to see you again.'

'And you. Please call me Jack,' he replied, offering his hand. As he walked into the bar the soles of his shoes stuck to the wooden floor. He noticed the brass rail around the bar had not been cleaned and looked as sticky as the ground he walked on.

They went into a small office with barely enough room for the two of them to sit. After some pleasantries Miss Gosling said, 'Jack, I'll get straight to the point; someone else has just been here and made me an offer that I am prepared to accept. As you know, your offer is simply not enough. However, if you were to match the other man's offer, I shall let you have the bar.'

'That's kind of you. But why would you do that?'

'Well… let's just say that I would feel more comfortable that you would look after the staff better. Although you don't know the other man, there is something about him that makes me nervous.'

'I understand,' said Jack, not really understanding. Yet what she had said resonated with the distant impression Jack had had of the man.

'So how much do I have to offer you to match him and secure the purchase?'

'Eighteen thousand five hundred pounds.'

Jack could not hide his reaction. His brazen guess at the bank was unfortunately spot on. The additional £4,500 that the mystery man in the black BMW had offered was more than Jack could see his way to affording, since the bank would not help. He had already stretched himself to offer £14,000 and he did not know how he could possibly find the required balance.

'Done,' he said, offering his hand again. 'But for that I want the stock.' He didn't but did not want to appear to be too keen. 'And I will give you £16,000 on completion and the balance after six months, provided everything in the accounts is as you say it is – which I'm sure it *is*, Miss Gosling, but I have to be sensible, don't I?'

'Don't you trust me, Jack? That is disappointing in one so young.'

'Yes, of course I do, but, well, you know. I have to be careful.'

'Well, I will throw in the stock, because that is what Mr Osbourne wanted too, but you will have to give me all the money on completion, please.'

Jack felt the blood drain from his cheeks. 'Is the other man who wants the bar called Osbourne?'

'Well, yes. I shouldn't have told you, but never mind. I don't suppose you know him, but please keep it to yourself. Now, perhaps you'd like to think about what I have said. But I really need to know where you stand by tomorrow morning as I want this all put away as the whole matter is not doing my health any good at all and—'

'OK, I agree,' interrupted Jack, now that he realised who the other bidder was.

'Oh, that's wonderful, Jack. You won't be disappointed. Now let me go and get my diary from downstairs and we can make some notes of what we have to do next.'

As she left the room, Jack noticed a business card on the small desk. *Benedict Osbourne, 41 Dean Street, Bristol.* Jack scrawled the address onto the sheet of paper on his lap as a childhood terror and the prospect of vengeance seeped into his mind.

*

'What are you up to?' asked George from the sitting-room doorway of the flat.

Jack didn't look up from the sheets of figures spread

over the table. 'Trying to figure out from where I can find the four and a half grand that the bank won't lend me. I think I can squeeze a couple out of the restaurant's cash flow by delaying the payment to a few of our suppliers. But that still leaves at least two grand to find from elsewhere.'

'Isn't that rather risky, pal, not to say reckless?' said George but with a grin on his face.

'Yes, but I've not got much choice. I had to up the ante to avoid the restaurant falling into the hands of an old enemy from prep school. You remember Osbourne and what he did to me, don't you? I'm determined to get even with him, so I couldn't let him get one over me on this one.'

'I remember him. I think he was expelled. But what did he do?'

CHAPTER 3

Twenty years earlier

As the first three weeks dragged by, Jack became less homesick. He began to make timid friendships with some of the other new boys. Some seemed more grown-up than him. Some had brothers at the school which made them seem more confident and at home. But still, Jack would sometimes find himself alone. He would stand at the top of the long winding drive, which the boys were not allowed beyond, and gaze in what he thought was the direction of home, hoping that just maybe he would catch a glimpse of his mother, twenty-five miles away. In this way Jack felt at once more connected to and yet more distant from his family. Why those who loved him had left him in this place, alone and unloved, was a mystery to him. It seemed cruel.

The worst moments were at night, when the boys went to bed. Although ten minutes past seven seemed early to Jack, and an odd time, he was always tired. It was when he was getting ready for bed that he missed his mother most. He noticed that some other boys went very quiet at this time too. The September evenings were still warm and after lights out, when the dormitory was obliged to become silent, Jack could hear the older boys playing outside. The echoes of their excited voices were muted by honey-coloured courtyards. A tennis ball thumped amiably on firm walls. A determined bee buzzed hopefully against a window, trying to escape. The church clock struck eight.

After breakfast the next day, Jack noticed a line of about eight boys nervously standing outside the headmaster's study.

'They're going to be whacked,' said Thomas, whose first name Jack now understood to be George.

'Why?' asked Jack.

'Caught talking after lights out.'

Jack had been warned by Matron that boys caught talking after lights out would be beaten but had not been prepared to witness the silent line of transgressors standing sheepishly outside the headmaster's study. Frightened that they might be inadvertently caught up in the punishment, Jack and George ran around the corner by the kitchen. The smell of fried bread sat heavily in the air.

'Let's wait here and see what they're like when they come out,' said George.

Not long later, the first two of the eleven-year-old boys ran around the corner, pulling at their shorts and laughing, perhaps with relief.

'Let's see your stripes, Osbourne,' said Robert Cookson, who had already exposed his bare behind. Two red marks about six inches long were angrily asserting themselves on each naked bottom.

'Wow, that stings,' said Cookson, wincing at Osbourne.

'Don't be so wet; he whacked me harder than you. He said he wasn't pleased to see me so soon after being whacked for ragging in the dorm last week.' Osbourne paused. 'What are you new bugs looking at?' he said angrily to Jack and George.

'Nothing,' they both said and ran off as fast as they could over the slippery brown linoleum towards the chapel.

Chapel seemed to Jack a dreary affair. There were too many hymns and two of something called psalms. Most of the boys seemed to mumble their way through these, while the choir and three of the masters sang as loudly as they could. The headmaster, at the front, in his gown with the red hood, sang all the hymns and psalms to the ceiling of the chapel, as if studying a large crack. Occasionally, and quite suddenly, he would look down at the boys, as if trying to catch two of them playing conkers at the back. Nobody dared to do anything nearly as dangerous as that. The worst offence would be talking during a psalm and even that would surely lead to a visit to the headmaster's study.

There was a small, fat master who played the organ, badly. The organ had pedals, and it seemed to Jack that his feet only just touched them. This, and Mr Smallwood's general incompetence, led to a large number of fluffed notes. The scrunching sound was hilarious to the boys, who tried in vain to suppress their giggles. The more they tried to curtail their laughter, for fear of being seen or heard, the more they wanted to laugh. This Sunday though, nobody was punished, the headmaster settling for a couple of scary scowls instead.

Even though there were no lessons on Sunday, after chapel the boys had to return to their classrooms for what was known as letter writing. On the inside of his new brown leather writing case, Jack had proudly written the words "Wirting Case", a spelling error that was to cause much amusement to his family for years to come. The boys were made to write a letter home to their parents, on blue Basildon Bond paper and with a fountain pen. Inevitably the ink would smudge, especially Jack's, who, being left-handed, pushed his small hand onto the still wet ink as he wrote the next word. Too many smudges and the master in charge would make the offender write the letter again. Eight-year-old boys were not used to fountain pens and so invariably desks and hands soon became covered in ink.

The letters were read by the master in charge, although one of the more sensitive ones made a deliberate show of turning the letter upside down, pretending just to check for neatness. So Jack felt that he could not tell his parents that he was unhappy and wanted to come home. Instead, he wrote: *It is OK here, sort of, but I really want to see you.* He then smudged the last two words with his fingers hoping that it would look as if it had been caused by tears falling onto the paper while Jack wrote.

But the trick did not lead to his rescue and so Jack remained incarcerated until the joy of the first leave-out weekend was upon him. The excitement amongst the boys was palpable and Jack could barely contain his own as he caught sight of the blue Hillman snaking its way up the long drive, past the ancient rhododendrons towards him. The huge smile across Jack's face was reflected in his father's as he got out of the car and they made their way towards each other. Jack ran towards his father but checked himself as he grew closer, anxious not to show too much enthusiasm to the other boys, and keen to ensure that his father did not kiss him, as he would ordinarily have done. Jack had not yet heard the expression stiff upper lip, but he was already learning to suppress his emotions in a way that was to influence his behaviour for the rest of his life.

*

Although Jack was frequently homesick in the first of his five years at St Cuthbert's, the incidences of this, as the headmaster had reassured Jack's concerned parents, slowly receded. Nonetheless, the excitement, security and comfort at being wrapped in the bosom of his family on the first day of the leave-out weekend always gave way to uneasiness and then dread on Sundays as the day progressed. After *The Black and White Minstrel Show* and crumpets for tea, Jack shed his home clothes. As his mother helped him into his little grey shorts Jack's shy, sunny smile was replaced by tears.

After a quick hug, Mrs Mayhew would bundle Jack into the front seat of the Hillman next to his father. The smell of old warm leather and the sound his father's choice of piano music on the radio mingled with the rolling motion of the estate car to numb the edges of Jack's anxiety. This was soon replaced by waves of dread when he noticed the clock on the dashboard. Only fifteen minutes to go until they reached the bottom of the long drive to school. The lodge crept into view, and the church clock struck seven.

The warm smile of Jack's mother was replaced by the whiskery gaze of Matron as she creaked her way towards him on the corridor outside his dormitory. Jack clutched at his new book of crossword puzzles and tried to smile. But she ignored him and creaked past, crutches and callipers supporting her unfortunate frame. As if in contrast, behind her glided Miss Watson, her long dark hair shimmering, recently washed and bouncing against the top of her shoulders. Her white uniform dress clung to her body, emphasising the curves of her hips and breasts. She put an affectionate arm around Jack, who managed a smile. Her perfume enlivened him as she steered him towards his dormitory.

'Come on, Jack, time for bed,' she cooed. Some older boys passing the door overheard her and made some sort of suggestive remark.

'That's quite enough of that,' she said, tossing her long hair and laughing. Jack thought he noticed her winking at one of the boys, but perhaps it was his imagination.

'See you later,' he said over his shoulder. Miss Watson did not reply but smiled gently to herself. At sixteen years old, Miss Watson seemed like a grown-up to Jack.

Now in the Easter term, the mornings were often bitterly cold. Ice would sometimes form on the inside of the dormitory windows as damp breath from the sleeping boys hit the frozen glass. When the bell rang to wake him, Jack knew that the warmth of the dip in his horsehair mattress would soon be traded for the sharp, cold air of an unheated dormitory. All the boys dressed as quickly as they could, shivering.

After a series of mildly tedious lessons, including the twice-weekly trudge through *Kennedy's Latin Primer* (compulsorily defaced as his Eating Primer), Jack and his now best friend, George Thomas, dashed from the classroom. They ran everywhere, as if to walk wasted time. After lunch there were no games, because the rugger pitches were still covered in snow. The previous day, the whole school had been taken tobogganing, but today the boys were free. So Jack and George ran quickly to join a snowball fight that was raging outside the dining room; but not for long. Some of the larger boys decided to pack the snowballs with stones and aim them at the smaller ones. George and Jack ran in opposite directions to avoid a gang of boys running at them, each with two stone-packed snowballs.

Jack decided that the safest plan was to retreat inside, where even the most daring of boys would not throw a single ball for fear of joining the line outside the headmaster's study after breakfast the next day. As he trotted towards his locker, near the classrooms, to reward himself with some sweets, two other boys ran towards him.

'Run, Mayhew,' said one. 'Osbourne has made an electric chair and is tying people to it and giving them shocks. Ryland and Smithson are kidnapping people to take to him.'

As Jack fled in panic, a recent nightmare returned to his nervous mind. He had watched a film on television (a once-a-week treat) in which a man had been tied to a chair with electrodes attached to his head. The man was screaming in terror, tears and sweat running down his grey face, his eyes huge, staring out of the black-and-white screen. At bedtime, George had explained that the man was being brainwashed. That night, Jack dreamed he was that man.

In his sleep he loudly cried, 'Help. Help.' This must have gone on for some time as the headmaster appeared in his brown tartan dressing gown at the door of the dormitory. The cord was tied firmly around his ample belly and his glasses were on crooked, as if he had pulled them on hurriedly.

'Who is making that noise?' he asked. 'You'll wake everyone up. Is that you, Mayhew?' He raised his voice. 'Mayhew?'

Jack cried 'Help' once more and then woke up with a start.

The headmaster was still standing at the door, staring at Jack. 'Be quiet,' Mr Banborough repeated and left the dormitory, closing the door behind him.

'Sorry, sir,' whimpered Jack, still shaking with fear at his nightmare.

So now Jack ran. As he did, two larger fifth-form boys spotted him. Smithson said to Ryland, 'He'll do,' and sprinted after Jack. They were about twenty yards behind him. At the end of the corridor they had already narrowed Jack's lead to fifteen yards and so Jack turned the corner and hid in one of the lavatories, standing on the seat. Both the floor and the seat he was standing on were wet. He heard Ryland and Smithson turn into the room where eight lavatories were lined up, side by side.

The old wooden doors had two-foot gaps between their bottom sill and the floor. There were no locks.

'I'm sure he went in here,' said one as the other kicked open the first door. Jack's little bare knees trembled as he balanced on the lavatory seat. The next door was booted open. Ryland looked under each door looking for feet. When he reached Jack's door, Jack could see Ryland's head but the older boy didn't see Jack standing on the seat. The door beside him was sent flying back on its hinges.

'I don't think he's here,' said Ryland.

'Just one more,' replied Smithson as he kicked open the door to Jack's cubicle.

Without a word, the boys grabbed Jack by both arms and twisted one hard up behind his back. Jack yelled but they pushed him in front of them back down the corridor.

The chair was in the middle of the fifth-form classroom. This was up some stairs, which themselves were behind a door. As Jack was hustled up the steps he screamed for help. But the door had been slammed behind him and no one heard him. Osbourne was fiddling with some wires as his gang pushed Jack onto the chair, holding him down.

'No, no, please don't,' pleaded Jack.

Osbourne looked down at him, laughing. His henchmen first tied Jack's arms behind the chair, tight. Jack kicked out at them but his feet made no useful contact with his assailants. The chair was of the type used by most institutions at the time. It had an all-metal frame to which were screwed a canvas seat and back. So Jack's arms were in contact with the metal frame. Jack's bare ankles were then tied, one by one, to the base of the metal frame so that his bare legs were also in contact.

Next to the chair was a car battery which was attached by some wires to a device with a handle on the end, which Osbourne called a generator. Seeing this, Jack began to cry tears of terror. Osbourne and the others laughed again. As he sniggered, Osbourne sharply turned the handle. A searing pain ran through Jack's body as the electric current made the muscles of his arms and legs jump in spasm. Jack yelled at the top of his voice.

'Do you want a go?' Osbourne asked Ryland.

'No, you do it,' he replied.

Osbourne cranked the handle again. This time the pain seemed to hit Jack's chest. He gasped and groaned as if he had been stamped on.

'Now his head,' muttered Osbourne.

'No, no, please...' wailed Jack, the memory of his dream adding to his terror.

Ryland and Smithson held one wire each to Jack's head.

'Don't touch each other, or the chair,' instructed Osbourne as he reached for the handle of the generator.

The door of the classroom opened. Mr Smallwood stood in the opening, trying to take in what he had seen. The boys dropped their instruments of torture and stared at Mr Smallwood. Jack shook.

Osbourne was never seen at the school again. Word went around the boys that he had been expelled. Jack's parents discussed taking him away from the school, but his grandmother counselled that this would not help him. St Cuthbert's was an exclusive prep school where the parents were interviewed for suitability, not the children. Jack should toughen up, and this would surely help him to do so. Now that Osbourne had gone, Jack would be looked after and might even acquire some hero status among his contemporaries. *And anyway, perhaps one day*, thought Jack, *I will get the opportunity to pay him back.* Bullies are cowards in the end, said Granny. His father made some remark about revenge being a dish best served cold. *Yes,* thought Jack. *One day I will pay him back...*

...ONE.

*

'He tied me to a metal chair and electrocuted me. That's what he did,' said Jack.

'Yeah, sure he did,' replied George. 'And Kennedy was shot by Osbourne too. Pull the other one.'

'He did, George. I told you at the time and you didn't believe me then. Why would I make it up? Anyway, any ideas?'

'What, for your revenge?'

'No. About how to raise another four and a half grand.'

'Well, there are those no-status expensive loans that the life-assurance salesmen who come into Arthur's are always talking about.'

'Yes, I've talked to Desmond. He showed me the application forms. Interest of twenty per cent per annum – no thanks. Any other ideas?'

George failed to come up with anything else, so Jack pulled on his jacket and headed off towards his car. When he arrived at the restaurant Jane was in the bar, polishing glasses. She was approaching forty from the wrong side, as Gloria Swanson had once remarked about herself, had short brown hair and a slightly portly figure. Jane liked to describe herself as "rounded". She always wore a skirt, sometimes and unfashionably rather too short. Her thighs were plump, so that the skirt tended to ride up. She had to regularly pull it down, wriggling her hips as she did so. She had a slight and soft Yorkshire accent, which Jack found quite appealing. She only just qualified as a staff member by the usual measure but her outgoing personality and ready laugh swung the panel in her favour. The panel consisted of George and Jack and since Jack had a casting vote, he always got his way.

'Jane, are you free for a drink after work today? I think your appraisal is overdue,' said Jack.

'Jack, you don't do appraisals, at least not the sort commonly run by personnel departments. But I hear that most of the other staff have been on the receiving end of your version and so no thanks,' she said with a laugh.

Jack was shocked that she had turned him down but not quite so shocked that the girls had been talking to each other. He only occasionally had misgivings about his present behaviour with women. George had said that he felt Jack was exploitative. But, Jack wondered, who was exploiting whom? These women had minds of their own, didn't they? And if they rejected him, he could cope. Couldn't he?

Jack gave a slight bow, smiled and walked over to the other side of the bar, where George was talking to some customers. As he moved away from them Jack muttered, 'Jane is coming out with me later so no point you asking her.'

George laughed. 'I might have to bribe her then.'

At the end of the lunchtime shift and with the

restaurant empty, George intercepted Jane whilst she was removing her apron. It was spotted with gravy and red wine. She was an enthusiastic waitress but her exuberance led to rather more spillages and broken glasses than the rest of the staff put together.

'Ooo, dear, I s'pose I 'ad better wash that again,' she said in her north Yorkshire lilt.

'Jane, could you do me a favour, please?' Jane looked quizzical and raised an eyebrow. 'Could you help me with the stocktake? I've got to do it now as it's the month end. I trust you and of course I'll make sure that Jack pays you for the overtime. It should take about three hours.' Jane always needed extra money.

'Yeah, sure. That has to be more profitable than Jack's "appraisal", which I politely turned down anyway,' Jane replied, laughing again.

'*Touché*,' muttered George to himself. 'And if there is a surplus, we can always drink it.' Jane liked to drink.

Stocktaking was generally a monthly routine at Arthur's but both the frequency and confidence in the results were sporadic. Acting on those was even less certain. But Jack was keen to get into the habit as when he left the running of the restaurant to someone else, after he had bought Jason's, it would become more important. Theft in the restaurant and bar trade was frequent. Cash and stocks of drink would go missing. Drinks would be given away to friends. The only way of detecting if this had taken place, that Jack understood, was to take stock. Comparing the result with the takings and cost of sales would give him an idea of whether his staff were being honest. That is, it would do if he did not make excuses for any discrepancy, which he usually did. In more professionally run operations, managers and others were frequently dismissed if there was a stock shortfall. These were regular at Arthur's, but nobody had lost their job. Jack gave food and drink away to friends frequently and since no cash was put through the till for this, the stocktake results were usually meaningless. But Jack persisted *pour encourager les autres*, as his housemaster at Worchester used to say.

After two hours, the stocktake was complete and George had calculated that there was, as usual, a small shortfall.

'Jane, you will be pleased to hear that there is a surplus and so we can have a couple of bottles of wine on the house.'

'Eee, I'm right pleased,' intoned Jane, exaggerating her accent.

'There seems to be some spare champagne,' replied George, uncorking a bottle from the fridge. 'And that reminds me of a joke. A Yorkshireman who had lost his wife went to a local engraver and asked him, "Please could you engrave *Lord, she was thine* on my wife's headstone?" "Yes, of course," said the engraver, "it will be ready tomorrow." So the following day the man went to inspect the headstone. It read *Lord, she was thin*. The man said, "Well, that's no good; you've left off the 'e'." "Oh, I'm sorry," said the engraver, "come back tomorrow and I'll have it fixed." So the man returned the next day. The headstone read, *Eee, Lord, she was thin*.'

Even without the benefit of a drink Jane laughed almost uncontrollably. Later, after a bottle of champagne, which she drank mostly herself, everything to her seemed funny.

'Eh, George,' she slurred, leaning back in one of the comfortable armchairs in the bar, out of sight from the window. 'Would you like to appraise me...? Jack seemed keen, but I told him no... Know what I mean...?'

Jane grabbed George's shirt and pulled him towards her so hard that he landed on top of her, the chair fell backwards and the two of them tumbled onto the floor. Jane was not a woman to be denied and with the bottom of her skirt already above her waist she plunged her hand down George's trousers with one hand and undid them with the other.

A few minutes later, the lock on the door of the restaurant made its familiar sound of resistance. The door then swung open to let Jack in. Hidden from view on the floor, Jane rearranged her clothes and made a cursory attempt at adjusting her hair, trying to suppress yet another laugh. George tucked his shirt back into his trousers, and quickly put on his shoes.

He walked around the corner towards the front door of the restaurant where Jack was standing looking at the stocktake figures.

'Stock showed the usual shortfall. And I've done Jane's appraisal for you,' he said as he opened the door of the restaurant.

Jack furrowed his brow as George stepped onto the busy street and closed the door behind him.

Soon after seven, Steven Gregson breezed into the restaurant as if he owned it, rather than as if he were applying for a job. He had thick dark straight hair with dark eyebrows and eyes to match. Rings around his eyes betrayed some late nights. But he managed a broad smile, set in a square jaw and full lips. His eyes did not smile with him, though, and so the overall effect on Jack was faintly disconcerting.

Steven already had bold plans for change, the need for which Jack questioned. Arthur's was successful, so why change it? Steve stated bluntly that he would increase the profitability of the restaurant but only if he were permitted to change the formula to the one he knew would work and had worked for him previously.

'What happened to your last restaurant?' asked Jack.

'We had a fire. The insurance company wouldn't pay up and so I lost everything.'

'Why wouldn't they pay?'

'Well, they thought someone might have started the fire deliberately and so they were entitled not to.'

'What bad luck. So you need a job.'

'Yes, I do, frankly. But my work rate is high, most of my old customers will come back and my formula is successful. So you will find that I pay for myself. I understand that you need someone soon because you are opening another place? I can start right away if you like.'

Jack felt uneasy.

'Well, let me think about it. I'll get back to you later in the week.'

Jack had noticed that several people who came into the bar seemed to know Steve. Most of them smiled or waved at him. More than one made remarks that indicated to Jack they thought Steve was taking over. A couple locked their heads together conspiratorially, glancing at both

Jack and Steve. Jack would have liked to have known what they were saying.

*

What an upstart: Jack plainly has no idea at all how to run a restaurant, Steven thought as he left the building. He, Steve, with his experience and connections, his fan club, could improve the profits of that place. He might even let Jack have some of it. But then…? Jack would never realise what was truly going on. Would he? And he'd plainly done no research into what happened to Steve's last place…

Steven knew that he was thought to be too charismatic and handsome. Women were drawn to him. And he knew more about restaurants than Jack. *This is going to be easy*, he thought. *Just need a few things to throw Jack off the scent.* Steven gave a chuckle as he kicked at a pile of leaves and pulled his black coat around his strong frame. He brushed his black hair away from his determined eyes and strode firmly and powerfully ahead.

*

Jack was feeling vulnerable. He thought Steve might be right for Arthur's and yet he wasn't sure he could trust him. Why did he always need to turn to women at times like this? he wondered. For affirmation of his manhood perhaps? For approbation when he doubted himself?

Mona's daughter Sian was on duty at Arthur's that day. So that evening Jack invited her and one of his other staff, Tabitha, to Romulus and Remus, a nightclub popular

50

with other eighteen- to twenty-five-year-olds in town. And there was a reason for inviting Sian with someone else. If his idea for what might take place at the end of the evening came to fruition, Sian would not want to tell her mother. The possibility that an adolescent fantasy might be his undoing touched only the smallest recess of Jack's maturing mind.

The nightclub throbbed to the music of Human League and Kool & the Gang. Purple and dazzling white light synchronised with the rhythm and fused with a heady mixture of rum and Coke so that later in the evening the two girls appeared to be dancing in a trance. Jack could only make himself heard by putting his mouth right up to the girls' ears and shouting. They smiled at him together and exchanged glances when he used that excuse to nibble both their earlobes.

'I've got a present for you both,' he yelled.

'What is it?' they both mouthed.

Jack felt inside the pocket of his leather jacket, which he had draped over the back of a chair. He carefully pulled out a small transparent plastic bag and cupped it into his hand. He showed his palm to the girls, making sure that nobody else could see. They shrieked when they spotted the white powder inside the bag and grabbed it eagerly from Jack.

'Wow, thanks. See you in a minute,' they bellowed as they headed off to the Ladies, stumbling on their high heels as they went.

The girls squeezed into the same cubicle and locked the door. They carefully laid two parallel lines of the cocaine on the top of the lavatory cistern and tidied them up with the edge of a credit card. Tabitha rolled two £5 notes into tight tubes and handed one to Sian.

'On three,' she whispered. 'One, two, three.'

Both heads ducked simultaneously with the fivers inserted into their nostrils and snorted both lines, inhaling deeply before stifling sneezes. Their faces flushed and they burst out of the cubicle with a mutual determination to seduce Jack, as he had hoped.

They were almost identically dressed in silver: glittering, tight, short dresses of the type that Jack's father referred to as pelmets. They approached Jack together and pulled him to the dance floor. With a girl latched to each hip, they ground their pelvises into his legs in time to "Don't You Want Me?" as they sang along with Human League, looking at Jack. The looks in their eyes were those of women rather older and more experienced than their eighteen years as they flung their arms backwards, legs either side of Jack's, so that Jack had to hold them both around the waist to stop them falling.

As the music stopped, Tabitha shouted in Jack's ear, 'Why don't you take us back to your place?'

Without answering, Jack picked up his jacket, took them both by the hand and headed to the exit. Jack had remained sober and not taken cocaine. It had been given to him by Jonas beside the swimming pool at one of his wild house parties. Jonas had wanted to pair him off with Rachel and had hoped that Jack taking coke would make his task easier. But Jack had simply kept it. And Jonas failed in his task.

Sian and Tabitha sat on top of each other on the passenger seat of Jack's MGB, Tabitha astride Sian, facing her. Tabitha's dress was hitched up to her waist so that Jack could see the left cheek of her bottom, framed by the black silk lace of her tiny knickers. Thin sides, said George, was always a good sign. Big knickers, not so much.

'Look, Jack,' said Tabitha, vigorously kissing Sian on the lips, and searching her mouth with her tongue. Jack tried, not always successfully, to keep his eyes on the road. They both sang loudly to "Don't You Want Me?".

Once in the flat, Jack opened a bottle of champagne, which the girls proceeded to drink straight from the bottle, pouring the foaming liquid into each other's mouths and then Jack's. They both started singing again, this time looking at Jack and dancing closely and intimately with each other. They hugged and kneaded each other's bottoms, began to kiss each other and fell onto the sofa. Jack sat on the edge of the table watching them as Tabitha pulled off Sian's dress and then stood to remove hers. Neither girl was wearing a bra, but both were wearing black G-strings. Tabitha bent over Sian to remove hers, removed her own, and leaned over with her back to Jack. She knelt in front of Sian, who was still on the sofa, opened her legs with both hands, dropped her mouth directly onto Sian's crotch and began to lick her gently. Sian threw her head back, her lips slightly open, and closed her eyes. She then opened them and looked at Jack, while Tabitha continued to lick her. Jack could bear it no longer. Leaving his shirt on, he took off his shoes and socks and pulled off his trousers and underpants in one movement. Sian smiled as she saw his manhood and looked at Tabitha. Jack knelt behind her, gently pulled one cheek of her bottom aside and pushed inside her. Tabitha came quickly. Sian sounded as though she was about to as well and so Jack lifted Sian's legs to lay her on the sofa and mounted her. Tabitha knelt over Sian kissing her lips and caressing her firm small breasts with both hands. When she took one of Sian's nipples gently in her mouth and softly rubbed her with her right hand, both Jack and Sian came and the three of them collapsed on top of each other, their sweat mingling.

George opened the door to the sitting room, said blandly, 'Sorry, folks,' and closed it again. Jack heard his bedroom door shut, but not before he also heard a muffled chuckle.

*

To supplement his income, Steve traded second-hand cars. Generally they needed work done prior to being sold on to trusting customers. Indeed, he preferred such vehicles. The profit margins were greater, after all. Steve's approach to the refurbishment of cars ready for resale was purely cosmetic. He had his own small garage. It was equipped with a simple paint-spray gun and a set of other old tools. Much rust was removed from decaying car bodies, covered with glass fibre and hidden from view by thick layers of paint. No warranty was provided and they were sold as seen. 'Suckers,' Steve would chuckle to himself. Of course, as his activities would be a breach of the terms of his bankruptcy, his trustees knew nothing of his supplementary income.

He was unconcerned about his reputation as a car dealer as he did not expect his customers to return. And they seldom connected him with his restaurant. Cars would frequently not proceed more than a few miles before boiling over. But there was no comeback on Steve.

*

Amongst the usual junk mail, the postman delivered two brown envelopes. The first contained the expected letter from Barclays Bank confirming to Jack that the bank would offer him a loan of £14,000 to buy Jason's on the terms discussed. The second was a letter from Avon and Somerset police giving details of his alleged driving offence and inviting him to confirm that he was the driver. Jack knew that because he had nine points on his licence, he would need to defend himself in court if he were to have any hope of keeping it.

He had asked around about Steven. Almost all the opinions were positive. Steve would keep the restaurant full and had the experience to run the place without Jack's involvement. But a couple of remarks puzzled him: "Steve will make Arthur's his" and "We were never quite sure what really happened at his last place".

But plans for the acquisition of the next restaurant were moving quickly and so, pushing his doubts from his mind, Jack resolved to confirm his job offer to Steven.

CHAPTER 4

As the red second hand swept to twelve, at exactly ten o'clock, a side door opened and an elderly-looking man wearing what looked like faded Oxford subfusc asked those present to all stand. Three magistrates shuffled into the court and mounted the dais as if there were insufficient space between their long desk and the chairs behind. Jack noted two women and one man. Mr Prendergast, his ruddy-faced solicitor, had warned him that if he were asked to take the stand, he should be respectful and on no account flirt with any of the magistrates, no matter how amenable they might seem. There was no risk on this occasion. Of the two women on the bench, one reminded him of his matron at prep school, complete with whiskers and an ill-fitting featureless dress, and the other looked like a traffic warden. Small, tight mouth, sunken cheeks, large glasses and short mid-brown hair.

The courtroom smelled faintly of cheap disinfectant. Jack tried not to imagine what sweaty criminal backsides had occupied his seat in the weeks preceding his own trial today. The varnished wood felt slightly damp and sticky. The side of his chair and the front of the desk were roughened by the fingernails of tense occupants, with grimy patches where nervous hands had clasped. Chewing gum filled some of the cracks under the desk in front of him; some was squashed on the floor, round lumps of anxiety.

As Mr Prendergast expected, Jack was initially asked to confirm his name and address. The details of his traffic offence were read to the court and Jack was asked how he pleaded.

'Guilty,' said Jack sheepishly.

'Sit down, please, Mr Mayhew,' said the chairman of the bench, a slim middle-aged man with penetrating blue eyes. As the prosecution barrister outlined the case for the Crown, Jack noticed with guarded relief that he seemed not only young, but inexperienced. When the barrister had finished his brief submission the chairman of the bench intoned, 'Mr Prendergast,' inviting Jack's solicitor to speak.

'Sir, my client is truly sorry for committing this offence. Although he has pleaded guilty he wishes you to know, in mitigation, that his view of the traffic light was obstructed by a lorry. As you now know, he has nine points on his licence and so he risks losing it. I am here today to plead exceptional hardship and so to ask you to be lenient on my client in your decision in relation to sentence.'

The chairman of the bench gave Jack a long stare over the top of his spectacles.

'Sir, my client is an entrepreneur who has created jobs in the area. He currently employs twenty-five people in his restaurant, Arthur's, here in Bath.'

Jack looked uncomfortably across at his solicitor. Arthur's only had twelve staff and Prendergast had not asked him how many he employed.

'He uses his car every day to buy provisions such as meat and vegetables for sale in the restaurant. Were he to lose his driving licence he would not be able to carry out this important duty and so his restaurant would fail, leaving a trail of local creditors. Twenty-five people would lose their jobs.'

Jack felt even more uncomfortable. He had never used his car to buy meat or vegetables and he had not told his solicitor that he had. They were always delivered. Still, the thought of Jack driving his convertible MG with the hood down stacked high with vegetables would no doubt be cause for much mirth back home, whatever the result in court.

'And so I ask the court respectfully for leniency. Indeed, in the public interest, I hope you will agree with me that a stiff fine would be more appropriate.'

'Has the Crown anything to say?' asked the chairman.

The prosecuting barrister shook his head.

'Very well. We shall adjourn to discuss this.'

The man in the Oxford subfusc woke up and announced, 'All rise,' as those with the power in their hands shuffled their way back through the now open door. Mr Prendergast, who now had rather more dandruff on the collar of his crumpled suit than when he arrived in court, gave Jack a cheerful, red-faced grin.

*

'Now Jason's is open and Steve has established his new restaurant on your premises I'm going back to London.' George's voice crackled a little as it emerged from the dirty phone pressed to Jack's ear in a side room at the court. 'I've been offered a job bond dealing that I think I am going to accept.'

'Well done, pal,' Jack replied. 'I knew you'd go back sometime. But I thought you might return to academia... Anyway, thanks for all your help...' Jack paused. 'I'm not sure I like your implication though.'

'What?'

'That Steve has fixed up his own restaurant in mine. What do you mean?'

'Well, you were warned. He has changed the menu as you know and made some decor changes that you agreed. Are you certain you've done the right thing? Steve strikes me as a little too sure of himself. And the circumstances of the demise of his last restaurant seem a little odd, don't you think? The place is regularly full but with people who seem to know him. They generally think the place is his.'

'We all have our ups and downs, George. It seems to me Steve had some bad luck. He is well known and knows what he is doing. I'm not too bothered because the takings are at least as high as they were when I was there and the staff bill is about the same. The last stocktake showed a small loss but nothing more than usual.'

'Well, I leave at the end of this week. I would keep a close eye on the place if I were you.'

'You're not me, mate. Relax. It will all be fine.'

As Jack put down the phone, he resolved to pay

some unexpected visits to Arthur's and take stock more carefully.

*

'All rise,' said the man clothes-hanging the subfusc. The magistrates shuffled back into court, this time wearing some stern expressions on their faces.

Doesn't look good, thought Jack.

The chairman of the bench was about to speak when the prosecuting barrister stood and said, 'Sir, I beg to inform you that my clerk has passed me some new evidence which I feel has a bearing on this case. Although the defendant has pleaded guilty and you have adjourned to consider sentence, the Crown believes that you should hear this evidence.'

The two women wingers shook their heads whilst the chairman of the bench replied, 'Mr Saunders, I know this is one of your first appearances at court but you should know that this is very irregular. Nonetheless, you may proceed.'

'We have been passed an anonymous note from someone claiming to be an employee of the defendant's and signed by one other stating that he or she believes that the defendant had been drinking alcohol shortly before the offence was committed. In view of this we respectfully remind the court that disqualification for this offence is mandatory and that they may impose a driving ban of perhaps two years.'

Mr Prendergast rose to his feet. 'Sir, this is inadmissible. May we have a short adjournment so that I can discuss this hearsay with my client?'

'Indeed you may. The court will adjourn for fifteen minutes.'

Mr Prendergast motioned to Jack to follow him out of the court. When they were in a small anteroom he said, 'Don't worry, Jack, the court should not accept this as evidence. It is merely hearsay. But I have two questions. Firstly, is this true? And secondly, have you upset some of your staff?'

Jack looked uneasy. 'Well, the answer to the first question is absolutely not. It was about ten o'clock in the morning when I was caught and I had had nothing to drink since the night before. As far as your second question is concerned, well, I don't think so. Aside from the chef, who is French and regularly drunk himself, all my staff are women and I think I am on very good terms with all of them. Look, it would be a disaster for me if I were to lose my licence for any time at all, let alone two years.' But Jack couldn't help wondering whether his enthusiasm for the opposite sex had had some unintended consequences.

'I assumed that would be your answer, but I wanted to check before I tell the court.'

What you have told the court already had no resemblance to the truth, so why break what I assume is the habit of a lifetime? thought Jack.

'Sir,' continued Mr Prendergast, once they were back inside the court, 'my client would like to assure the court that he had not had a drop to drink for twenty-four hours before the offence and that was only a pint of shandy. The offence was of course committed at ten o'clock in the morning and my client is not in the habit of imbibing any alcoholic beverage until after eight in the evening and never drinks when he is on duty, as he was the night before. I would also remind the court respectfully that this note does not constitute allowable evidence and is by no means sufficient to have the slightest bearing on the case and so should be dismissed.'

'Mr Saunders. Anything to add?'

'No, sir.'

'Very well. The court will take a further fifteen-minute adjournment.'

*

'Steve's,' said a male voice answering the restaurant phone.

'Who's that?' asked Jack.

'It's Steve, Jack. Didn't you recognise my voice?'

'Well, I thought I did but I was a bit taken aback by how you answered the phone. The restaurant is called Arthur's.'

'The thing is, Jack, people are calling the place Steve's and so I'm just going with the flow. The customer is always right, you know…'

'I'd rather you didn't change the name without consulting me,' Jack said, irritated. 'How's it going?'

'Haven't you seen the figures?'

'Yes, but what's behind those?'

'I'm not quite sure what you mean, Jack. It's going well, as I said it would. People seem to like the new menu, and the margins and income are higher than when you were running the place. Please don't tell me you are unhappy with that.'

'There was a stock shortfall.'

'Oh, come on, Jack, you know how unreliable those figures are. And you told me yourself that there was always a shortfall when you were here.'

Yes, because we were giving drink away to friends, thought Jack, but didn't reply as Mr Prendergast re-entered the small anteroom next to the court and pointed at the clock.

'I must go now. I will come and see you soon.'

*

'Mr Saunders, we have considered the additional information that you have submitted to the court. As you are aware, this does not constitute evidence and so we are bound to ignore it.' The chairman turned to Jack and asked him to stand and then to a quietly smiling Mr Prendergast said, 'Mr Prendergast, we have given due consideration to your plea in mitigation. We have considered your client's previous good character and his undoubted contribution to the local economy. We note the risk to the livelihoods of his staff and the knock-on effect to suppliers in the event that his restaurant ceased to trade. But…'

Jack looked over to Mr Prendergast, who was now not smiling.

'…we also note the success of the establishment and the relatively high income of your client. We therefore fine him £350 and endorse his licence with three points. This takes his total to twelve. Having regard to all of the circumstances, however, we shall not disqualify him from driving.'

Jack managed to keep a serious face, despite his inner joy and desire to laugh out loud at the bench's over-estimation of his contribution to the local economy, said, 'Thank you' to the chairman and left the court with Mr Prendergast.

Jack wanted to say something like he was glad he had not had to make the plea in mitigation himself, as even he would not have had the chutzpah to say what his solicitor had done, particularly not on oath, but instead, he gave him a warm smile, shook him by the hand, thanked him and walked tall towards his MG, a free man.

*

Not deterred by what he had heard at the court, Jack decided to celebrate with one of his staff. After all, they liked him, didn't they? And an evening with him was entirely voluntary, wasn't it?

When Jack picked Sandy up after her shift, she was wearing the shortest of skirts, as usual. Her black shirt barely restrained her very ample young braless breasts. Her father, with whom she lived and who was a regular customer at the restaurant, did not approve. But since to dress like this was uniform, his daughter was an employee and he had regular gigs playing the guitar at Arthur's, he wasn't really in a position to complain. He might have complained however, if he knew of Jack's intentions. Sandy was eighteen.

Sandy drank a whole bottle of champagne, which Jack had bought her to reward what he had described as a brilliant last six months' performance. The more she drank, the more her breasts found their way towards the outside of her shirt. She had boasted to the other staff that she didn't often wear knickers and this Jack could not get out of his mind as she fidgeted on her bar stool.

Both floors of the wine bar had been busy, with many customers sitting outside on the pavement in the spring sunshine. But now it was quiet. Mick Jagger belted out 'Satisfaction' and Sandy smiled suggestively at Jack.

'I need to go to the Ladies,' she said. Then she whispered in Jack's ear and put her hand in his. 'Want to come with me?'

Jack stood and looked around him. He saw nobody he knew. He followed Sandy down the winding spiral staircase where a young man craned his neck to look up her skirt. The Ladies were around the corner, down a couple more steps. As Sandy staggered through the outer door towards the first empty cubicle, there was a flush from the one next to it. The door opened as Jack stepped backwards into the corridor. A middle-aged lady strutted past him and gave him an old-fashioned look. Sandy stood at the open door of her cubicle and lifted her skirt towards Jack. Yes, no knickers, just a blonde, tidily trimmed bush.

Jack took one more look around him and then quickly joined Sandy in her cubicle. She was giggling and plainly drunk. She put one leg up on the lavatory bowl. Jack held her naked firm bottom with his left hand and pushed his way into her. Sandy giggled again and gave a little shriek. Jack put his hand over her mouth. She bit his finger but Jack did not dare to remove his hand. Pulling her bottom hard towards him he continued quite roughly until it was over. Sandy slumped on Jack's strong shoulder and he lowered her gently to the lavatory seat. He then straightened his clothing, listened to check there was nobody in the entrance to the Ladies, opened the cubicle door and closed it behind him, leaving Sandy slumped on the seat. As he left the Ladies, two women in their forties were arriving. They looked quizzically at Jack.

'Sorry, wrong loo!' he said.

As Jack climbed the stairs he found himself wondering about his present relationships with women and recalling what George had said about his behaviour. The thought troubled him and so he pushed it out of his mind.

*

Steven Gregson decided to abandon Arthur's for the weekend. After all, he needed time off at Jack's expense, didn't he? Some weeks ago, a customer had offered him the use of his small cottage near Inverness, perhaps to repay Steven for his generous hospitality at Arthur's. With an eye on the cottage, Steven had never given this customer a bill. He sat at the edge of the loch gazing into the pitch-black, still water. This was his favourite spot after dark. Nobody could see him. The midges that irked him during the day had disappeared and the salmon no longer jumped for flies as they headed up the river at the corner of the loch. Stillness.

But Steven's mind was not still. He brooded. The calm of the night no longer assuaged his anger. Why should Jack be successful? What did Jack have that he did not?

What irritated him the most was that Jack had offered to help him when Jack realised that he was bankrupt.

'What makes you think you can help me?' he had asked. 'You don't even know what a trustee in bankruptcy is.'

Alice, Steven's wife, had remarked that he seemed jealous of Jack. Steven had reacted badly. 'You even behave like Macbeth when you are in Scotland,' she had said.

Out, out, brief candle, he thought.

CHAPTER 5

Mona was more mature than the others and so Jack resolved to take her somewhere expensive and sophisticated. And she was Sian's mother. It had long been one of his fantasies to bed both a mother and daughter but he wondered how female jealousies between mother and daughter would work.

Mona seemed pleasantly surprised to be asked out for dinner with Jack, and Jack was pleased that such an attractive woman in her early forties would come out with him, being a dozen or so years younger than her. But Jack was capable of seeming mature for his years when required, and this was one of those times. And of course, women usually thought him to be handsome.

The Close was the most expensive and luxurious restaurant in the area and in a town blessed with a relatively large number of good places to eat. It was dimly lit, which Jack figured would put Mona at her ease in the company of a younger man. Not that he found the few wrinkles around her eyes unattractive. He expected that, like Elizabeth Taylor, she had earned every one of them. He smiled as he remembered George's remark that older women who had been married were so much more desirable, as they had had sex hundreds of times.

The evening crackled with lively conversation. The candlelight played softly on Mona's warm and affectionate face. It was calm and relaxed and there was a sparkle to her shining blue eyes, without a trace of sadness or anxiety. Unlike the women of Jack's age who had a tendency to be shrill, uncertain and overexcited, Mona had a mature yet gentle confidence. Her demeanour was not challenging, unlike some of the others. She laughed readily at Jack's stories and gave him warm smiles, looking directly into his eyes when he asked her about the more personal aspects of her life. Her ex-husband, Sian's father, had been an actor of some note. He was a regular leading man in the movies and so had not been short of opportunities to stray. This he did once too often and Mona threw him out. She was, she confessed to Jack, heartbroken. There had been men since, but nothing serious. She admitted to being choosy and later that George had asked her out the day before, but she had declined. Jack managed to suppress a triumphant clenched fist.

To Jack's surprise, Mona asked him in for coffee when he dropped her off at her rather splendid Regency house. She reminded Jack quickly that Sian was on the late shift at Arthur's and so wouldn't be back for an hour.

'Sian is very protective of me, and, well, you being my boss and hers might make life complicated. So I haven't told her about our date and it would be best if you don't either. Do you agree?'

'Of course. Thanks for the offer, but I think I had better get back to the restaurant to see how the late shift is going. And don't worry, I will keep mum,' said Jack, pleased with his pun but not sure that Mona got it.

'OK. Thank you so much for a lovely evening,' she said, giving Jack a gentle but brief kiss on the lips. 'Goodnight.'

As Jack drove away, pleased that he had played moderately hard to get, he noticed in the mirror that Mona watched the car until out of sight. He drove past Arthur's on his way home as a pizza flew out of the kitchen window followed by the usual set of expletives. Jack decided to drive on.

*

Jack put down his crossword and looked at the staff rota. Mona was not in until the next day but he was keen to see her before then. She was sensitive and warm but had been badly hurt by her husband. She possessed a beauty from which radiated a warning that she was to be handled with care. And Jack noticed he felt something towards her that he had not experienced before. He had treated most of his other girlfriends either as part of a game, or as a conquest, or as the sort of friend with whom you could enjoy a laugh in the pub. But Mona stirred something else in him. She seemed vulnerable and too mature to be caught up with Jack's boorish and insensitive behaviour. One of George's favourite quotes crossed his mind: *Wise men are harmless: for they do no harm, either to themselves or to others.*

After their second date, Mona asked Jack back to her house. It was elegant and well furnished. It made Jack feel his flat was rather too bohemian: shabby student rather than shabby fashionable. He had agreed to come back for coffee but was determined not to push matters too far too quickly. She put on some classical piano music that he recognised and made some coffee in a large porcelain pot.

'Would you like a drink?' she asked.

'Umm, yes, please. What have you got?'

'Silly boy. Most things.'

'Oh, a whisky would be great, please.'

Mona moved over to a large corner cupboard and took down two large and heavy-looking cut-glass tumblers and a bottle of Talisker malt whisky. She had worn a neatly cut black dress that evening which accentuated the curve of her waist and hips. The dress was cut tight into her thighs so that Jack thought he could make out the clasp of some stockings.

'This OK?' she said, gently waving the bottle and raising an eyebrow.

'Lovely. Thanks.'

'Ice?'

'Yes, please.' Mona dropped the ice into the two glasses and poured the whisky without speaking. The open fire burned brightly whilst the sensual first movement of Rachmaninov's second piano concerto soothed Jack into the corner of the sofa. When Mona turned to him, a glass in each hand, he felt both warm and secure. Her smile as she approached made him feel a tenderness to which he was not accustomed.

'What?' she asked smoothly.

'I dunno. I was just thinking how beautiful you look.'

She sat on the deep-pile carpet at his feet and leaned

on the base of the sofa, not touching him. The top of her head moved gently as she talked without looking up. Jack could smell Chanel No. 5. He said something that made her laugh and she placed her left hand on his foot, just for a moment, and then removed it. They fell silent as the music came to a climax. As it did, Mona turned her face towards Jack.

'Do you like this? I think it is very sexy. Orgasmic even,' she added as she turned away.

Jack felt a tension deep inside him and took a breath.

'Yes, I know the piece. And I think I know what you mean.'

He put his right hand on Mona's left shoulder and bent down towards her. She turned to face him and looked unblinkingly into his eyes, lips slightly apart. The front door banged as someone entered the house. A voice called, 'Hi, Mum,' and steps sounded on the staircase.

Mona leaped to her feet and whispered, 'It's Sian. She's gone upstairs but I'm afraid you'll have to leave. Remember, I don't want her to know I'm seeing you. I'm so sorry. Come out this way.'

The words "I'm seeing you" resonated in Jack's ears as Mona led him to the French windows that opened onto the garden.

'Can I see you tomorrow?' whispered Jack as Mona ushered him through the open door.

'Yes, but it will have to be at your flat because Sian may be here. Is that OK?'

'Of course. I think you know where it is,' said Jack. 'Goodnight.' He put his arm gently around Mona's slim waist and pulled her towards him.

'What are you doing out there, Mum?' said Sian from the other end of the room.

'Just letting the cat out, darling,' she replied as Jack disappeared into the shadows, his heart heavy with the effect of his closeness to Mona and his mind anxious at the thought of having to make the flat respectable by the following evening.

*

'Well, Mona has already turned me down once but I have a cunning plan which I intend to put into effect tonight as she is working with me,' said George, stuffing a small plastic bag of white powder into his pocket.

Not cunning enough, thought Jack. And he wished they were not chasing the same woman.

'I don't think plying Mona with Charlie will work, but we shall see,' said Jack with a slightly smug expression on his face.

Jack spent more time cleaning the flat than he had ever done in his life. Washing up, normally piled high in the sink until an absence of clean implements forced some action, was completed. A shop assistant advised Jack on which bath and sink cleaning materials to use and dirty clothes were hidden in a wardrobe. An unopened tin of furniture polish that his mother had given him hopefully three years before was pressed into action and his bedroom mirror was buffed up, just in case.

Jack had decided to cook, as this had worked before. The flat smelled of garlic and herbs and when the doorbell rang, he felt an unaccustomed nervousness. An intoxicating fusion of shining blue eyes, thick blonde hair and Chanel No. 5 greeted Jack at the door. She was wearing a loose-fitting sheer black blouse through which Jack could make out a low-cut black bra and neat breasts. A small dark tartan skirt was held together with a large Highland kilt pin. Before he could ask her to come in, Mona dropped the bag she was carrying and draped her arms around Jack's neck. Pressing her body against his, she said, 'Evening, gorgeous.' Their kiss was urgent yet gentle. Mona ruffled Jack's hair as if he were a little boy. He stroked hers as if she were Venus.

After a bottle of Veuve Clicquot, Jack served his pot-roasted chicken. Short red candles lit Mona's face in the way Jack remembered on their first date. He had decanted a bottle of Château Beychevelle an hour earlier and this Mona appeared to appreciate. She swilled the red velvet claret around the glass and looked inquisitively at Jack.

'Tell me about your school days. You mentioned that someone had bullied you.'

'Yes, they did. Tied me to a metal chair and electrocuted me. But I will get even with him one day.'

'I'm sure you will. Were you happy otherwise?'

'Well, I was quite homesick at the beginning. The matron had had polio and wore callipers on her legs and used crutches. I was frightened of her. I later learned she was quite nice but I didn't realise at the time. One day in my first term we were given gooseberries, which I hated. "Goosegogs" we called them. But we had to eat everything we were given. I said I didn't like gooseberries and asked the master in charge if I could leave them. He said no and made me eat them. I was nearly sick with each one.

I can see them in my bowl now, green and slimy, with small brown pips and hairy skin. All the other boys were allowed to go and I sat on my own looking at my bowl, sobbing. When the master came back in he noticed I had not finished and told me again that I could not leave the table until I had. I wiped my eyes hoping he had not seen me crying. When he left the room again, I got out my hanky, wrapped the remaining gooseberries into it and put it, running in juice, into the pocket of my shorts.

'I didn't understand why my parents had left me there. I missed them and asked them if I could come home. We had to write to them every Sunday and in one letter I smudged the ink hoping they would think it was caused by my tears. It didn't work though.'

'That's awful,' said Mona, reaching across the table and holding Jack's hand. She noticed there were tears in Jack's eyes.

'Sorry. I still get a lump in my throat if I talk about it.'

Neither of them felt like eating the chocolate pudding that Jack had made. They were distracted by unvoiced thoughts. Mona got up from the table and without speaking left the room. Jack sat nervously at the table. She then returned and stood in front of him. She pulled off her blouse and stared at Jack with a half-smile, one side of her mouth lifted, almost shy. She held his hand and gently pulled him to his feet. Jack kissed her softly, removed her bra with one hand and led her to his bedroom where he unclipped her tartan skirt and let it fall to the floor. She was naked.

Their lovemaking was tender and slow. Afterwards, they lay, limbs entwined, silent, unmoving, moved and warm. Her breath was shallow and sweet, her hair damp with passion and feminine musk. The light from the red bedside lamp emphasised the soft glow of the top of Mona's chest. Jack thought that this was probably the first time he had made love to a woman. The others were girls. And with them it had been just sex.

CHAPTER 6

A gentle autumn gave way to a winter that was particularly harsh. Snow that appeared at once white and blue lay deep on the fields between Bath and Bristol. Long shadows softened the already gentle slopes of the hillsides. Sheep huddled together, grateful for their dirty winter coats protecting them from the icy east wind that seemed to have lost none of its severity on its way across the country from Siberia. Jack had to drive his MG carefully on the sometimes glassy roads, the car not being built to deal with the treacherous conditions. *Time for a change*, thought Jack.

Jason's was usually packed with youthful customers who appreciated the loud, pulsating music of the day. But although it was profitable, the surplus disappeared into supporting Arthur's, which, since the summer, seemed to be suffering a downturn. Income had dropped, yet staff wages had not. Steve's explanations over the last few weeks had puzzled Jack and so he was on his way to pay a surprise visit to Arthur's. It was a Thursday evening, when turnover had recently been less than on Thursdays the previous year.

Jack could not find a place to park outside the restaurant. Expensive cars lined the street on both sides. He left his MG at the bottom of the road and, pulling the collar of his long black woollen coat around him, walked purposefully up towards the restaurant on the opposite side of the road. The smell of garlic and the sound of gentle music filled the air. From his position behind a tree, Jack could see that Arthur's was packed with people. Some were standing near the bar waiting for tables. He caught sight of Steve glad-handing some prosperous-looking men and flirtatiously kissing the cheeks of their glamorous companions, making appreciative remarks about their Chanel handbags. Jack changed his mind about going in. Instead, he would wait for the turnover figures to arrive the following Monday. Given what he saw, they should show a large increase on the previous week.

Instead of surprising Steve at the restaurant, he decided to risk surprising Mona at her house. He knew her daughter Sian was working that evening and so with luck Mona would be in and pleased to see him. She was – and dressed only in a loose kimono. Although he had seen her the previous weekend, she flung her arms around him as if they had not been together for several weeks. She smelled faintly of soap and her thick blonde hair was damp.

'I've just had a bath and was going to have an early night,' she said, blue eyes flashing, grinning and tossing her hair.

'Suits me,' replied Jack as he pulled her up the stairs.

Some minutes later, as they lay relaxed and enveloped in each other's arms, Jack asked, 'Do you remember I told you that during my trial there was a note that the prosecution handed to the magistrates which claimed I had been drinking when I jumped the red light?'

'I do. What about it?'

'Well, I never discovered who wrote it. Do you think there is any way you could find out? I'm uneasy about Arthur's. I can't put my finger on it and I'm wondering if there is any connection.'

'That's not something you normally have trouble with…'

'Ha, ha. Thank you, but what do you think?'

Mona unwrapped herself from Jack and made her way towards the bathroom. He admired the contours of her long back, the shape of her waist and her small, tight muscular behind.

'I'll ask around,' she said, turning and smiling at Jack as she closed the door behind her.

*

The post arrived before Jack left for Jason's on Monday morning. The usual large white envelope nestled amongst the brown ones containing bills. The figures from Arthur's for the previous week made Jack lean back on the hall windowsill in surprise. All the takings were down on the previous month and in particular the income for the Thursday he had visited was half what it had been the month before. But he had seen that the restaurant had been full.

Jack picked up the phone.

'Steve here, how can I help?'

'Steve, I've seen the figures for last week. Tell me about Thursday.'

'As you can see, it wasn't a great night.'

'But I walked past that evening and noticed the place was full.'

There was a pause.

'Could you hold on a second, Jack? There's someone at the door.'

Steve seemed to cover the phone with his hand and Jack could hear a muffled conversation.

'Have you been spying on me, Jack?'

'What do you mean?'

Steve's tone was abrupt and aggressive. 'You know what I mean. Why didn't you say you were coming? And why didn't you come in?'

'Please don't make me feel guilty about walking past my own restaurant. It *is* my restaurant, remember.'

'The place may have been full, Jack, but people aren't spending the money. They go for cheap items of food and hardly drink anything.'

'They didn't look like cheapskates to me.'

'Sorry, Jack, but I have to go. There are customers to serve.' The line went dead.

Steve stood motionless in his empty office, staring at the figures on his desk. Jack's questioning needed to be stopped. An idea took shape in Steve's head.

He did not know much about the mechanics of the cars he cosmetically refurbished. But he understood enough to know where the brake pipes were fitted.

'Hi, Jack,' said a warm voice on the phone.

'Hi, Mona. Glad you've called.'

'Why? You sound gloomy.'

'I just had a worrying conversation with Steve. Not only was he quite rude but he claimed that the reason the sales figures were down on Thursday is because even though the place was full that evening, people aren't spending the money. And I don't believe him.'

'Mmm. Well, there is something else you are not going to like. I think I've found out who was behind that note alleging you had been drinking that found its way into court.'

'Go on.'

'I asked Sian. She said that some of the girls thought that you had treated them badly by, well… I think the expression "humping and dumping them" was used. And she says she thinks they wanted some revenge on you.'

'Who was it?'

'Sian says it was Vicky and Beryl. They both left just before your court case, didn't they?'

Jack tried to hide his awkwardness. He wondered whether Sian had admitted her threesome with him, her and Tabitha.

'And there's more. Sian says that Steve put them up to it.'

Jack let out an audible sigh. 'Why would he do that?'

'Why do you think?'

'Cash would be great if you have it,' said Steven. Of course Paddy had it. It was race week in Cheltenham and although they had watched the racing on a pub television, this table of Irish punters had plainly had a good day. 'I'll tell you what, your bill is five hundred and ninety. Give me five hundred in cash and we will call it quits.' The man whom Steven had called Paddy all evening (even though his name was Seamus) gave a large grin and thrust a fistful of notes into Steven's hand, with a wink. As Steven turned and walked away from the table, he pushed the notes into his pocket and ripped up the bill. Jack would be none the wiser.

*

That Sunday, Jack drove past Arthur's at lunchtime. The sign on the door said

"Closed". He had not agreed to close the restaurant on any day, let alone on one of its traditionally busy days. Jack parked his car opposite, walked over the road and peered through the window. At the back of the restaurant was Steve, serving food to some people Jack recognised as Steve's wife and family.

Trying to control his temper, Jack walked into the restaurant.

'Hello, Jack,' said Steve, looking shifty.

'Why is the restaurant closed?'

'Well, takings have been poor lately on Sunday and so it is hardly worth the staff coming in. So I said they could have today off.'

Jack stood unspeaking while Steve's wife stopped

cutting up her son's beef, turned to Jack and smiled broadly.

'Hi, Jack. How are you?'

'Oh, and you said I could feed myself, as part of my salary,' Steve chipped in, before Jack could answer.

'I said you could feed yourself, but—'

'Well, I'm not having anything and so I am giving it to my family.'

'So I see. I will see you next week,' said Jack as he turned and left the restaurant, angry, bewildered and unsure of his next move.

*

The following day, Jack picked up the phone to the restaurant. Sian answered.

'Hi, Sian. Is Steve there?'

'No, he hasn't come in yet. Can I give him a message?'

'Yes, please. If he does come in.' Jack immediately regretted the implication. 'When he comes in, please tell him that there is going to be a stocktake this Friday. Tell him we are bringing our year end forward and so we need one now. Thanks.'

Jack dialled the external stocktakers.

'Could you put me through to James, please? It's Jack Mayhew.'

'Putting you through.'

'Jack, what can I do for you?'

'James, I know our regular stocktake isn't due for a while but I'd like you to arrange for one this Friday. And please could you make it especially thorough.'

'Of course. We shall be there first thing Friday morning, before the first customers arrive. Is everything OK?'

'I'm not sure… Thanks.'

*

Jack wasn't very keen on Cat Stevens, but Mona was and so he put *Catch Bull at Four* on his turntable while he prepared dinner for two in his flat. Plenty of red wine and herbs reduced around two whole partridges, a gift from one of his pals who had been shooting in North Yorkshire. Jack hoped that one day he would be able to accept his friend's invitation to join him, but he was unable to afford such an extravagant day, for the moment at least.

'I've arranged an additional big stocktake for tomorrow. I'm sure Steve is up to something and I want some ammunition,' said Jack, gazing at Mona who was sprawled on the floor, glass of white wine in hand.

Cat Stevens sang "Can't Keep It In" and Mona tapped her feet.

'That reminds me, Jack, do you want to tell me a bit about your murky sexual past?'

'Nothing to tell really. Anyway, it was before you came into my life.'

'Please, at least tell me that it didn't involve Sian. I'm thinking that I should tell her about you and me and I don't want to find that you have done a mother and daughter number.'

'I'd better get that,' said Jack, saved by the bell of the telephone.

A male voice said, 'Mr Mayhew?'

'Yes.'

'This is Detective Inspector Burt. I am phoning about the fire at your restaurant in town earlier today.'

'Fire? What fire?'

'Didn't you know there had been a fire at – what was it called – Arthur's?'

'No, I did not. Why didn't somebody tell me?'

'I can't answer that, sir. We assumed that your manager, Mr Gregson, would have told you. There has been extensive damage, I'm sorry to say.'

Jack looked at the floor and then at Mona. 'Was anyone hurt?'

'No. According to the fire brigade, the building was empty at the time. And according to them it seems to have started in the stockroom. Most of the wine and food has been destroyed. But the reason I am speaking to you is that they also think that the fire was started deliberately.' The detective paused. Jack gripped the phone. 'Can we come and see you, or would you prefer to come to the police station…? Mr Mayhew…?'

'I'll come to you,' said Jack almost in a whisper as he replaced the receiver.

'Steve,' he said as he slumped on the sofa.

*

Bath Police Station did not share the gracious Georgian architecture of most of the rest of the town. Jack didn't like sixties brutalist design although he somehow felt it was appropriate for the purpose of the building in which he now sat. Light blue plastic stacking chairs lined the rear wall of the waiting room and there was a smell of institutional floor-cleaning fluid. The blinds at the window were faded and hung haphazardly. The door, which had wired glass at the window, opened to reveal a man in a dark suit with worn shiny trousers.

'Mr Mayhew?'

'Yes?'

'I am Detective Inspector Burt. Would you come with me, please?'

DI Burt's office was poky. A second man, introduced to Jack as another police officer, sat on the far side of the small desk, which had a chair in front of it where Jack was invited to sit.

There was something that looked like the sort of tape recorder that Jack had seen on the television on the side of the desk.

'Sir, would you mind if we recorded our conversation, please? It is so much easier than taking notes,' asked the detective.

'Of course not. I've got nothing to hide.'

'Good. Thank you.'

The other policeman switched on the machine, gave the date and the names of those present and smiled at Jack.

'Mr Mayhew, how has Arthur's been doing lately?'

'Fine, thanks. Why do you ask?'

'We have heard that it has not been doing particularly well.'

'How did you know that?'

The police officers looked at Jack, smiling.

'Well, actually, income has been down. I have been rather worried about it.'

'I'm sure you have,' said the detective.

'Look, I don't know why you are asking me this. I thought you were going to help me find out who did this.'

'That is what we are trying to do, sir. Where were you earlier today?'

'I've been at my other restaurant, in Bristol.'

'Jason's.'

'Yes, that's right. And then I went back to my flat in town here.'

'At what time did you arrive and leave Jason's?'

'I got there at about 9 a.m. and left at about six, to go back to my flat.'

'Yes, that's where we called you. Are you sure you were at Jason's all that time?'

'Yes, why?'

'Well, we have information that you went to Arthur's at about 8.30 a.m. and left at about 9.30 a.m. That's right, isn't it? And the fire was first spotted at nine forty-five.'

'No, it is not right. And what sort of information do you have?'

'The fire brigade says the fire was started deliberately. It started soon after you left the building. And the restaurant is in some financial difficulty. Have you anything to say?'

Jack looked blankly at the police officer, feeling bewildered.

'Jack Mayhew, I am arresting you on suspicion of arson. Anything you say may be used in evidence…'

*

'Mona, I've been arrested. Do you know any solicitors specialising in crime apart from that chap who defended me on my driving offence?'

'What did you say? You can't have been. What for?'

'The police think I set fire to Arthur's. They say they have evidence that I was there this morning, just before the fire started. Someone has obviously set me up and I have a good idea who it might be.'

'No, I don't know any of those sorts of solicitors. I don't have your criminal tendencies.'

'That's not funny, Mona. If I can't prove my innocence I might go to jail. Could you call Mr Prendergast for me and ask him to come to Bath Police Station. The police are keeping me here until my solicitor arrives. They seem to think that I will leave the country. I have to go now. This isn't a private phone and my money is about to run out.'

The line went dead and Jack was left on his own in a small bare room. After what seemed about two hours, the door opened and a uniformed police officer ushered in Mr Prendergast. He was wearing the same shabby suit that he had on the last time they met and looked not only as though he had not washed his hair since then but as if he had been up most of the previous night.

'What have you been doing now, young man?'

Jack hated being called "young man".

As Jack opened his mouth his solicitor said, 'Look, the police are not entitled to keep you here. I've got you released and I will get bail granted formally in the morning. Please tell me you are innocent.'

Jack looked at him, open-mouthed.

'Yes, I thought so. Now come with me to my office and tell me your version of events, and who you think may have set you up, and indeed set light to your restaurant, if that is not the same person.'

*

'Jack, the staff at Jason's have supported your alibi as to your whereabouts on Thursday and the police have dropped the charges against you,' said Mr Prendergast down the phone. 'Furthermore, I have got them to tell me who effectively accused you. You were right, it was Steve Gregson. I think you may find that they now direct their attention to him – if they can find him, that is. Nobody has seen him since Wednesday evening and his wife says she doesn't know where he is. That probably explains why you have not been able to get hold of him either. Of course, nobody has been at the restaurant since the fire, except for the fire brigade and the police.'

'Thank you,' said Jack, putting down the phone and slumping into the nearest chair.

The phone rang again. Mr Prendergast said, 'By the way, the police were very interested in what I told them about the sales figures, and Steve's behaviour. They were particularly interested when I told them that you had arranged a stocktake to be carried out the day after the fire. Do you think that Steve thought you were on to him and so destroyed the stock, thereby destroying the evidence that he was on the fiddle?'

'Could be.'

'Anyway, I have got an insider at the police station who has promised to keep me informed. They are not supposed to but they don't call me Clouseau for nothing, you know.'

'Inspector Clouseau was a policeman, not a lawyer.'

'Was he? Oh well.'

'And a buffoon,' said Jack after he had hung up.

Jack had another problem to contend with as a result of the closure of Arthur's. He was having difficulty paying his bills. Things were already tight before the fire, but now that he had no income he could not pay his creditors. And the insurance company would not pay out whilst there was a suspicion of arson. He had called the bank, but they would not extend his overdraft any further.

*

A pair of pliers would be enough. Perhaps with a wire cutter. The first two nights that Steve observed Jack's car, it was parked on a hill. Steve's simple plan would obviously not work in those circumstances. On the third night it was parked on the flat and, importantly, on a dark stretch of road with no street lights. And no moon.

Steve waited until after three o'clock in the morning, when the population of Bath was safely out of sight and nightclub traffic had largely passed. Lovers in the back seats of cars had deserted the lane. Rain pelted the dark street. Steve decided that should there be a passer-by, they were less likely to stop, because of the late hour and the rain. If they did, Steve had his excuse ready. "Just dropped my keys." And a cheery wave of thanks. The lonely lane was deserted.

Pulling up the hood of his jacket and straightening his gloves, Steve lay on his back and pulled himself under the front of the car. He felt for the first brake pipe. It severed easily and brake fluid dribbled on to his already wet face. Steve smiled. The front nearside wheel of the car sat in a puddle. Muddy rainwater and leaves soaked into his collar and smeared the side of his face as he cut the second brake pipe. Steve then retreated to the relative shelter of a nearby tree and looked around for signs of life. A police car raced past the end of the lane. *Go catch some proper criminals*, thought Steve.

The two rear brake pipes were cut more easily and so Steve was soon away from the car and walking towards his own, parked half a mile away. *Job done*, he thought.

*

Although the sun now shone brightly the next morning, the roads were still wet. The lights were all green as Jack passed through the town and out to the long winding hill that led into the countryside. Rodrigo's guitar concerto reminded him of Arcadian days at Oxford. As the second movement started, he turned up the volume. Turning the wheel to the right he gave the brakes a slight squeeze. They seemed soft. The car gained speed as it made its way swiftly down the hill. Jack moved the car onto the right-hand side of the road to overtake a lorry. As he did so a bus appeared from a side street and so Jack pushed the brake pedal to slow the car to move back to the left. The brake pedal hit the floor. The car continued to speed up down the hill towards the bus. Wrestling with the steering wheel,

Jack managed to squeeze between the bus and the front of the lorry. The bend in the road tightened. Jack tried to straighten the car so as to follow the bend and jabbed at the useless brakes again. The rear tyres shrieked as the MG veered to the right and then to the left towards a tree. Events slowed in Jack's mind to a fraction of their actual pace, but at sixty miles per hour, the tree loomed large towards the car. The MG glanced off the side of the tree, through a hedge and turned over onto its back, spinning violently on the wet grass as it did so.

Silence.

*

Mona's face appeared out of focus to Jack, as though in a dream. She mouthed words that he could not hear. Eventually both the image and the words became clearer. She smiled and tightened her grip on Jack's hand.

'Thank God,' she said.

Jack looked at his unfamiliar surroundings and appeared puzzled.

'You're in Bristol General Hospital,' she said. 'Do you remember what happened?'

'I remember a tree. And the brakes not working.'

'Yes. The police say somebody had cut the brake pipes. Don't worry now. But they want to know who you think might have done that.'

'I can think of one person,' said Jack as he fell back into a deep sleep. In his recurring dream he was a little boy. His mother would smile at him, then turn her back and leave him. Alone. And sad.

Mona offered her daughter a glass of wine and poured herself a large one. The logs in the fire crackled and hissed as the heat drove moisture out of the wood. The smell of pine filled the air and Mona tried unsuccessfully to relax on the edge of the sofa.

'How was your day, darling?' she asked her daughter.

'Oh, OK. But since Arthur's closed it isn't the same. Where I am now isn't nearly as good and I don't like the people as much. Mind you, Steve was a bit creepy. And nobody seems to know where he is. Some people are saying that he probably started the fire because of what happened before.'

'What happened before?'

'Well, I don't know if it is true, but there is a rumour going around that he started a fire in his last restaurant and that he went bust because the insurance company didn't pay him. I don't know why they would do that. I mean, what's the point of insurance if they don't pay you?'

'If they think that you started a fire deliberately they are not going to pay you, are they?'

'Well, I think that's mean.'

'Sian, do you think that Jack knows about this rumour? It might be useful if he does.'

'No idea. Jack doesn't really talk to me these days. He used to.' Sian looked at the floor with a wistful smile that turned into a small pout.

Mona cleared her throat, nervously. 'Darling, there is something I want to tell you. I hope you will think it is good news.'

'Oh, what, Mummy?'

'I have been seeing quite a lot of somebody. I suppose you could call him my boyfriend.'

Sian leaped to her feet, moved over to her mother and wrapped her arms around her. 'Mummy, that's lovely. Is he nice?'

'Well, I obviously think so, otherwise I wouldn't be seeing him, would I?'

'I s'pose not. What's his name?'

'It's Jack.'

Sian laughed. 'Well, that's a coincidence. Same name as the other Jack, but he'd be a bit young for you!'

'No, it *is* Jack.'

'What…? Jack Mayhew…? It can't be. Mummy. It can't be.'

'It is, darling. I thought you would be pleased.'

'Pleased? Pleased?' Sian stood up and quickly left the room, slamming the door behind her.

After a minute, as a mother would, Mona started to climb the stairs towards Sian's room. She heard sobs from inside.

*

'Jack, it is Mr Jones here, from the bank. How are you?'

'Not great, thanks. As you know, things are rather tough.' He decided not to add that someone had also tried to kill him.

'Yes. Jack, I have some bad news, I'm afraid. The bank has decided to call in their loan. I did try to persuade them not to but, well, you know how things are…'

Jack paused. 'Why? I'm sure the insurance company will pay out soon and then all will be well.'

'The trouble is that the figures you have provided over the last few months already gave the bank cause for concern. And now the fire. And, well, we hear that the insurance company won't pay out anytime soon, if ever, due to the possibility of arson. I have had faith in you, Jack, as you know, but, well... I'm sorry, but the bank has to look after its interests. I'm sure you will understand.'

'But I will lose everything I have. My flat, the business, everything. Is there nothing I can do?'

'I'm afraid not. You will need to arrange for someone to value all the assets charged to the bank, unless you would like me to recommend someone, that is.'

'No. That's OK. I'll do it. I'd better go now.' Jack hung up, eyes wide and holding his breath.

The phone rang again.

'Jack, I have some news,' said Mr Prendergast. 'The police say they have two witnesses who saw Steve Gregson go into the restaurant on Thursday morning and leave about fifteen minutes before the fire was first spotted.'

'Who saw him?' asked Jack, rather flatly.

'The manager of the pub opposite and one of his staff. So, Mr Gregson is now the prime suspect. And my man at the fraud squad has given me a possible explanation of why the restaurant was full and yet the income being reported to you and banked had been dropping. Apparently, there's a well-known wheeze in the trade called "skimming". The proprietor gets to pay the overheads and the staff and for all the supplies. The manager puts some of the takings through the till but pockets the rest. One way of telling if this is happening is through a stocktake. If the margins are below what you expect, it gives you a clue. They think that is what Steve Gregson was doing. So it seems that your hunch was right... Jack?'

'Yes, I'm here... It's all a bit late. The bank have called in their loan. I've lost everything. I may even go personally bankrupt.'

'Oh, I am sorry Umm. Well, I had better get on... Bye.'

Jack sat alone in his flat, his head in his hands. The image of Osbourne tying him to the electric chair at prep school crept into his mind. His grandmother had said that perhaps one day Jack would get the opportunity to pay him back. His father had commented that revenge was a dish best served cold. The dish was very cold in relation to his revenge on Osbourne. And now Steve Gregson. Yes, revenge would be best served as a cold dish...

...TWO.

CHAPTER 7

The offices of Jack's accountant, Russell and Co., were housed on the ground floor of a post-war single-storey building with a pebble-dash finish. It had once been painted cream. The dark green wooden window frames needed attention and there were brown stains at the corners where decades of dirt from above had marked the walls. Mr Russell's secretary opened the door to Jack and ushered him towards their shared office. The mid-brown carpet was worn and slightly sticky. There was a smell of damp. Jack was pleased that he did not usually have to visit his accountant, most of the business being carried out by post and telephone. But today he needed advice. He was unsure whether Mr Russell would be able to help, but Jack had nowhere else to turn.

Mr Russell's desk was covered in bulging brown card and lever-arch files, as was the floor. Boxes of similar files were stacked around the walls bearing faded white labels on which were written the names of the clients. Jack noticed two marked "In receivership" and one marked "Compulsory winding-up". *Have I come to this?* he thought.

Mr Russell extended a clammy hand and offered Jack a seat on a chair covered with a stained orange cushion.

'Sorry, Jack, it's not looking good,' he announced, peering at Jack through thick NHS horn-rimmed spectacles.

'How bad is it?' said Jack quietly.

'I'm afraid it is as you feared. Due to the fact that you cannot pay your creditors on time because of the problems at Arthur's you are now technically insolvent. And as the bank want their money back you have no option but to appoint a receiver to liquidate the remaining assets of both restaurants. Although Arthur's is closed due to the fire, you can no longer trade anyway at either restaurant due to the company's insolvency.'

'Where does that leave me?' asked Jack.

'Well, the liquidation of the assets is unlikely to cover all the bank's loan and so they will look to the sale of your flat and then your personal guarantee to make up the difference. How much equity do you have in the flat?'

'Almost none, as I mortgaged it up to the hilt to fund the business. My car is leased and I don't have any other means of paying them off.' Jack paused and then, looking dejected, asked, 'Will they make me bankrupt?'

There was a silence. Mr Russell removed his glasses and a grubby handkerchief from his pocket and tried to give them a shine. While he was doing so he squinted at Jack. 'It is unlikely. They don't like doing that. But to avoid it you will have to come up with an offer in a full and final settlement.'

'How can I do that? I don't have any money. Obviously no bank will lend me any.'

'Well, I'm going to have to let you think about that. In the meantime, you will need to tell the staff that the restaurants are now closed, that therefore they no longer have jobs and that furthermore there is no money for redundancy compensation.' Mr Russell paused again and added, 'I'm sure you understand that as you can't pay me there is not much else I can do for you. Sorry.'

Jack looked at the floor, stood and tried to smile as he shook his ex-accountant's hand. As he turned to leave, Mr Russell said, 'Good luck, Jack. Excuse the pun but you've just caught a cold. Don't worry, you won't die from it.'

That's not a pun and neither is it funny, thought Jack as he closed the door behind him.

Jack's staff took his announcement with a mixture of anger, disappointment and tears. When he admitted that the company had no money to pay their wages, let alone redundancy money, one man took the tape deck from under Jack's nose and marched out of Jason's with it under his arm, muttering darkly as he left. The vegetable supplier arrived with his delivery to be told the news. When he learned that the restaurant was in a limited company and so he would not be paid for the previous month's supply, he looked hopelessly at Jack and forlornly at the large tray of cherries in his hands and murmured something about life not being a bowl of these.

After the announcement at Arthur's, he was left alone in the restaurant as the light faded. Even those girls whom he had thought he had befriended left him there, some muttering to each other that it served him right. Sian looked at him tearfully, said nothing and left with her friend for the pub over the road. Steve, of course, was nowhere to be seen.

Jack had not spoken to Mona since he had been released from hospital, although he had tried to do so, without success. She had not come into Arthur's that day and so Jack tried to call her from the restaurant telephone. The line was dead. He went to the phone box opposite and dialled her number.

'Mona speaking.'

'Hi there,' said Jack, trying to sound less gloomy than he felt. Mona hung up.

Jack craved female company to soothe his anxiety and yearned for someone to give him some sympathy now his world had imploded. He thought that at least Mona would be able to provide that comfort, even though she and her daughter had lost their jobs owing to his misfortune. Why would she not speak to him?

Having the use of a car provided by the insurance company, Jack drove slowly to Mona's house gathering his thoughts. He rang the brass doorbell and waited. He rang it again and continued to wait. Thinking that Mona had gone out in the fifteen minutes between his calling her and arriving at her front door, he turned to leave. At that moment Mona opened the door and stood expressionless on the threshold.

'I don't want to see you any more, Jack,' she said.

An empty shudder tumbled down Jack's already drained body. 'Why?' he almost whispered, trying to behave manfully.

'You know why, Jack. Now please leave me and my daughter alone.'

Mona tried to close the door but Jack gently placed his foot in the way.

'I don't understand. I had hoped you would be sympathetic. I mean, please don't be hard on me for fouling up my business.'

'It's nothing to do with that, you silly boy. And that is what you are.'

'Please let me in and talk to me properly, even if it is to say goodbye.'

Mona sighed and opened the door. Jack tried to kiss her but she turned away.

Jack wasn't offered a seat. Standing in the hallway, Mona said, 'You have broken my daughter's heart. And you have disappointed me. Worse than that, you have betrayed both of us. What sort of woman do you think I am? I had thought you were mature for your age, but I was wrong. You are an arrogant, selfish little boy who needed to be taught a lesson. I'm not surprised you have lost your businesses. You have been naive and foolish. You managed to seduce me and my daughter, and by the sound of it a few other poor girls, because of your unfortunate good looks and what we mistook for charm. I should have known better. Regrettably, my daughter did not.'

'Mona, please,' pleaded Jack.

'I haven't finished yet,' she said. 'Several of the girls have spoken to me about your behaviour. Are you trying to take your revenge on the entire female sex because your mother dumped you at boarding school when you were eight? Or are you just very needy for the same reason, chasing every bit of comfort a woman can give you whenever you can? What on earth happened to that decent, promising young man that George told me about who led the moral way at school and seemed to be admired by everybody?'

Jack winced as he fought his feelings. 'I suppose he tried to wear the mask of adulthood...' he said meekly.

'Well, it's a pathetic mask, Jack, and there is nothing adult about it. My advice to you is to leave this town, as you have upset so many people. And don't you dare contact either me or my daughter again.' Mona lowered her voice, and her head. 'Now get out of my house.'

Jack stretched out his hand to try to touch Mona's arm, but she moved away.

'Mona, I am so, so sorry,' he said, turning and then trudging down the elegant steps towards his car. As he made his way through the traffic and the rain towards what was still, for a short while, his flat, he could hardly see through his tears. Once in his flat, alone, he sobbed, once more the little boy abandoned at school by the woman he loved.

*

Jack parked his car at the end of the road where Mona lived, as he had every day for a week, and waited, hoping for a glimpse of her. Sometimes he tried to concentrate on a crossword to help to pass the time, keeping an eye on the road in front of him. The previous day he had caught sight of her. He had thought she had seen him and crossed the road to avoid him but he couldn't be sure. Jack looked in the car mirror. He was pale, his cheeks sunken and his hitherto bright blue eyes looked dull and vacant. For the first second after he awoke each morning he felt fine. Then his true feelings came crashing into his psyche like a tidal wave, crushing his enthusiasm for life. He curled up in a ball and tried to return to the oblivion from where he'd come. When sleep did not anaesthetise him, he lay awake but unable to get out of bed. At night, fuelled by whisky, he resisted his bed as to sleep would bring him closer to the morning feeling of despair. He no longer listened to music, as to do so reminded him of Mona. He had no work to distract him and so he lay on his sofa for hours on end watching daytime television. As most of his friends were his staff, whom he had either emotionally abused or who had lost their livelihoods at his hands, he was deserted by them. He felt he could cope with losing his business and his money as they might one day be replaced. But the loss of Mona had crushed him.

Jack had taken to ignoring the telephone, leaving the answerphone to take messages, to which he seldom replied. On the morning George telephoned, Jack was curled up in bed hoping the world would pass him by and not heap further vengeance upon him. The blackness was thick in his mind, but through it he heard George's sympathetic voice. His was a familiar voice that he had known almost all his life, reassuring, soothing even. Jack could not hear George's message, but he felt inclined to return his call later that day, when the morning gloom had lifted slightly.

'Hi, Jack,' George said brightly but slightly hesitantly. 'I thought you had died.'

A pause. 'Well, sometimes I feel as though that would be an option,' replied Jack weakly.

'Mmm, you don't sound great. I thought I would come and visit whilst you still have somewhere for me to stay. Sorry, that was insensitive. This weekend any good?'

'Sure. I've nothing much on, if that's what you mean.'

'OK. Cheer up. This too shall pass, as my mother used to say.'

When George arrived, he was alarmed by what he saw. No longer the image of a Greek god, Jack was drawn and thin. His previously luxuriant blond hair was unwashed and matted. His eyes appeared to have sunk into their sockets and had dark rings around them. His normally upright and slightly swaggering gait had lapsed into a stoop. His clothes were frayed and baggy, rather than the sharp ones he habitually wore before.

George tried to hide his shock. During the weekend it emerged that Jack's apparent depression was only partly associated with the loss of his business. Losing Mona had diminished him to a point George did not think possible.

'I am guessing that Mona was not just another conquest,' said George, looking Jack in the eye. Jack nodded.

'And the other girls… you know… None of them will speak to me. Not just because I was stupid enough to mismanage things so that they lost their jobs, but, well, they obviously talked to each other about my behaviour… with them…'

'Well, I did try to tell you. At the risk of quoting Greek philosophers at you again, remember Seneca? *Everything that fills up tragedies, everything that overturns cities and kingdoms, is the struggle of wives and mistresses.* It's a maxim in the City that if you shag the payroll you are asking for trouble. And actually, Jack, it isn't you. That wasn't the behaviour I had come to know and respect. I should have tried harder to deter you.'

Jack raised an eyebrow at George, thinking: *Hypocrite*, but said, 'Did you know Steve?'

'What do you mean?'

'Did you know Steve before you mentioned him to me as a possible manager? And did you know he was a crook?'

'No and no. Of course not. I'm your friend, remember?'

'Sorry. I think I've become paranoid. Seems like the whole world is against me…'

'Sure. I understand. But I was your friend then and I'm your friend now. What we have to do is get you somewhere to live after the bank have taken the flat, which you told me could be as soon as next week, get you some work and some cash and, dare I say, a woman. That always cheers you up.' George looked squarely at Jack. 'Here's a grand. Please, take it.'

'No, I can't take your money.'

'Please. You've done a lot for me over the years,' said George, thrusting a cheque into Jack's hand. 'Can your mum help you in any way?'

'I haven't told her. But I plan to see her next week,' replied Jack, forcing a thin grin. 'Thanks. I'll pay you back.'

'No need. I probably owe you.'

As George made the coffee, his mind cast back to their earliest school days. Jack's attachment to his mother seemed to him to be at the root of his friend's homesickness. All the boys suffered up to a point. But Jack found it harder than most. And when a pretty girl smiled at him, he appeared to fall immediately in love.

*

Jack's parents came from a generation and class to whom bankruptcy would be anathema. Catherine's mother had been educated at Benenden and sent her daughter to Roedean. Thereafter a smart finishing school in the Alps had taught his mother not how to cook but how to construct a menu for others so to do. She had spent more time learning to ski and to engage in polite conversation than on domestic duties. After all, there would be staff, wouldn't there?

In the event there *were* staff, but sadly no cook. Catherine's family, for three generations, had made money from an upmarket chain of tailors, with a flagship store in Regent Street, but the business had been taken over in the early 1950s by an asset stripper, leaving the family angry and not badly off but not as rich as they had been. The days of a tribe of servants, indoor and outdoor, and a Rolls-Royce, had ended in Catherine's mother's generation. Catherine had to make do with a cleaner, a gardener and a series of au pair girls. The latter had brief tenures, either because they were too beautiful to be sure Jack's father was not distracted, or were more interested in other, simultaneously held jobs. Indeed, Catherine dismissed one girl from Scotland when she discovered that she was entertaining kerb crawlers in town on her evenings off.

Catherine nearly died of polio in the 1957 outbreak. She and his father had been told that she would never walk again. But as Jack's family was made of determined stock, she did. The hospital had feared that Jack, then a year old, had perhaps had polio too, but there had been no sign of any symptoms.

Jack's father had been a high-street solicitor. He reluctantly took over the family firm, having read law at Cambridge, although he would have preferred to read engineering at Imperial College. Life for the Mayhew family had been very comfortable but not ridiculously affluent. So Jack's feeling of entitlement was not as evident as that of his mother and father. Indeed, since leaving Oxford he had resolved to restore the family's fortune.

'Darling, you look terrible,' said Catherine, greeting Jack at the door of the Georgian vicarage that had been his family home for as long as he could remember. Brutus, the golden retriever, wagged his tail at Jack so hard that it thumped against Jack's legs. 'You're not looking after yourself. Come into the kitchen and I'll give you a nice bowl of soup and then a thick juicy steak. How about that?'

'Mum, I'm not really hungry.'

'Oh dear. Women trouble, darling? Is it that pretty girl Tabitha? She's so delightfully chatty – we always have a good laugh when I am at Arthur's. She really is very sweet. I encouraged her to drop in whenever she's nearby. She was giving you the eye when I was last at Arthur's. Do be careful with your staff, darling.'

Jack paused, but tried to avoid his mother's gaze. She could always tell if he was not telling her the full story.

'No, Mum, not her.'

'Did I mention that she had popped in to see me here the other week? If I didn't, I should have done. She arrived with a suitcase, which I thought was odd. A rather smart one. She settled herself at the kitchen table and we shared a bottle of Muscadet; then another. It seemed as though she didn't want to leave and as, well, I liked her company and she had had too much to drink I let her stay the night. Funny thing was, though, in the middle of the night I heard footsteps on the stairs. I opened my bedroom door and there she was, creeping down the steps, in different and – I couldn't help noticing – rather revealing clothes. And off she went. The bed had never been slept in.'

'Where did she go?' asked Jack.

'I've no idea. Perhaps to see one of her admirers. From what she said, she certainly seems to live the high life outside the restaurant. What you pay her couldn't give her the lifestyle she appears to enjoy.'

'Yes, I think she has some wealthy boyfriends,' said Jack. He moved the conversation on to give his mother an edited version of his last few months. The problems with Steve, the fire and the consequent demise of his business. Pride and a wish not to disappoint his mother deterred him from mentioning the full financial extent of his problems. Neither did he mention Mona, or any other women.

'You poor darling. But look, failure is not falling over, as your father used to say, misquoting someone – I forget who. Failure is not getting up again. And you are going to get up again, aren't you…' This wasn't a question but an instruction. Since his father died, Jack's mother had become quite independently strong. As with most families of a certain type, she had relied on his father, not just financially, but organisationally. He had provided for Catherine well, but most of his estate was bound in trust and so not freely available. His father was shrewd and had not only put his money out of reach of the tax man but also anyone other than his immediate family and in particular any suitors of his still glamorous widow who he feared might fancy more than simply her.

'So, what are your plans for after you have got up and dusted yourself off?'

'I don't know yet. I'll think of something,' replied Jack, aware that this was the only truthful answer that would be acceptable.

'Well, I'm sure you will think of something soon. You'll need to as I don't think the trust will be able to help you.'

'That won't be necessary anyway,' said Jack, too proud to admit that cash from the trust would be extremely welcome.

Two months later

The morning sun pierced the autumn mist to allow a sharp blue sky to enliven the pale Georgian facades of the street where Mona lived. The smell of damp leaves reminded Jack of school days while the broad, grand melody and thick harmonies of the *Fantasia on a Theme by Thomas Tallis* infused his limp consciousness. He imagined that it was on just such a morning that Vaughan Williams might have composed this hauntingly English piece. Jack's mood reverted to its usual emptiness as he drove to the opposite end of the road where Mona lived. He parked in a different place and waited. He waited an hour. Mona did not appear and so Jack drove, with no particular aim, towards Bristol. *Make the most of it*, thought Jack. He had to hand back his car to the leasing company the following day.

Jack found himself inadvertently approaching the area around Jason's, which he wanted to avoid. He had no idea what the bank's receivers had done to the restaurant or whether it was trading or closed. So he turned right into Dean Street. The name triggered a distant reaction in his memory. Dean Street, Dean Street. A short traffic jam slowed his progress which gave him the chance to open the glove compartment. He rummaged around for what he was looking for and pulled out a sheet of crumpled paper. On it was written *41 Dean Street, Bristol* and, after a dash, in large letters, was the word *Osbourne*.

The odd numbers of the houses were on his side of the street. He passed 49, 47, 45. He had not been conscious of noticing any attractive women for some weeks, but to his left, coming out of number 41, was a dark-haired, slim woman in her mid-thirties. Her face looked familiar. As she walked slowly down the steps outside the house, she looked towards Jack's car, and then at Jack. Her blue-green eyes drilled into his, just for a second, and then looked away. She stood at the side of the road, waiting to cross as Jack's car drew level with her. She looked at Jack again. Her eyes appeared to widen as Jack returned her gaze. He gripped the steering wheel and looked ahead as images of his prep school flashed through his mind. As he passed her, she crossed the road behind him, and looked back at Jack's car as she walked. Jack parked his car hurriedly, causing the driver of the car behind to sound his horn and gesticulate angrily. Jack leaped out of his car and across the road, narrowly missing the oncoming traffic. Noticing the commotion, the woman looked around and stopped as she saw Jack approach her. She raised an eyebrow and smiled faintly as he stood opposite her and noticed familiar perfume.

'Angela?' he said.

'Yes,' she replied, inclining her head and looking closely at him. 'Is it really you, Jack?'

Then they both spoke at once. 'What are you doing here?' they chimed, smiling broadly at each other.

'I live near here,' said Jack, almost saying, forgetting the truth, that he worked in the area.

'Well, so do I,' she replied, which seemed obvious to Jack, as he had seen her coming out of her house and locking the door behind her. 'How are you? You are just as handsome as I thought you would be.'

'Oh, it's a long story,' said Jack, looking at the ground, not as confident as he had been a few months previously despite noting there was no ring on her wedding-ring finger.

'Well, why don't we go for a coffee and you can tell me all about it? And indeed, all about the last fifteen or so years since I last saw you.'

Jack hesitated and looked at the house from where Angela had emerged. Would Osbourne be at home? He looked tentatively at the large bay window for signs, hoping that he was neither at home nor able to see him with Angela. Seducing the man's girlfriend was not the revenge he sought.

'Oh, we won't go in; let's go to the cafe down the end of the road,' she said.

'Lead the way,' said Jack, relieved but curious as to why Angela did not want to give him coffee in her house opposite. After crossing the road to lock his car, Jack joined Angela at her side. She was as playful as she had been when Jack was thirteen, the last time he saw her, although he now could appreciate her flirtation through the lens of experience.

CHAPTER 8

Sixteen years earlier

Angela Watson was, by any measure, a beauty. She was five-foot five with dark, curling shoulder-length hair, flashing blue-green eyes and a warm, faintly mischievous smile. She was slim and with a neat bottom and breasts, the tops of which were occasionally visible, much to the excitement of the older boys. Such exposure was irregular in a boys' prep school and convention expected that she would only be seen trussed up in her all-white under-matron's uniform. But the boys sometimes spied on her off duty, which could be a thrilling game on long Sunday afternoons. She did not appear to have a boyfriend, or at least that was what the boys fantasised. She was perfect.

So the boys thought. However, they were not aware that she had been expelled from her own school the term before she joined St Cuthbert's, and neither were her present employers. They were certainly not aware that her misdemeanours had involved a keen sexual interest in those younger than herself. She had been caught in bed with barely pubescent girls, twice, but the school had put this down to innocent exploration. But when she was caught again, this time with two boys, Angela's parents were summoned to take her away.

This was especially embarrassing for her father, the Reverend James Watson of the parish of St Bede's, near Redhill in Surrey. But he managed to hush the matter up, as was the way of the church in the 1960s. There was a slick system for covering up sexual indiscretions and this the Reverend Watson employed assiduously. Rather as if Angela had become pregnant, when she would have been despatched to Switzerland before the bump appeared, she was to be sent away. The wisdom of sending her to a boys' prep school might have been questioned by most casual observers, but the vicar felt that as assistant matron of St Cuthbert's, which was run by his old Cambridge chum, "Bandy" Banborough, she would be safe. The question of whether the pupils would be, let alone the younger masters, seemed to be of no concern.

By the time Jack was thirteen he was taller and more physically mature than his peers. He had broad, muscular shoulders and a strong back. He had developed a fine jawline, which, together with his thick fair hair, tossed back in lengthy streaks over the top of his head, made him look handsome beyond his years. He had learned to use his flashing blue eyes and winning smile to good effect and had started to notice girls much older than him steal admiring glances. The other boys, still genitally hairless, had noticed in the showers the hallmarks of maturing masculinity.

In earlier years, Jack had regularly endured the pain of being one of the last to be chosen by the captains of the two rugby teams of the afternoon. Even his great friend George was usually chosen ahead of him, even though he was so myopic that he could hardly see the ball, let alone catch it. But George had the advantage of being tall and so was useful in the scrum, which had the added benefit that he was never far from the ball.

Before taking up his place in the pack, in his very first game of rugby, George had been sent out to the wing, being a fairly fast runner. He refused to remove his glasses until Mr Snelson, the first-year games master, insisted. It was a dull grey afternoon and as the ball came out of the scrum and was passed clumsily towards him, it appeared through the mist of his short sight and hit him square on the nose.

'You're supposed to catch it,' said Mr Snelson.

'But I couldn't see it,' complained George, rubbing his nose and finding a smear of blood.

'Gosh, I didn't realise you were that blind. Swap places with Elsworthy and get into the scrum.'

Now, almost five years later, Jack's physique had developed markedly. He looked older than his years. He was no longer last to be picked – he was captain of the first fifteen and used his strength to good effect at number eight. As the only boy in the team whose voice had broken, Jack was a commanding presence on the field. George was still being made to play, but only in the team which never engaged any other schools. He could still not see the ball and found no pleasure in his muddy place in the scrum in what seemed to him to be permanently wet and windy weather.

During the last two school matches, Jack had seen Miss Watson standing alone on the touchline. Today, her voice could be heard above the cheers of the other boys as Jack, ball in hand, drove his mates over the opposing line and touched down for a try. As Jack stood up from the mud, sweating, out of breath and receiving slaps on the back from his teammates, he noticed Miss Watson clapping and cheering. She flashed a broad smile at him and yelled, 'Well done, Jack!'

Two of the other boys heard. One said, 'Mayhew, she called you Jack!' Jack had heard but said nothing and blushed slightly as he trotted back to the halfway line. As he did so, he noticed that Miss Watson's eyes had not left him. He also noticed the curve of her waist and the roundness of her neat breasts, the tops slightly exposed despite the cold weather. Jack was quickly distracted from his maturing basic instincts as the opposition kicked off and his full-back grasped for the ball.

St Cuthbert's' unbeaten run continued as at full time the score was ten–five, Jack having scored both tries. At tea, Miss Watson was helping to supervise.

'Jack, I thought you all played marvellously.' Jack smiled. 'Especially you,' she added, looking almost coy under her dark fringe. Jack could smell her perfume as she touched his arm lightly and then turned away.

'Oooo!' said one of his teammates, who had spotted the gesture.

'Shut up,' hissed Jack, turning slightly red. But he could not resist the smile on a pretty face. And he craved female affection.

*

Angela Watson had initiated a small group activity which she called the Country Ramblers. Mr Griffiths, the young head of English, had made some remark about the Shakespearean appropriateness of the name, but the allusion was lost on the boys. The rambles took place on a Thursday afternoon, when there were no games. Not only was the group small, just four boys, but it seemed that Miss Watson was able to choose who could join. Jack was invited first.

'Who else would you like me to invite, Jack?' asked Miss Watson in a hushed tone in the dormitory corridor, using Jack's first name again.

'Umm. How about Thomas, Grayson and Elsworthy?' suggested Jack, conscious that none of them played in the first fifteen, and, crucially, none was quite so mature and none paid Miss Watson much attention.

'OK,' said Miss Watson. 'Our first trip is this Thursday. We will go up on the hills.'

As Thursday morning arrived, Jack felt an unfamiliar sense of excitement. He was used to and relished the thrill of impending liberation. Four years of incarceration, albeit in a hundred acres or so, magnified the joy of escape into the countryside. He wondered what the prisoners of Alcatraz might have felt when freed from their island fortress in the bay of San Francisco. But this time there was another emotion which infused his soul and distracted him from Mr Griffiths' attempt to explain the use and meaning of the subjunctive. The vision of Miss Watson, smiling and calling him Jack, seemed to spark an intense new feeling in him; a longing, but for what, he was unsure.

When up on the hills that afternoon, the breeze was light and fresh. The early spring sun was just strong enough to warm the skin. Bees fought over the first of the pollen. A tractor throbbed in the distance. The boys and Miss Watson chatted animatedly, all excited but for their different reasons. Each time one of the other boys walked next to her, Jack would manoeuvre himself so that he would be at her side again. He was not conscious of why, but it seemed natural that way. Indeed, when George drifted up a different path with her so that she and Jack were temporarily separated, he felt a stab of jealousy of the type he had not experienced before. When their paths met again, Miss Watson shot a glance and a broad smile at Jack, which he reciprocated with a deep sense of joy. The sun played on Miss Watson's face, her eyes seemed to flash at Jack and the wind gently blew her long hair around her bare neck and shoulders.

As they made their way down the steep, winding path back to Miss Watson's car, the other boys were up ahead, running and tumbling their way. Miss Watson was behind Jack. She seemed to slip on the path, although gently, and as she stumbled Jack broke her fall. She grabbed Jack around the shoulders and gasped his name as she fell. Jack was strong and so held her up, grabbing her slim waist firmly. As he did so her shirt rode up and his arm made contact with her braless breast. Her balance regained, Jack removed his arm swiftly, although he noticed, reluctantly. Their faces were six inches apart. Miss Watson's dark pupils dilated.

'Sorry, Jack,' she whispered, looking directly into his blue eyes. Jack could manage only an embarrassed smile. 'We had better go. The others will be waiting for us.'

That night the faint smell of Miss Watson's perfume on his arm and the brief but glorious image of her breast kept Jack awake.

Jack thought about Angela, as he now called her when out of earshot of the others, almost permanently. When he awoke she was smiling at him through the warmth of his blanket and when he was in bed at night he almost resented the boys' attempts to talk to him before lights out as it distracted him from these more important thoughts. There were exceptions. One night, Grayson, fed up that Jack's usual exuberance seemed muted, started a slipper fight. His soft tartan slipper missed Jack and landed on his bed. Jack leaped up, grabbed Grayson's slipper and hurled it across the dormitory, catching Grayson on the arm. As Grayson bent to retrieve his slipper, Jack followed by throwing his own, the usual red leather one with the hard sole, which caught Grayson square on the jaw. Pandemonium followed, with most of the other eight boys joining in. George threw his slipper at Elsworthy, which missed and hit the dormitory door as the headmaster appeared from behind it. Everyone froze.

'Come and see me after breakfast, all of you,' he said. The boys knew what that meant. All eight collected three stripes on their backsides which they compared painfully in the classroom corridor before chapel.

After chapel, the art class was taken by Angela Watson, as the art mistress was indisposed. During the lesson Elsworthy dropped his pencil on the floor. It rolled towards her, stopping at her feet. She was bending over a table showing another boy how to mix the shade of green he wanted. Elsworthy scrambled to retrieve his pencil, hoping that Miss Watson would not notice. As he did so he could not resist a glance up Miss Watson's skirt. A tuft of black pubic hair was visible between her leg and her knickers. Elsworthy's gaze lasted a second too long and Miss Watson moved her legs, almost standing on him. 'What are you doing?' she asked.

'Oh, just getting my pencil,' he replied. 'I dropped it.'

During the next few minutes Elsworthy shared the exciting news with Jack and George. George contrived to drop his pencil two minutes later and was able to confirm the most erotic sighting he had ever experienced. A tuft of pubic hair. Jack was in two minds. He had dreamed of Angela's most private of places, yet these were his own dreams, not to be shared with George or Elsworthy. Yet he could not resist the roll of his own pencil. The sight made him momentarily breathless. Had she noticed?

The art mistress was still away later in the week. The three boys had their pencils ready to avail themselves of a further view. George went first as he was worried Miss Watson would notice and curtail the boys' fun. He could not believe his eyes. Miss Watson was naked under her skirt. Not just a tuft of black hair, but a neatly trimmed bush encasing the fold of her lips. On sharing the news with Jack, Jack threw two pencils on the floor for good measure and almost audibly gasped at what he saw. He stood up and when Elsworthy tried the same trick, Jack grabbed him round the neck and pulled him away. He then flew at George and punched him hard in the face, sending him crashing into a chair beside Miss Watson.

'Jack, what are you doing? Stop it. You had better go outside and cool off,' she said.

Jack said nothing, but as he left the classroom, Angela turned towards him and, with her back to the rest of the class, smiled and winked at him.

That weekend, Jack was walking back from winning the home rugger match, which as usual Angela had watched. She caught up with him and said quietly to him, 'Jack, when you have had your shower and after tea, please come up to my room. I have something to show you.'

'OK,' said Jack, a little too enthusiastically.

'Make sure nobody sees you. You'll get us both in trouble.' She smiled.

In the shower Jack consciously ensured all traces of mud were removed from his face and hair. After he had shaken the hand of the opposing team captain and waved off the team, George said, 'Hey, Mayhew, let's go.'

'No, it's OK, I've got to write the match report and give it in by six o'clock.'

George pulled a face and scampered off.

When he was out of sight, Jack turned and made his way back towards the main building, in which were the dormitories and Angela's room. He looked over his shoulder to check nobody was following him or could see where he was going. As he started to climb the stairs, Mr Snelson was leaving Angela's room. Jack turned to retrace his steps.

'Mayhew, well played today. Another triumph. I thought you kept the pack together very well and of course your try is sure to be remembered for weeks to come. Miss Watson was certainly impressed. I have just had tea with her.'

'Thank you, sir,' said Jack, standing at the bottom of the stairs.

Mr Snelson whistled rather too happily as he passed and had a spring in his step. Jack wondered why as he waited until he was out of sight. Jack then leaped up the stairs, taking two of them at a time until he reached Angela's room. He knocked on the door.

'Come in.'

Jack opened the door rather hesitantly.

'Oh, there you are. Where have you been?' she said, closing the door behind them. Jack noticed that she locked it.

'I had to wave off the other team. Anyway, Mr Snelson was in here.'

'Yes, I thought it was you when he knocked. I was *very* disappointed it wasn't…!' she said, rather too convincingly. 'Come and sit down.'

The room smelled of now familiar perfume. The window was open. The curtains rustled in the breeze. There was only one chair in the little bedroom and so Angela sat on her small bed, leaning back on one arm. She was wearing a miniskirt, which hardly covered her bottom. Jack noticed that she was not wearing a bra. He could see her neat nipples, which appeared to be firm against her tight white shirt. Jack sat on the other end of the bed to her.

'Come closer, Jack.'

Jack stood up, trying to conceal the bulge in his trousers, and sat as close as he dared. Without speaking, Angela took Jack's hand and placed it high up on her bare leg. With her other hand she drew him close to her and rubbed her lips gently against his. Hers were soft, warm and a little moist. Jack did not move at first, anxious not to make a mistake. Her lips became gently more insistent, parted and allowed her tongue to part his own. Jack started to slowly move his lips against hers and Angela responded. She pushed her tongue sensitively between his lips and searched the edges of his young mouth. She breathed into it, now more eager.

Angela took Jack's hand, which was on her leg, and gently pushed it up her skirt. Jack's fingers touched the edge of her soft hair.

'I know you have seen it. I thought you might want to touch it,' she said gently.

Jack moved his fingers hesitantly further. He felt the soft opening of her femininity and the wetness of her curling hairs. Jack was hard against his trousers. Angela moved her hand and cupped it over his bulge.

'You naughty boy.'

As Angela moved to unzip Jack's trousers his warm fluid pumped into his pants. Trying to stifle his gasps, Jack leaped up, turned his back on Angela, unlocked the door and fled from the room without a word. As he ran uncomfortably towards his dormitory, he heard Angela's bedroom door close gently behind him.

'What were you doing in Miss Watson's room?' enquired a familiar adult voice.

'Nothing, sir,' replied Jack.

'Well, you must have been doing something,' said Mr Banborough, making his way towards Angela's room.

After Miss Watson hurriedly left the school, Jack consoled himself by not washing the fingers of his right hand. The sweet smell of Angela made him understand for the first time the words of a Groucho Marx song 'Heaven's Above'.

CHAPTER 9

Jack easily passed his common entrance exam to Worchester, one of the most respected public schools of the day. His father had said that he should have sat for a scholarship, but his mother did not want him to endure such pressure, or the possibility of failure. She thought Jack was still such a sensitive boy, but had not fully appreciated how much he had grown up. Emotional and physical knocks he could now take, toughened by five years' boarding.

By the time Jack was sixteen, three years later, he had already represented the school in the first rugby fifteen on several occasions and in his favourite position of number eight. At six-foot one, he was taller than most of the opposing scrum. He had a deep, commanding voice and a strong, muscular body. His jaw had become more angular and his cheekbones more pronounced than in his earlier teens. His eyes were sometimes dazzlingly blue and his straight fair hair was thick and swept back from his face. He would toss his hair when he spied the regular admiring glances from ladies of all ages or run his strong hands through it confidently. 'Like a Greek god,' as his mother's friend had whispered.

When he was a new boy, Jack had dodged the worst excesses of the prefects. Many of the stories passed round the senior boys at his prep school about fagging turned out to be true. In his first week he heard the command "Somebody" being bellowed from the lavatories (or "rears" as they were descriptively called) at least three times. Fortunately, there had been a fag closer than him and so he avoided the humiliation of having to warm the prefect's lavatory seat prior to it being used. Jack was assigned to fag for one particular prefect, Erdington, who was deputy head of house. His duties included cleaning Erdington's study and shining his black shoes. When asked to empty Erdington's "wagger" Jack was relieved to discover that this only meant his wastepaper basket. But Erdington was relatively civilised and so treated Jack well. He even gave him a florin now and again. Some of the other boys were not so lucky. And of course Jack had not forgotten his treatment at the hands of Osbourne.

So when Jack became head of house he became determined that fagging should stop. The term before, he had witnessed his predecessor, Richard Lambert, beat a boy for smoking. The head of house was expected to administer such punishments along with other penalties such as writing lines or cleaning for lesser misdemeanours.

The irony was that Lambert himself smoked (and later became senior partner of one of England's largest firms of lawyers). Earlier that term, when the dry earth at night was still warm from the September sun, Lambert and Jack decided to visit their girlfriends. At night. In their dormitories at the girls' school. Such excursions were hazardous, as to be caught would mean expulsion from the school, not just of themselves but the girls too. And expulsion would surely mean Richard Lambert sacrificing his almost certain place at Oxford. But that was all part of the excitement.

After the junior boys had gone to bed, Jack and Richard, armed with two packets of Players No. 6 – "Numbies" – made their way silently down the corridor to the changing rooms, past the "rears" and to the back door. A bright silvery moon lit their way down the drive and out onto the road behind. They talked in excited whispers as they walked smartly, skirting the school grounds, smoking their Numbies and feeling liberated. Jack did not enjoy the cheap, acrid taste of these cigarettes, but at least they were more tolerable than that of the laughably and inaptly named Woodbines. Sweet honeysuckle they were not.

The first of the autumn leaves crackled beneath their feet. The soft wind rustled the trees above as the boys' excitement mounted and they approached the grey walls of Lordsbury School for Girls. A downstairs light shone from one side of the building but all the lights upstairs appeared to be off. Jack was not sure how Richard knew in which dormitory the girls slept. But he pointed to a large, partly open Victorian sash window on the second floor. A black-painted fire-escape ladder rose vertically from the flower bed up to the window.

Richard and Jack pushed their way past the rose bushes surrounding the base of the ladder, their dark trousers protecting them from the thorns, which appeared to be inadequate sentries, asleep whilst on duty protecting unwelcome intruders from climbing the fire escape. The boys looked around furtively before grasping the fire escape firmly with both hands. The moon cast shadows of the boys onto the wall as they slowly climbed the ladder. A dog barked from inside the house. Jack and Richard froze. The dog barked again.

'Be quiet, Guinness,' said a firm, mature female voice from the direction of the lighted room. The boys then gingerly climbed on, past the first floor and towards the second. As they passed the first floor, they could hear voices of young girls talking quietly inside. Fortunately, the curtains were closed. The curtains were also closed over the window they needed on the second floor. The lower window was open about four inches. The curtains were blowing in the wind. When they reached it they stopped. They could hear rather older female voices. One they did not recognise, but the other two were those of Jenny and Sophia, Richard's and Jack's girlfriends.

'Shall I knock?' whispered Richard into Jack's ear. Jack tried to suppress a giggle. Richard put one hand under the open window and tried to pull it up. It did not move.

'What was that?' asked Jenny.

'What?' chorused the others.

'That noise from the window.'

'Oh, it's Sir Galahad at last coming to ravish you. Wouldn't you just love that?' said Sophia in a lascivious tone.

'Well yes, I would. In fact, I'm desperate, as you know. And I know you are too, little Miss Hot Pants. You hardly keep your knickers in the freezer, do you?'

'For God's sake, stop it. I'm turned on just thinking about it.'

Jack's eyes widened and he jabbed Richard in the ribs, pointing persuasively at the window.

Richard grabbed it again and gave it a strong pull upwards. This time the window rattled open about three feet. There was a screech from inside and Richard and Jack threw themselves on their stomachs through the window and onto the wooden floor below.

The girls shrieked again but this time their shrieks dissolved into excited laughter. There were six girls in the dormitory; Jenny, Sophia and Olivia plus three the boys did not know. Those three muttered earnestly, 'Get out, get out,' and 'For Christ's sake, we'll all be expelled,' and 'Oh please go, my dad will kill me, and then I shall never pass my A levels.'

Jenny and Sophia leaped out of bed in their long Laura Ashley nightgowns and threw their arms around Richard and Jack respectively. Olivia pulled back the bed covers and stood excitedly on her bed with her arms outstretched, grinning at the boys. Her brown hair was dishevelled and fell in twists down her back and across her shoulders. Jack, who by now was distracted from his girlfriend, could make out Olivia's bush, nestled above two long legs jumping gently on the bed, her young breasts bouncing to the rhythm as she fell backwards onto her mattress. With her legs wide apart, but her nighty securely covering her womanhood, she said, 'Come and get me, boys, I'm all yours. Both of you.'

'Shit,' said Jack and, taking Sophia's wrists, which had hardened their grasp since Olivia's invitation, he freed himself from her and made for the open window.

Jenny laughed uncontrollably as Richard followed him.

'Come back, come back,' Olivia pleaded between muffled bursts of laughter.

'No, for Christ's sake, leave, before we are all caught and expelled,' said one of the others.

Without another word, Jack and Richard climbed through the still-open window, pulling down one side of the curtain in their haste. With a smile and a wave, they left and commenced their descent of the fire escape, rather more quickly than they had ascended.

As they reached the bottom, Jack slipped and fell into the rose bed. Guinness started to bark, this time more earnestly.

'What now?' enquired a voice.

Guinness barked more determinedly.

'Oh all right, out you go.' The bolts of the front door slid aside and, out of sight of the boys, the door opened. Guinness appeared and barked fiercely at the boys.

'Shush,' said Jack, pleading with the dog.

'Run,' said Richard, a slight air of panic in his voice for the first time.

As they both ran, the front door opened and Miss Jenkinson, the housemistress, appeared at the doorway, her grey bun and stocky figure silhouetted against the light.

'Hey, you two. What do you think you are doing? Come here at once!'

Without looking around, Jack and Richard ran down the drive of the house with Guinness scampering after them, now not barking but enjoying the game.

As they left the drive, Guinness stopped and Miss Jenkinson shouted at him to return.

'Good boy, Guinness. Now all I have to do is find out who those Worchester boys were.'

*

Six across, thought Jack, wrestling with the final clue of *The Times* crossword. Four letters. Shakespearean private aircraft divides the kingdom. Jack smiled as he wrote the word "Lear" and Rupert swaggered through the open door of the prefects' sitting room. Jack had been waiting for him to join the others. He put aside his copy of the newspaper, stood up and announced, 'OK, guys, I've discussed this with Charlie' – the nickname of Charles Bragg, their young housemaster – 'and he has agreed that I can abolish fagging. And I shall be the first head of house not to beat a boy.'

'Oh come on, Jack,' said Rupert, speaking up for the other prefects, who were open-mouthed at Jack's pronouncement, 'we've waited four years to have our own fag. We had to do it. Why shouldn't they?'

'Rupert, this is the 1970s. We have had Woodstock, flower power, peace and love. How can we still expect small boys to clean our shoes, let alone warm our bog seat and have another boy beat them?'

'Because we had to – and it didn't do us any harm, anyway.'

The other prefects muttered in agreement. The smell of toast and melting butter infused the prefects' sitting room. This together with the sound of Lou Reed easing its way from the record player softened the hostile atmosphere.

'Do you want another piece of "tosst"?' Rupert asked Jack in his favourite northern accent and glaring at him whilst stabbing his bread hard with a toasting fork.

'At least we don't roast the new boys in front of this fire, like they did at Rugby a few years ago. They've got off lightly, if you ask me.'

'Well, chaps, I'm not asking you. This is not a democracy – yet. And so we are doing it, starting now. There will be no announcement. We shall just stop.'

'Bollocks,' said Rupert, butter dripping down his chin. 'I knew this sort of thing would happen if Charlie made you head of house.'

Jack picked up the worn leather-bound prefects' minute book from under the loaf of bread, opened it and began to read. 'Listen. *1912. Easter term. According to Mr Douglas's wishes it was decided that no Prefect should talk to Inferiors in the dormitories.*

'And *Simonton received four cuts for using "water closet" language. It seemed obvious the remark was intended for a Prefect but he denied it.*

'And *1915. Summer term. Jameson received four cuts for calling Brown, who had just been made a Prefect, a "dirty cad" with no provocation whatsoever.*

'And *Johnson, Barry and Treverton were licked for having on the previous night talked disgustingly in Johnson's study.*'

The five prefects could contain their mirth no longer.

'Who did the licking?' asked Rupert, choking on his toast.

'You know both that and "cuts" meant beating. Don't

be an arse,' said Jack. 'The point is, we don't seem to have come very far since 1912, do we?'

'Well, if you get an Oxford interview before Christmas as you hope, don't tell them that you have been responsible for destroying over a hundred years of tradition, will you? Because they will show you the door. The one about dons changing a lightbulb is not just a joke, you know.'

'What lightbulb?' asked Cedric Smythson, who was failing to keep up, as usual.

'How many Oxford dons does it take to change a light bulb? *Change...*?' Rupert reminded them.

'Actually, they may just credit me with some intellectual stamina when I tell them how I have had to stand up to you lot. Come on, we'd better get back. I've got double economics.'

'More bollocks,' muttered Rupert, who was more of a scientist.

So Jack buried a tradition that had indeed endured over a hundred years, much to the pride of his mother. In his final school report Charlie Bragg described Jack as an...

...immensely civilised head of house who is showing considerable leadership skills. He has not disappointed me. Indeed, he has grown in the job to a point that I can see a great future for him. My knowledge of Jack's nocturnal adventures at Lordsbury School for Girls went no further. I would have regretted losing a future head of house so cheaply. But, erunt homines hominibus! I wish Jack the warmest of luck at Oxford and in his future career.

CHAPTER 10

Patrick Osbourne, Benedict's father, preferred taking a run-up, cricket bat in hand, when administering the regular beatings that his son endured. He would wear his MCC tie whilst performing his fatherly duty, before returning it to its place draped over the cricket bat in the corner of his study. The run-up on this occasion was longer than usual, such was Benedict's father's anger at having his son expelled, and for unspeakable bullying. He himself was bullied at school; he was told to toughen up. Yet he showed his son no mercy.

Whilst Patrick either beat or ignored his son, Benedict's mother laid on him only verbal abuse. To her, he was and would always be a failure. And she told him so. Regularly. His two sisters of course could do no wrong. They were bright, beautiful, spoilt with horses and lavish parties and Cambridge-bound. Benedict could not compete. 'You will never succeed at anything,' she would remind him. And so when the school telephoned to ask that he be picked up and never to return, Benedict's mother's only words to her son as he appeared at the front door, having been dropped off by a taxi, were 'What did I tell you? A total failure.'

Twenty-one years later, Benedict Osbourne left the house by the back door and drove his Mercedes to Jason's for his meeting with the receiver. He had been annoyed at failing to purchase the restaurant when it was available last time, but pleased that whoever had bought it had obviously overpaid and gone bust as a result. He allowed himself a one-sided smirk at the thought that he would now pick up the site for half of what he had offered previously.

*

Angela Watson and Jack exchanged stories of the previous sixteen years over several cups of coffee. Angela laughed at Jack's tales of his time at Worchester, his abolition of fagging and exploits up the fire escape of the girls' school. She did not seem surprised that he had got into Oxford or that he had been head of house.

'You were always going to be a leader of men,' she said, looking at him over her cup of coffee, a twinkle in her eye.

They reminisced fondly over their days together at prep school although skirting around what remained the most interesting parts to them personally. Jack wondered how Angela now felt about her behaviour. For his part, he remembered the incident with both affection and amusement. And excitement. He was struck by how the age difference between them had narrowed and was reminded of Mona. He had always liked older women.

Being embarrassed, Jack mentioned his business interests only obliquely, not admitting their failure. As his period of promiscuity had been part of his undoing and he had become ashamed of it anyway, there was no mention of that either.

A plan to get even with Osbourne began to form in Jack's mind while they were talking. He could probably get access to Osbourne and Angela's house through Angela. But how could he avoid hurting her either physically or emotionally? After all, she was likely to be in bed with Osbourne at the time of day he was considering. And the thought of that puzzled him. Had Osbourne become a decent fellow? he wondered. If not, as he expected, what was Angela doing with him? Could he perhaps save her from him at the same time as evening the score on the electrocution?

'You've gone distant on me,' said Angela. 'A penny for them.'

'I haven't heard that expression since my parents used it! No, it's OK, I was just distracted by something.'

'Well, I had better be going. How about lunch sometime?' said Angela.

Jack tried to hide his surprise and delight at the invitation and managed to reply vaguely. In truth he hoped that their meeting would be clandestine so that Osbourne would not be aware of it. As he said goodbye to Angela he kissed her tenderly on the cheek. As she reciprocated, he noticed again the same perfume that she had used all those years ago. Not wanting to risk calling her house when Osbourne was in, he gave her his telephone number, hoping that she would call him in the next week. After that he would not be at the flat. It was to be repossessed by the bank the following Monday. And after that, Jack had no idea where he was going to live.

*

George Thomas stared at the screen in front of him and made a sign at the broker opposite. They had learned earlier that after what was being called Big Bang, they would each have at least three screens to watch and all trading to speak of would be made from their desks, electronically. The younger ones amongst them figured that the mid-eighties would herald financial opportunities that would dwarf those presently available on the trading floor. The older ones, of course, talked of Armageddon and the Wild West.

George had been summoned to a boardroom to sit in on a meeting with an accountant in his forties who fancied himself as a turnround operator, someone who could improve the fortunes of loss-making companies. This man was Clement Slimbridge and he was looking for opportunities. He had qualified at one of the second-division firms of accountants and did not look like making partner at his present firm. George could see why. Slimbridge wore a brown suit with a cream nylon shirt and a novelty tie, for which he apologised, quipping that, well, he had to wear it because his daughter had given it to him for his birthday. Brown shoes. He was thin and laughed loudly at awkward moments and especially at his own jokes. He had slightly buck teeth over large lips, of the Australian cultural attaché variety, as worn by Barry

Humphries. His acne had not cleared up the way it should have done by his age, and his hair was greasy.

Why am I here? wrote George on a notepad in front of his boss, Tim. *I'm a trader; not corporate finance.*

Just to make up the numbers, wrote Tim in reply.

George rolled his eyes and tried not to sigh as Slimbridge stuttered though a prepared speech detailing his achievements.

When the meeting broke up and George returned to his desk, one of the other traders was telling a joke.

'A man rather the worse for wear was leaving a nightclub when a lady of the night approached him and asked, "Do you want super sex?". The man thought for a while and then replied, "Um, well, what sort of soup is it?".'

Everyone laughed except Slimbridge, who clearly wasn't sure if he was meant to.

*

'Jack Mayhew.'

'Hello, Jack. It's Angela,' said the soft voice on the phone. 'How about tomorrow?'

'How about tomorrow, what?' asked Jack, trying to remain cool.

'Lunch in town.'

'I'll just look at my diary.' Jack put his hand over the mouthpiece and looked out of the window for a full ten seconds. 'Yup, that looks fine. I'll move something to another day.' He had nothing planned. 'Shall I choose somewhere? I'll call you back.' He wanted to be as sure as possible not to bump into Osbourne.

'Lovely. Let me know,' said Angela and hung up.

Jack looked around his flat at the packing cases full of his possessions. How was it possible to have felt pain and emptiness simultaneously? But now the darkness that had enveloped him for the last few weeks had begun to evaporate in the light that radiated from Angela. Van Morrison had understood. From the darkness to the "Bright Side of the Road".

*

Jack was at the restaurant early so as to ensure that he could choose a table that afforded some privacy. After twenty minutes, Angela arrived. As she walked past other tables, several men turned to admire her tight figure and lush long, dark hair. Jack stood to welcome her and noted the familiar perfume as he kissed her cheek. The aroma hauled him back to those walks on the hills and her tiny bedroom at school. The restaurant was busy and Jack had chosen a table in the corner where he could sit with his back to the room but where he could see the entrance in an adjacent mirror.

After a bottle of Muscadet chosen by Angela, Jack turned the conversation towards what he thought of as the purpose of their meeting.

'How long have you known Benedict Osbourne?'

'About two years. But how do you know I know him at all?' said Angela with a surprised tone.

'Well, I assumed that you did as you were coming out of his house,' replied Jack, realising his mistake and what Angela's next question would be.

Sure enough: 'But how do you know that is his house?'

'Let's just say I stumbled on his address some time ago.'

Angela gazed into her glass of Muscadet and there was a brief, awkward silence amid the noise of the restaurant. A waiter filled their glasses, seemed on the point of asking for the third time if everything was all right but apparently thought better of it and left them alone.

'What's the matter?' said Jack, and then asked, perhaps a little too hopefully, 'Aren't you very happy together?' He reached across the table and took her hand.

'Together?' gasped Angela. She laughed.

'What's so funny?' asked Jack.

'We aren't together. I'm his secretary,' said Angela, laughing more, 'although he pompously calls me his private and personal assistant. I can't imagine anyone in their right mind being with him in that way. He is a shit and treats me terribly. And I have to look after the horrible reptiles he keeps. But he pays well and I need a job. That's hilarious! Together!'

Jack laughed too, and put his head in his hands, running them through his thick blond hair. 'I can't tell you how pleased I am to hear that. Aside from the obvious, that makes my plan much easier to complete.'

'What plan?' asked Angela.

*

'The cash in that envelope represents my only and therefore final offer,' said Osbourne, throwing a large brown envelope down onto the small desk in front of him.

139

The bank's receiver looked down at the envelope but did not touch it.

'Final sealed bids are due by 5 p.m. this evening. So I cannot accept whatever it is you have attempted to give me until then. If you would care to seal the envelope I shall open it after 5 p.m.'

'How can I trust you not to take some or all of the money?' asked Osbourne, looking down his nose at the respectable-looking accountant.

'Mr Osbourne,' said the man, after taking a deep breath, clearly trying to remain polite. 'I act for the bank, am a partner in my firm and a Fellow of the Institute of Chartered Accountants. If you do not trust me I invite you to remove your cash and return at 5 p.m.'

'Fine,' said Osbourne, taking the envelope off the desk. 'I shall return at four fifty-five. I am a busy man and so I hope I am not wasting my time.'

The receiver gave a small bow as Osbourne turned and left, closing the door behind him with a little too much force.

'Please tell me that that dreadful man is not going to steal this place,' said the trainee.

'I fear he might. So far his is the only offer, but I wasn't going to tell him that, of course.'

At 4.55 p.m. the door of the restaurant swung open and Osbourne swaggered up the stairs to the small office of Jason's.

'Well?'

'Good evening, Mr Osbourne. Well, what?' replied the receiver, inclining his head towards Osbourne.

'Had any other offers?'

'I'm afraid I am not at liberty to tell you that, Mr Osbourne. But if you wish to make an offer you have three minutes to make it.'

'Here,' said Osbourne, placing the envelope on the desk and pushing it towards the receiver.

'Thank you. I shall assess the bids, discuss them with the bank and let you know the outcome by this time tomorrow.'

'Why can't you let me know now?' said Osbourne somewhat aggressively.

'We have a process to follow, sir. Would you like me to count the money in front of you and give you a receipt?'

'Yes. But be quick as I have to leave.'

The receiver counted the notes, mainly used, and wrote down the figure of £3,500 on a slip of paper and gave it to Osbourne.

'I just want to confirm that this offer is for the remaining stock, fixtures and fittings. You will need to agree terms for a lease, if you want one, with the freeholder,' said the receiver.

'Yes, it is.'

'Would you like to offer any more?'

'No. As I said, this is my only offer. Do I need to?'

'We shall be in touch tomorrow. Good evening, Mr Osbourne.'

Osbourne left without saying goodbye.

*

Angela's first-floor flat was small but comfortable. Rose-scented candles sat half burned on the mantelpiece. Jack was surprised to note rather too much pink, including a worn-looking pink bear on her bed. It puzzled him that an attractive, relatively confident woman in her thirties should still surround herself with such relics of her childhood. This was a female space, with no sign of a masculine influence. He would have to change that, if he were to move in.

'How do you like your coffee?' asked Angela from the tiny kitchen next to the sitting room.

'Strong and black, like—'

'Yeah, yeah, like your women. I know…'

'Sorry.'

Jack had told Angela in the cafe what Osbourne had done to him at prep school. His gang that chased him. The electric chair. But as he needed time to think it through, he had not told her anything about his plan for revenge.

'Tell me more about Benedict Osbourne. Does he have a wife, or a girlfriend?'

'No, not as far as I know. And I think I would know. As I told you, I can't imagine any woman in her right mind fancying him. Not that he is bad-looking, but he treats everyone with disdain. He looks down on most men and treats women with no consideration. He has made the occasional improper suggestion to me, usually if I take him coffee to his bedroom. I decided the best plan was to ignore him, rather than reply.'

Jack thought for a moment. 'So he fancies you?'

'Well, it seems so.'

'Who wouldn't?' said Jack, smiling and raising an eyebrow.

'Well, I remember you did once…'

'I wondered how long it would take you to mention that. It seemed to me to be mutual. But then I was just a boy.'

Angela initially said nothing, but gave Jack a long look, deep into his eyes. Jack returned the gaze and then looked away.

Angela looked uncomfortable, then said, 'You know, at the time, you didn't seem like a boy to me. You seemed like a young man. In fact, you were. You were far more grown-up than the others. I was young too... you didn't seem much younger than me. So what we did, the relationship we had, didn't feel wrong. It felt natural.'

'To me too... When you are alone in his house one day, do you think you could let me in?' asked Jack, changing the subject.

'OK. But why?'

'I just want to have a look round. And then I will tell you about my plan.'

*

Angela opened the back door of Osbourne's house and urged Jack to hurry inside. The house smelled of stale tobacco and a salamander's cage which stood nearby. In the hall were framed photographs of Osbourne at his public school. School teams. Perhaps unsurprisingly there were no photographs of his prep school. Questions might arise which could force him to admit that he had been expelled and then he would have to lie as to the reason. But Angela had confirmed that this was not a challenge for Benedict Osbourne.

'Can I see upstairs?' asked Jack.

'Now why would you want to do that?' quipped Angela.

As she led the way, Jack chanced a small smack on her bottom. Angela did not react.

Jack noticed a large double bed, with a metal bedstead. Black silk sheets.

'Is this his?'

'Yes. I know. Black silk sheets. Just in case. He says blondes look good on them. Look, I found these the other day. Wishful thinking perhaps.'

Angela opened a bedside cabinet and removed a pair of handcuffs.

'Is there a key?' asked Jack.

Angela removed a key from one of the handcuffs and waved it at Jack with a little smile and a quizzical look.

'Does the bedside light work?'

'He would sack me if it didn't,' replied Angela, switching it on and then off. 'Why?'

'Let's go. I don't need to see any more.'

*

The ironmonger's shop reminded Jack of the television series *Open All Hours*. And it was Arkwright who served him. The one who had the stutter. Jack resisted the temptation to ask if they had "N E Os, or Xs" and had to suppress a giggle at the thought. Instead, he bought six yards of thin electrical cable, some insulating tape, a small screwdriver, some wire strippers and a timing switch.

At precisely 11.30 a.m., Jack walked past Osbourne's house and glanced at the large bay window. Angela waved at him, with her right hand and thumb extended. So Jack crossed the road and walked briskly to the back door, where Angela was waiting.

Once upstairs he put on some thin gloves and unplugged the bedside lamp. Through the stalk of the lamp he threaded two wires up to the switch, which he had dismantled. He unscrewed the small clamps which held the lamp's positive and negative wires, inserted his wires next to them and then turned the screws hard clockwise so that they gripped all four wires. He fed the new wires down the back of the bedside table, under the rug and then up to the bottom of each leg of the head end of the metal bedstead. He stripped a foot of insulation from each wire and wrapped them tightly round each leg of the bedstead. He then secured the wires with insulating tape. Finally, Jack plugged in the timer, set the light to come on at 6 p.m. and returned downstairs to Angela.

He smiled at Angela and gave her a kiss on the cheek.

'See you later. Six thirty,' said Jack as he left.

Angela left Osbourne's house at three o'clock to change, having reached a break in her work. She returned at four, dressed in hot pants and a tight white top with a plunging neckline. No bra. She went to Osbourne's bedside table, removed the handcuffs and waited for him to return from what he had described to her as a long lunch to celebrate his acquisition of Jason's. He would be drunk. At 5.05 p.m. Osbourne returned home. Angela stood with her bottom on the rail of the Aga and gave him a small smile. Osbourne's eyes widened. His tie was loose around his neck and he carried his suit jacket over his arm. He leered at Angela.

'My, to what do I owe this pleasure? Are you going out?'

'No, I'm staying in. With you. I thought it was about time I was honest with you.'

'You little hussy. What took you so long?' he said, swaggering towards her.

'I think we should have a drink first. Don't you?' she said, putting her hand up to Osbourne's chest to stop his further advance. 'And then, for a change, I shall give the orders.'

'Ratherrr...' he intoned, like an aggressive Bertie Wooster.

Osbourne opened a bottle of champagne, poured himself a glass, poured another for Angela and ambled purposefully over to her.

'Just give me the glass and go over there. And sit down,' she said, widening her stance slightly and leaning back on the Aga rail so that her pelvis thrust forwards. 'You will do as you are told. I'm going to punish you. You are to say nothing.' Angela drank her champagne and glared at Osbourne.

'Oh, please do. I promise to be good.' Osbourne sniggered and leered again at Angela.

'Give me some more champagne. And then sit down again,' she commanded.

Angela looked at her watch. Five thirty.

'Now go upstairs, take off all your clothes, and lie on your back on your bed. I shall drink the rest of the champagne and then come upstairs to do to you what you deserve.'

'Bloody great. I mean, yes, of course. Anything you say.'

Osbourne staggered up the stairs, missing the top step. He fell into his bedroom. Angela poured the rest of the bottle of champagne down the sink and waited.

At five forty-five, Angela walked up the stairs into Osbourne's bedroom. He had done as she had instructed. And was unsurprisingly attentive. Angela stood at the bottom of the bed and dangled the handcuffs. Osbourne smiled.

'Give me your left hand.' She handcuffed it to the bedstead.

'Now give me your right hand.' She did the same.

Five fifty. 'Now I am going to go downstairs. For some more champagne. When I return I shall be naked.'

Angela turned and left Osbourne. She went downstairs, quietly opened the back door, left the house and closed the door behind her.

At six, Jack and Angela, at opposite ends of the street, could hear Osbourne's screams. They seemed to last longer than Jack had expected before the trip switch blew and Osbourne's house plunged into darkness.

*

The next morning, Osbourne hammered on the communal front door of Angela's flat. Eventually it opened and Angela's elderly neighbour appeared, looking anxiously at the aggressive-looking man in front of her.

'I've come to see Angela Watson,' he said.

'I'm afraid you're too late. They left last night,' the lady replied.

'Going where?'

'I don't know. They packed up over the last couple of days and have moved somewhere else. I'm awfully sorry but I don't know where to and they haven't left a forwarding address.'

'You say "they". Who was she with?'

'A charming young man called Jack Mayhew.'

Some miles away, in Angela's car, Jack smiled to himself as he thought: *ONE DOWN.*

CHAPTER 11

The meeting room of Macfarlane's Bank smelled of the polished wood and leather that made up most of the interior. The chairman's personal collection of Scottish seventeenth- and eighteenth-century oil paintings hung confidently on the walls around a substantial walnut boardroom table. Large leather chairs on sturdy chrome legs automatically returned to their central position when its occupants swivelled and left them unoccupied. A large chiming brass carriage clock ticked reliably above an Italian marble mantelpiece. The ambience of the room reflected the culture of the bank. Solid, neat, reliable, trustworthy, experienced and never in a hurry.

'I don't think we shall have much trouble raising the money for this turnround,' said Slimbridge through wet lips. 'But having recently met you, I thought you'd like first refusal.'

'Dare we observe that your projections look rather, well, like hockey sticks?' asked Tim, although the question was a rhetorical one. 'And how much are you proposing to invest yourself? I can't see any reference to that.'

'We are going to factor the debt and invest the cash back into the company in return for shares in my name.'

'But the cash receipt from selling the debt to the factoring business isn't your money. It belongs to the company.'

'I will add it to the director's loan account.'

There was a long pause whilst Tim and George exchanged glances before Tim said quietly, 'As the company stands at present, the cash receipt is required in the business; but I just wonder how you think that cash properly represents an injection by yourself in return for shares. We think the business needs new money, not recycled money already locked in the business.'

'That's why we've come to see you. It's a great opportunity,' replied Slimbridge, wiping his wet lips on his sleeve and making a slight snorting sound.

'I'll just have a chat with George outside for a moment. Do help yourself to some more coffee. Would you like some more biscuits?' asked Tim, looking down at the empty plate.

'Please. Seem to have scoffed the lot. No lunch!'

'I'll send for some. Please excuse us,' said Tim, standing and nodding slightly to George in the direction of the door.

As soon as the door was closed behind them George said in a stage whisper, 'Tim, that guy is a crook. I wouldn't trust him as far as I could throw him, and that is not very far. What an arse the man is.'

'Don't worry. I didn't take to him when he came here last time. I am just pretending to be discussing the deal with you. We'll go back in in ten minutes and make our excuses for not investing. Some other sucker probably will. The City is awash with cash and chaps wet behind the ears with an eye on the bonus pool. I'm just going to make a call on something else and then we will go back in.'

Behind the closed door of the boardroom, James, Slimbridge's unqualified accountant, said quietly, 'Maybe we should cut the cash requirement a little.'

'Yes, where can we squeeze? I know, push the creditor days out from ninety to one hundred and twenty. That should do it,' instructed Slimbridge.

'I thought ninety was a bit steep given that suppliers are not going to be keen to advance any credit to this business at all, but let's...' James tailed off as Tim and George re-entered the room.

'Gentlemen,' said Tim, not bothering to sit down, 'we think the risk profile on this one is not good for us. I'm sorry. Many thanks, though, for giving us the opportunity. George will show you out.'

On his return George muttered, 'What a shyster,' and asked, 'You're in corporate finance, but I'm a bond trader. So same question as last time: why did you need me?'

'Oh. Just to make up the numbers,' replied Tim, smiling at him, pleased with the repeat of his joke, and administering a playful thump on the shoulder.

*

'Why Cheltenham?' asked Jack.

'Not too far from where I know and not too near to bump into Benedict Osbourne,' replied Angela over the noise of her shaking blue Ford Anglia.

'Very wise. And didn't you have this car when you were my matron?' asked Jack, emphasising the word matron as if he were Leslie Phillips in a *Carry On* film.

'Yes, I did! Fancy remembering that,' replied Angela, laughing and tossing her hair.

'Must be one of the oldest in the country. Are you sure we are going to get there?'

'Be careful. Since you lost your car you can't complain. And have you decided where you are going to live yet?'

'Well, I have some ideas,' said Jack, gazing out of the window, uncertain whether now was the right time.

The flat Angela had rented in the Montpellier area of Cheltenham was not dissimilar in style to the one Jack had had in Bath. Behind the elegant Regency facade lay a faintly squalid shared entrance hall, off which stood a cream-coloured door. Attached was a brass figure five that had been screwed on poorly so that the number was crooked. There was, as usual, a faint smell of damp. The floor tiles – a later addition, Victorian – were dirty. The remains of dead leaves lay in the corners of the hall. Jack wondered how long they had been there. Once inside, though, the furnished flat appeared newly painted, cream again, and clean. A large bay window in the sitting room let in the bright morning sun. At the end of the room was a small kitchenette. Jack could see one bedroom with a double bed.

Angela had already moved most of her few possessions into the flat and Jack helped her with the rest. The old pink teddy bear fell out of the top of the box Jack was carrying.

'Be careful of Wilberforce. He is very old. Do you remember him spying on us when you came to my room that time at school? I put him under my bed so he wouldn't report me.'

'Can't say I did. You were the only detail on my mind.'

'How sweet,' said Angela, looking over her shoulder and under her eyebrows, smiling at Jack. 'Coffee?'

'I thought you might prefer this,' said Jack, producing a bottle of champagne from his bag. 'House-warming present.'

'Why yes, Jack. I would prefer that. Champagne at eleven in the morning. How decadent.'

'The French say that's the best time to drink it,' said Jack, opening the bottle carefully. 'It's not that cold, I'm afraid.'

As Jack handed Angela a full glass, she grasped his hand as well as the glass and moved towards him. She held it a little too long. As she released his hand and took the glass she looked up at Jack and pushed her tongue on to her top lip, licking it briefly.

'Let's sit over here,' she said, moving to the sofa by the large window, sitting and patting the seat beside her.

There was a silence. Jack looked at her. Even with no make-up and hair ruffled and untidy from the move, Angela was still attractive. Her eyes shone and the light from the bay window played on her dark brown hair. She wore tight dark blue jeans and a T-shirt with "The Eagles" written on the front in their unmistakable brown logo.

'"Hotel California",' she said. 'Now you are here, you have no alternative but to stay.'

'You mean that?' said Jack, standing to reach for the bottle.

'Well that's what the Eagles reckon, isn't it?' she said in a teasing tone.

Jack ensured that Angela drank most of the champagne.

When Jack sat down again, he was closer to Angela. She gently put her hand on his knee. Jack moved his hand onto her thigh and looked at her.

'Remember the last time?' asked Angela with her familiar raised eyebrow.

'You weren't wearing trousers then.'

'That can be fixed,' said Angela.

As they kissed, Jack felt a tenderness he had missed. Angela moved her hand down to his crotch and felt the bulge beneath his trousers. As she slowly opened the buttons of his flies, she said, 'Don't do what you did last time.'

'I'll try not to,' Jack replied as Angela opened her mouth and went down on him.

*

Despite having spent the afternoon between the sofa and the bedroom and the evening sun now casting a red glow on the sitting-room wall, Angela displayed only one kind of hunger. Her appetite for Jack's body was voracious, as if she had reserved her pent-up need for him since he was a schoolboy until it was at last satisfied in a series of shuddering explosions. Yet Jack's thoughts by dusk were of food. How could this be? he thought. This was his fantasy come true. And the pain of his break-up with Mona was fading with each expression of Angela's own hunger. She rolled off him, breathless and her hair damp with sweat.

'What?' she asked as Jack gazed at her with a lopsided grin.

'Aren't you hungry?'

'Yes, but you stay there. I'll go. I could do with some air…!'

*

Benedict Osbourne pulled the collar of his coat up around his neck while the rain, driven by a north wind, lashed his body with a soaking determination. Gloomy dusk intensified into a dark night. A leaf blew into his face, sticking to his cheek. Osbourne waited. And waited. A black cat crossed the street, slunk up towards him and sat near his right foot, staring up at him. Osbourne kicked it away, making sharp contact with his foot.

Much later, as Angela left the flat, Osbourne pushed himself further into the clump of trees opposite so that he would not be noticed. Angela's car reversed out of its parking space near the house and disappeared from view. The light from the bedroom window went out. Jack was alone. Osbourne felt the outside of his coat pocket and then crossed the road towards the flat. A dog barked as he reached the front door. Osbourne then eased his credit card between the edge of the front door and its frame, pushing gently against the curve of the lock. The card bent as the catch slid back. The door appeared to stick and so Osbourne leaned on it, increasingly heavily. It opened with a creak and a scratching sound as it scuffed across the Victorian tiles. He froze. 'Back already?' said Jack as he turned over and went back to sleep. Osbourne left the door unclosed, waited a few minutes and then moved slowly up the stairs to where Jack lay asleep.

*

Angela reached a smart-looking Indian restaurant which advertised the best Indian food outside Bengal and parked her car. There was a short queue of expectant diners and so she sat on a plush red velvet chair and waited to order her takeaway.

*

Jack awoke with a start, conscious of a hard object pushing into his left temple. 'Don't move,' said Osbourne, tightening his grip around the handle of a gun. Jack flinched as out of the corner of his eye he glimpsed the steel barrel.

'Now slowly get out of bed and sit on that chair,' said Osbourne, pointing with his free hand at a small wooden chair in the corner of the bedroom. Naked, and now breathing heavily, Jack stood and moved slowly towards the chair, the gun not leaving his temple. Osbourne had prepared a webbed strap, already buckled so that he could drop it with one hand over Jack's head and around the chair. He tied Jack to it tightly.

Osbourne moved to the edge of the bed and sat on it gently, not averting his gaze from Jack. He laid the pistol next to him on the bed. Jack glanced at him and then the gun, as if planning his next move.

'We've been here before, haven't we, Mayhew?'

Osbourne gazed absentmindedly at his shoes, wet from the rain. 'A long time ago. Although this time you are in rather more danger. Don't you think?'

Jack did not answer.

'Both my parents think I am a failure. They always have,' he said. 'But you aren't, are you? Oh no. Blue-eyed boy. Head of house. Oxford. Successful business. Pretty girlfriends. Well. Nothing is forever.'

'What do you want?' asked Jack.

Osbourne began to recall his school days as if in a dream. He looked glazed and at times vacant. His story was punctuated by "Well, I'm not a failure, am I?" and "I'll show them".

Noticing an open bottle of red wine and two glasses on a table near the door, Osbourne rose from the bed, inspected the bottle and poured himself a drink. 'Want some?' he asked. Jack shook his head. Minutes passed. Osbourne poured another glass of wine and then drained the bottle. He stared at Jack.

'You see, the thing is, I have not had your advantages. My sisters have. They're a bit like you. Things have gone well for them. My parents like that...' Osbourne's voice dropped as he stared again at his shoes. 'Still, I have a very partial solution.' Osbourne felt in his trouser pocket and pulled out a single sheet of typed paper and a pen.

'Sign here.'

'What is it?'

'It's your promise to pay me £50,000 per year for the next ten years. That should go some way towards compensating me for taking Jason's from under my nose;

but not for getting me expelled from school. I'll think of something else for that.'

Jack wondered if Osbourne really believed that his expulsion was not his own fault. There was something manic in his manner. A twitch. A tightly crazed laugh. 'I have no money. As you know, I lost everything,' Jack said.

'You will have. You have time. And you are always successful in the end, aren't you, Mayhew?'

'I can't sign that,' said Jack.

Osbourne rose from the bed and walked slowly towards Jack, levelling the gun at Jack's face. Then, placing the barrel of the gun on Jack's forehead, he said, 'I think you are going to change your mind, aren't you, Mayhew?'

Jack tried to move his head away from the hard steel of the gun barrel, but Osbourne followed his every movement.

Bringing his face close to Jack's and waving a pen in front of his eyes, Osbourne cocked the trigger and said, 'I will count to three. One… two… three.'

Still pointing the gun at Jack's head, Osbourne smiled. 'Don't worry. Just one of my silly games. It's not loaded. I'm sorry. I'm sorry for what I did to you at school. And I'm sorry if I have frightened you now. Just one of my silly games.'

Jack was surprised to be able to hear the shot. But he felt nothing other than the weight of Osbourne's body hitting him. The two of them toppled the chair on which Jack was strapped and crashed to the ground. The blood in Jack's eyes prevented him from seeing clearly the two armed police officers who pulled Osbourne's lifeless body off him. They hoisted Jack up from the floor, still strapped to the chair, and untied him. Angela appeared at the doorway. She stood for a few seconds, immobile with shock. The police laid Osbourne flat on the floor, muttered something to Angela and gently tried to usher her away from the scene. Pulling her arms free of their grasp she flung herself towards Jack and cradled him in her lap.

Shortly afterwards, the two police officers joined a third in the street below, a siren wailed and blue flashing lights appeared as an ambulance arrived.

*

Jack took some days to begin to recover from the shock of what had happened to him. And he felt emotionally conflicted. His revenge on Osbourne was not supposed to lead to his death. Jack had even felt he could forgive him. After all, Osbourne's torture of Jack was a schoolboy prank, repaid later in kind. But now Jack's forgiveness was muddled with guilt. And as his memory of the incident flashed back at him he tried to work out how the police knew of Osbourne's presence. And why were they armed? Angela was equally puzzled but reminded him that the police had said they would provide an explanation when Jack was ready to talk to them. They had agreed to come to the flat.

'Benedict Osbourne was a very disturbed young man,' said the WPC with the fixed but kindly smile of the welfare professional. Jack thought the police must have many unpleasant duties of this type to perform.

'We have had reports of him threatening people before. And so we have been keeping an eye on him for some time.'

'But how did you know he was here?' asked Angela.

'He drew a gun on somebody yesterday. We followed him here with the intention of arresting him. Of course, we had to be careful as we thought he might be armed. So we were armed too.'

Jack looked bewildered. 'But why didn't you just arrest him once you got here, instead of shooting him dead? He told me the gun wasn't loaded. Just one of his silly pranks, he said.'

'We shot because when we arrived, he was pointing a gun at your head.'

'But it wasn't loaded.'

'Jack. It was.'

CHAPTER 12

Jack needed a job. And to eat. He walked to the nearby parade of shops and returned with cod and chips wrapped in a recent copy of the *Birmingham Evening Mail*.

'Why don't you apply for that?' asked Angela, pointing at a small, boxed advertisement in the Situations Vacant section, covered in chip fat.

'Because it is in the Black Country, in an engineering group and for a job I know nothing about. I'm not an engineer, don't like Birmingham and aside from some rather thin MBA theory I know nothing about business development. I'd be about as useful as a barber on the steps of the guillotine.' *But I need a job*, he thought.

*

Jack borrowed Angela's old car and parked it well away from the group head office where he was to attend his interview. Thick, yellow-edged smoke from the neighbouring foundries blotted out the sun and hung in the air, infecting it with an acrid smell. A large building with no roof stood forlornly next to where he had parked. Metal roof supports stood twisted, no longer supporting anything at all. Jack imagined the activity that had until recently occupied the space between the crumbling factory walls. The noise of metal being pressed, formed, bashed, cut and sawn. Workmen shouting above the din. The click, click of welding machines. Sirens. Flashing lights. Thump. Clunk. Clang.

At the top of a set of steps worn by a thousand boots, above a large red door in need of paint, an engraved sign of chipped and weathered stone declared: "Arnold Foundries Group Ltd 1858". At that time, the entrance would have been impressive, thought Jack. He imagined the entrepreneurs of the Industrial Revolution who by now had consolidated their positions. Large rotund men in heavy wool suits and waistcoats. A thick gold watch chain threaded into a breast pocket and securing a heavy fob watch with a gnarled and chunky winder. These men were now rich, their workers short-lived, dirty and poor.

Jack announced his arrival to the presentable lady at the reception. He was asked to take a seat, but worried that his newly cleaned suit would pick up some of the grey dust which appeared to line every surface. The receptionist noticed him run his finger over the front edge of her desk.

'Foundry soot. The new chimney is supposed to have stopped it but... well. You know. Times are hard. I hope you aren't asthmatic.'

A middle-aged lady in a tweed suit and neat, short grey curled hair appeared at the doorway.

'I'm Mrs Braithwaite, Mr Carey's PA. Mr Carey is running late, so you had better come upstairs and I will give you a cup of coffee,' she said in a broad Black Country accent.

She poured, from a filter coffee pot, a cup of black liquid that looked and tasted as if all the water had been boiled out of it the previous day. Mrs Braithwaite noticed Jack's slight wince as he gulped the strong, astringent liquid.

'Sorry, would you like some sugar? I think we have some somewhere. None of us takes it.'

Jack was reminded of an earlier television advertisement for M&B bitter "for the men of the Midlands" and wondered if that applied to this drink they mistook for coffee.

'No thanks, I'm fine.' Jack paused, thinking of something to say as Mrs Braithwaite bashed away at her typewriter, peering at a sheet of paper on her desk and muttering about Mr Carey's poor handwriting. 'It's nice to be back in Birmingham. I haven't been here for a while,' he said weakly.

'Birmingham?' said Mrs Braithwaite, looking aghast at Jack. 'This isn't Birmingham. You'd better not make that mistake around here. This is the Black Country and don't you forget it. Birmingham ends at the Albion Ground up the road. West Brom isn't in Birmingham. Birmingham...' she mumbled, shaking her head and looking back down at her work.

'Oh, I'm so sorry. Of course. How silly of me. I won't make that mistake again,' said Jack, feeling sure that he would. *They do speak differently to Brummies*, he thought. *It is a more tuneful and less harsh accent.* Jack's mother thought the Birmingham accent was the ugliest in the country. This was less ugly, more comical.

Jack's interview was scheduled for 10.30 a.m. At ten forty-five he was offered another cup of coffee, which he politely declined, not having managed to finish the first one. He wondered whether he could convince those interviewing him that his restaurant experience added to his more recent MBA would be sufficient to win him the job. The phone on the secretary's desk rang.

'Sandra Braithwaite,' she said, with a hard "a". Then, toning down her thick accent somewhat, she replied to the person on the other end of the telephone, 'No, he isn't here yet.' Then, 'Yes, of course I will tell you when he arrives.'

At five past eleven Jack could hear female laughter downstairs and steps being taken two at a time. Then through the open door to the outer office where Jack was sitting strode a tall, slim man in his late thirties. But he looked older. The skin of his face was pockmarked as if he had suffered from bad acne in his teens. His light grey suit looked as though it had been tailored for him. His shoes were black and well-polished. Brown hair showed the first hint of grey at the temples. As he placed his two black leather briefcases on the floor beside him he quickly adjusted his short fringe, almost nervously. He appeared to be forcing his lips tightly closed, not in a pout but in a manner that added to his air of concentration. Slightly close-set eyes looked at Jack briefly and then at Mrs Braithwaite.

'Mr Carey, this is Jack Mayhew. He is here for his interview. I have put the papers in the boardroom. I'll call Mr Marwick and tell him you are here, and bring you a cup of coffee.'

Smiling for the first time, Bill Carey, deputy chief

executive of Arnold Foundries Group plc, stretched out his hand towards Jack and introduced himself as Jack stood. Mr Carey's handshake was firm and as it gripped Jack's, Carey's eyes burnt purposefully into his, as if searching for something, but which had the effect of showing who was in charge.

'May I call you Jack?' he asked.

'Of course,' Jack replied, surprised at Carey's informality. Carey did not, however, ask Jack to call him Bill.

Jack followed Carey down a narrow dark corridor and into the group boardroom. Twelve old chairs covered in worn green leather, some ripped, surrounded a large oak table. The edges of the table were grimy, the thin varnish having been worn by the sweat of nervous hands. The grey carpet was worn and not clean. But what struck Jack hardest was the smell: acrid, pungent and metallic.

As Jack sat at the table, on Carey's invitation, a slender middle-aged man of average height, with straight dark hair, black horn-rimmed glasses and a neat appearance, bustled into the room.

'Sorry, Bill. Have I missed anything?'

'No, we haven't started. Angus, this is Jack Mayhew.' Carey then sighed briskly and closed the dirty steel-framed window next to him. Through it Jack could see clouds of yellowish smoke belching from a tall chimney above a factory.

'That foundry smoke is really bad today. If the factory inspector gets wind of it again, we shall all be in trouble.'

'At least the foundry is still in business...' added Angus Marwick wistfully.

'For how much longer?' added Carey. 'Sorry, Jack, I don't want to put you off...' he continued, waiting for Jack's reply.

'Oh, that wouldn't put me off,' said Jack, reading the cue Carey had given him correctly.

Carey smiled. 'Good. I like your CV. Unusual.'

Meaning unusual to have someone with no suitable experience whatever applying for this type of job, thought Jack.

'How much debt are you in?' Carey asked, with a grin and a raised eyebrow.

'Bill, I don't think you can ask Mr Mayhew that. At least not at a first meeting,' chipped in Marwick, with a scoffing chuckle and straightening the full length of his dark grey polyester tie.

'Well...' said Jack, shuffling uncomfortably in his seat.

'You don't have to answer that,' said Carey. 'Let me tell you a bit about what is going on here. We are trying to complete a rescue of this company. Sandy Brockhouse was installed as rescue chairman and chief executive six months ago. The old board were asked by the banks to repay the overdraft by that Friday or accept Sandy as chairman. So they had no choice. Sandy showed half the board the exit in week one. I can't possibly say, but I suspect others will follow—'

'Bill...' interjected Marwick, suggesting Carey had gone too far again.

'Having completed his review with the aid of reporting accountants, Sandy closed four factories in the first three months, making 3,000 people redundant. The dole queues around here stretch to Dudley and back. Sandy appointed me as deputy chief executive last month and if I am a good boy he will make me chief executive sometime later this year. The group is still substantially in debt, such that each week Angus and I wonder how we are going to pay the remaining 6,000 employees. The Revenue hasn't been paid for three months and more closures will follow if we can afford the redundancy payments. It is a big if. Of course, the trade unions try to resist us every step of the way. I was a Labour councillor once but the sooner Mrs Thatcher succeeds in changing the employment legislation more in our favour the more likely we are to survive. But we are still here. And if I have anything to do with it we shall be next year, and the year after that.'

Carey gazed at Jack, trying to assess his reaction. 'Does any of what I have said sound familiar to you?' he asked, narrowing his eyes.

'Well, I have been through some tough times in the last year or two.'

'That's exactly why I wanted to see you. Judging by your CV you are obviously bright, and goodness knows we need bright people here. But as important, you are going to be used to muck and bullets. You have had your back against the wall and you are still standing. Tell me about the restaurant business.'

Carey and Marwick both leaned back in their chairs, looked at Jack and waited for his reply.

*

Jack had been distracted by thoughts of the unresolved issue of Steve Gregson, but now looked wide-eyed at the letter in his hands.

'What's the matter?' asked Angela, peering over her cup of coffee.

'They've offered me the job.'

'Well, I'm not surprised. You could do that restaurant job standing on your head.'

'No, I mean the one at Arnold Foundries. Development manager, whatever that means. That's nice. Bill Carey has written in black ink on the bottom: *Do join us.* I'm going to turn it down and take the restaurant job. I can't see myself working in a nearly bust engineering company. I don't know anything about engineering. Anyway, it might go bust on me. I've got enough problems as it is.'

Angela looked over Jack's shoulder at the letter. Her warm breath and spicy perfume distracted him for a moment.

'What do you think?' asked Jack.

'This,' replied Angela, taking him in her arms and kissing him passionately on the lips.

*

'It's Bill Carey,' said Angela, handing Jack the phone.

'What, again?' mouthed Jack.

'I'm wondering how you are getting on at the restaurant? We still need you and so I'm hoping not that well.'

'Fine, thanks,' lied Jack.

'Well, keep in touch. I think you are a flyer. You know where we are.' The phone went dead.

Jack gave Angela a long look while he thought through his options. The restaurant work was tedious. And he could not see how his ambitions could be satisfied there. On the other hand, the work at Arnold Foundries offered Jack a huge opportunity. Carey was keen to have him. He had said with a smile that there was something in Jack that reminded him of himself when he was younger. And the salary was much higher than that at the restaurant. Jack was not confident he could do the job, but Carey seemed to see things differently.

CHAPTER 13

Three months later

'This is Jack Mayhew,' said Carey to the short, middle-aged, grey-looking man with round shoulders in the chair opposite them. 'I think he may be able to help you. Please take him up to Sheffield and show him around the factory. How does tomorrow sound?'

The man manoeuvred his corpulent frame through the boardroom door and muttered, 'From the management book of lies: "I'm from head office, I'm here to help you".' *One of the old-school seventies' industrialists*, thought Jack. He imagined long lunches in the directors' box at the West Bromwich Albion football ground, while they discussed which average player to sponsor the following season.

'Name's Douglas Highcliffe,' said the man, holding out his hand. 'I'm the main board director responsible for Barnsley Stampings.'

That evening Jack studied the monthly accounts and management reports that Carey had given him in their first meeting since Jack joined Arnold Foundries plc. The company, Barnsley Stampings Ltd, had lost its biggest customer overnight. Jack worked out that this represented thirty-five per cent of the company's annual turnover. *How does Carey think I can fix that?* thought Jack. *And what is a metal pressings business doing in a foundries group, anyway?*

Soon after joining the motorway in Highcliffe's silver Daimler the next morning, they came to a standstill. Highcliffe announced that he did not have time to sit in a traffic jam and returned to his office, leaving Jack to explain to Carey what had happened.

Carey pursed his lips, narrowed his eyes and told Jack to go to Sheffield on his own.

'I will deal with Highcliffe and tell Bailey, the MD up there, to expect you in the morning. No excuses. Tell me what you think the day after.' The phone rang. 'Yes, put him through.' Carey's tone of voice changed. 'Sandy, how are you?' he greeted the chairman ingratiatingly and waved Jack away. Jack left Carey's office and passed three other senior managers, one of whom asked how long Carey was going to be, adding quietly that he had already been waiting an hour. The pretty but efficient-looking young secretary who had replaced Mrs Braithwaite scowled at the man who had spoken and made a note on her pad.

*

Four men in blue overalls eyed Jack's arrival suspiciously over thin clouds of the smoke of untipped cigarettes. Their yellow fingers betrayed decades of habit. *And decades of pawing over the bare-breasted beauty on page three of The Sun,* thought Jack. As the radio presenter intoned that Mrs Thatcher was unlikely to deviate from her tough monetarist stance, despite the problems it seemed to inflict on British industry, and pressure from "the wets", Jack switched off the car radio.

The sun confined its presence to newspapers alone. Grey skies and drizzle enveloped Jack as he locked his new company car, pulled his black coat around him and strode a little nervously towards a double glass door over which a grey and red plastic sign announced "Reception". One of the men in blue made a remark to the others as Jack passed, which resulted in unforced laughter.

Jack could hear the deep, heavy thump and ching as small pieces of pressed metal left the press and joined the hundreds of other identical parts bound for the motor industry. A hooter sounded as Jack pushed open the door and the men ambled slowly back into the factory.

A pale girl in her twenties sat behind a desk filing her nails and peered through her fringe at Jack, saying nothing.

'Good morning. I'm here to see Mr Bailey.'

'Ooo are ya?' said the "receptionist".

'Jack Mayhew. Am I not expected?'

'I don't know nuffink. I'm joost a trainee. Doreen, is Mr Bailey espectin' someone?' she shouted through an open door.

'Don't know. Ask him,' said a voice.

Jack noted the effectiveness of the "reception" and stood as an attractive woman in her forties, who introduced herself as Mr Bailey's secretary, arrived to take him up to his office. She gazed at Jack a little too long. As she and Jack made their way up the stairs, the secretary rolled her ample hips and Jack noticed her wink at the receptionist. Both women giggled.

Sidney "call me Sid" Bailey was tall and slender with black hair forced into place by rather too much Brylcreem. He wore an ill-fitting grey double-breasted suit that was probably once fashionable. He stood as Jack entered the room and bent awkwardly to extend a strangely knobbly right hand towards him.

'Good morning, young man. What can I do for you?'

Young man? and *What can I do for you?* thought Jack, uneasy at the patronising implication of both.

'Didn't Bill Carey tell you I was coming?' asked Jack, already knowing the truthful answer.

'Well, he might have said something about it. But we don't take much notice of him up here, you know. His interest is mainly in foundries, and in closing those.' Bailey gave a scoffing laugh. 'We have been quite successful here at Barnsley Stampings, you know. Without us the group would have gone bust months ago. D'ya know that?'

'Umm, well, I notice that you made a third of a million profit last year—'

'The only company in the group that did, by the way,' interjected Bailey.

'Yes, I know,' continued Jack. 'But I noticed that you have lost a lot of business recently.'

'Well. You say "a lot". It is just one customer,' said Bailey, looking out of the window and leaning back in his chair and scoffing again. Jack noticed his hand shake as he lit a cigarette and tossed the packet towards Jack by way of offering him one. Jack shook his head and smiled.

'Mr Bailey—'

'Sid, young man. Call me Sid.'

'Sid, that one customer accounts for thirty-five per cent of your business, doesn't it?'

Bailey plainly didn't know. 'Well, you could put it that way, I suppose. But what you don't realise, young man, is that we supply parts for the entire model life of a vehicle. And when the vehicle isn't made any more that work obviously ceases. But don't worry, we will get some other work. I'll go and see them and win some other business.'

'How will you do that?'

'I shall make them an offer they cannot possibly refuse.'

'You mean drop the price.'

'Exactly, young man. Tends to work, y'know.'

'Yes. It can do. But I also notice that your gross margins have been dropping over the last few months. So you can't really do that, can you?'

'Well… that's a matter for Dick, our finance man. And for Brian, our production chap, to bloody well get some cost out of that factory, as I have been telling him to for months – years. We can't compete otherwise. I've told him and told him. Does he listen? No, of course not. And then what happens? I get some youngster from head office coming up here asking questions and making me feel un-com-fort-able. I've been doing this job for seven years. And it is all about sales, this business. Sales, sales. The factory's job is to make the stuff to a profit. Geddit, Jack?'

Jack looked at Sid Bailey and took a deep breath. 'Could you introduce me to Dick, please? I want to spend some time getting more deeply into the numbers.'

'Yes, of course. Dorothy, please could you take this young man to see Dick and then get me Land Rover on the phone. I need to go and get that business back.'

Dorothy smiled warmly at Jack and walked rather too closely to him as they ambled up the glass- and aluminium-panelled corridor.

'Will you be wanting to stay the night up here? Shall I book you a hotel?' she asked, trying to smarten her accent.

'I am staying, but I've booked somewhere, thanks.'

'Oh, where?'

'The Grand in town. Is it OK?'

'Oh. The Grand,' said Dorothy with a lopsided grin. 'Well, I'm sure you will have a nice time there,' she added, grinning again. Jack was not sure why she winked at him.

*

Once in his hotel room Jack took a beer from the minibar and began to study the papers Dick had given him. He had made a casual remark about Sid's sales technique not helping profit margins and had also handed him three sets of the accounts of competitors. Jack glanced at these and noticed the businesses were all profitable and of similar size to Barnsley Stampings. He then left his room to find the restaurant for dinner.

The restaurant was neo-plush. Jack noticed that the decoration was of the type fashionable a decade previously further south. Dark carpets with bright orange swirls.

Unnecessary chandeliers. Candles on tables, dripping wax on to crisp but worn white linen. Waiters in shiny, ill-fitting suits looking as though they were Moss Bros hire cast-offs. A trolley with an unfeasibly large stainless-steel dome trundled from table to table offering puddings or "sweets", as the stout waitress preferred to call them, to the expectant customers. Black Forest gateau. Stewed prunes. Oranges in Cointreau. Her party piece appeared to be to pour the cream into a bowl from a ladle taking it high above her head to the delight and applause of the diners. Jack suspected that this trick had been perfected over years. "Years of self-denial", as his geography master at prep school would say as he startled the boys with his card tricks. A pianist with a poorly fitting dark toupee played flamboyantly in one corner of the room. At corner tables, middle-aged men in suits sat opposite women in tight dresses considerably younger than themselves. Neither behaved as if they were man and wife, and yet displayed a certain intimacy. Jack had no difficulty in imagining the scene that would take place sordidly and hurriedly in three hours' time.

Jack could not resist ordering Steak Diane. The waiter did not disappoint him with his flamboyant and inflammatory display as he stirred the brandy, flaming, into the sauce at the table. Of course, there was Blue Nun and Mateus Rosé on the wine list. Too smart for Hirondelle. A bottle of decent Châteauneuf-du-Pape on Arnold Foundries plc dulled Jack's thinking about the problems facing Barnsley Stampings. And as he left his table having signed the bill his attention was drawn by a blonde girl in a tight red dress, sitting alone near the bar. He sat on a small sofa opposite and ordered a brandy. Almost immediately, the girl came over to him and squeezed onto the sofa next to him. The strong scent of Oscar de la Renta preceded her.

'You on your own?' she suggested.

'Yes. You?'

'Well, yes. Aren't you the lucky one? I'm Georgia.' A flirtatious smile, a giggle and a hand on his knee.

They talked for a while. She asked for champagne. She tossed her long blonde hair and tilted her head whilst pretending to be fascinated by Jack's conversation. She laughed convincingly and often at what Jack thought only mildly amusing.

'You're funny. Shall we go to your room?'

Jack had already concluded that Georgia had another name, regularly worked the room and was professionally engaged in that capacity.

Jack smiled. 'I'm surprised you do this. I mean, why do you? You don't know me. I might be dangerous. There must be a lot of other things you could do.' As he spoke, Jack thought his missionary zeal would not be appreciated. 'And I'm afraid I don't pay for what you are offering. Sorry.'

'I don't need a lecture. And your room could be fun. I think you know that. And you are very handsome. You won't be disappointed.' Georgia stroked Jack's cheek with one hand and whilst she turned her back to the bar, put her other hand between Jack's legs.

Jack didn't move.

'Look, are we going to your room or not? I can't stay here otherwise.'

'No, I'm sorry. You are lovely. But. No. Thanks.'

Without looking round at Jack, or saying another word, Georgia stood and moved straight towards the table nearest the bar where another man was sitting alone. As she did so, Jack caught the eye of another girl, similarly dressed, who was deep in conversation with an Asian-looking man about twice her age. There was a moment's recognition, but no words were exchanged. It was Tabitha from Arthur's. He smiled at the memory of their brief liaison.

Tabitha and Jack having spotted each other, Jack moved over to the table where she was sitting. She moved slightly away from the man she was with.

'Hi, Tabitha.'

'Hi, Jack, what are you doing here?' They both spoke at once.

Jack explained briefly and Tabitha said rather vaguely that she was a self-employed estate agent but didn't introduce her companion, who smiled at Jack, nonetheless. The conversation between the three of them was uneasy and so Jack made his apologies and left. As he did so Tabitha wrote a telephone number and her address on a beer mat advertising John Smith's and thrust it into his hand. 'Great to see you, Jack. Give me a call sometime. It's my birthday next week. Remember?' she said, smiling at him. Jack smiled back and made his way to the lift.

With time on his hands, Jack called George from his bedroom. George was coming to Sheffield on business the following week and the two old friends had resolved to try to meet. Jack told George about his chance encounter with Tabitha and they agreed that when George was in Sheffield it would be fun for the three of them to sample the high life of the town, if it existed. George teased Jack about how friendly he had been with her in the Bath restaurant days. Jack did not need reminding of that, nor of the evening Tabitha had spent at his parents' house sharing several bottles of Muscadet with his mother around the kitchen table.

'Such a nice girl, Jack,' his mother had said. 'Knows how to drink, though…!'

*

Bill Carey had asked Jack to meet him at the foundry near Dudley to present his findings and suggested strategy for dealing with Barnsley Stampings. There was a hot smell in the corridor next to the factory where the production director's office was situated. The air caught the back of Jack's throat and made him cough. Two men passed each other ahead of him as one said to the other, 'Aw roit, Fred?'

'Aw roit ah,' came the reply. Jack had learned that this was the equivalent of the French "*Ça va?*", "*Oui, ça va.*" Or indeed the English "How are you, Fred?", "I'm well, thank you. You?", "Yes, very well, thank you."

The door of the foundry production director's office was open. Bill Carey sat uneasily on a small chair, blowing his nose and coughing. The production director was looking sheepish; frightened, even.

'So, fifty redundancies. On my desk by Monday, please. Come in, Jack. Can we use your office, Shaun?' Carey's statement was not a question. Shaun, the production director, left his office, uncertain of where to go.

Carey's stern expression evaporated as a secretary of about twenty-four years old entered the office. She was wearing an incongruously pretty skirt given the grimy, unattractive surroundings.

'Could we both have some coffee, please, Tanya? Thanks.' Carey winked at Jack as she left.

'So, Barnsley Stampings. What do you think?'

Jack was apprehensive. He felt that his analysis was right, but he was tentative in his delivery. 'Well, there is the obvious problem of the lost business to deal with. We're going to need to make about twenty-five per cent of the workforce redundant to stem the losses from that alone. And we should also cut some of the admin and managerial staff too. It may be our chance to get rid of some dead wood.'

Carey smiled for the first time. 'I can tell you who the first one of those will be,' he said.

Jack continued, 'But there is a more fundamental problem. Take a look at these.' He passed three sets of competitors' accounts over the table to Carey. A hooter sounded in the factory and immediately most of the presses were silenced. 'I've made a comparison between our direct wages per head and per pound of sales with these three competitors.' Jack passed over a page of A4 paper on which were typed four neat columns.

'Jesus Christ. We're stuffed,' said Carey, tightening his cheeks and narrowing his eyes. He looked at Jack.

'My idea is to cut both the direct workforce and staff overheads including management by twenty-five per cent and ask the balance of factory workers to take a pay cut of another twenty-five per cent. That way we will be paying them about the same per head as the competition.'

Carey took a long look at Jack and leaned back in his chair. 'There is only one problem,' he said eventually.

'What?'

'The MTU. The metal trades union up there. They have never accepted compulsory redundancies in their history. They won't go quietly. And they are certainly not going to accept a pay cut of any description, let alone one of twenty-five per cent.'

'I've thought of that,' said Jack. 'If we name those that are to leave, the others will know they are safe, for now at least; and so they will vote to accept the deal.'

'They won't, not if the MTU says they can't. But what about the next bit? They will never accept that,' added Carey, seeming uncharacteristically downhearted.

'I intend to explain the facts of life to the union and to the men directly. I shall show them what I have just shown you, quietly take them through it and ask *them* to tell *me* what should be done. It will be obvious even to them. And I shall warn them that if they don't agree we shall be forced to close the company and then they will all be out of a job.'

Carey smiled but shook his head. 'Let's see what Angus says. But I think I know what his reaction will be. Tanya,' he yelled through the wall. 'Please get Mr Marwick on the phone, right away.'

A minute later, Tanya appeared at the doorway. 'Mr Carey, Mr Marwick is in a meeting,' she said.

'Well, get him out. This won't wait,' snapped Carey. Tanya scuttled off, looking alarmed and bewildered.

The phone on Carey's desk rang. Jack heard the finance director's voice on the other end, sounding anxious and subdued. Bill Carey ran through Jack's plan. He heard Marwick say words to the effect that if this was not so serious it would be funny. He doubted whether Jack's MBA and experience was enough and reminded Carey that the cost of closing the company would be so high that the group, in its already fragile state, could not afford it.

'We can't afford not to let Jack do this,' said Carey. 'If he doesn't the losses will be so severe that the recovery of the whole group will be threatened. We may have to put out a profit warning as it is, but it would be much worse if we don't take this action.'

'But the bank won't let us do it. Remember we can hardly move without their permission.'

'We aren't going to tell them,' retorted Carey. There was a silence on the other end of the phone. 'Angus?' he said.

'Well, I'm not at all happy about it. I don't think it is a resigning matter, but nor do I think Jack has a chance of getting this past the MTU. And we can't afford a strike either. And, Bill, Jack has no experience of this at all. He is very young… And what will the chairman say?'

'OK, Angus. Thanks for your input,' replied Carey, hanging up the receiver.

'Right, we're doing it,' he said to Jack. 'I already have a broad idea, but I want you to work up the full cost of closure and I will run this past the chairman tonight. The stakes are high, but we have no choice.' Carey thought for a moment. 'I shall phone the MD up there tonight and put him out of his misery and appoint you in his place so that you have the requisite authority. I don't want you undermined. The MTU will have a go at that anyway. You head up there tonight and I shall call you later, when I have spoken to the chairman and fired Sid Bailey.' Carey stood and nodded his head as if confirming his intended actions to himself. He reached out his right hand to shake Jack's.

'Good luck, Jack. I'm reminded of the guy who told his car workers: "I have a thousand jobs at two dollars an hour; I have none at two dollars ten cents." Or something like that. Who was that? Jack Welch at GE, I think, or was it Chrysler?'

'Not sure,' said Jack, somewhat shocked at the speed of Carey's decision and at finding himself managing director of a troubled company he knew little about at the age of twenty-nine.

As Jack left the room, Carey sat at the small desk and gazed out of the window. *Success is shared, failure is personal,* he thought. *And perhaps Jack is indeed too young. So if it doesn't work, and it probably won't, I shall fire Jack. But we'll still have a great deal of explaining to do to the City when our results fall badly short and we are back in the hands of the banks. Jack Welch, the tough boss of the American engineering group GE, had a nickname: Neutron Jack. When Jack leaves the factory all the people have gone and only the shell of the building remains.*

*

Jack arranged to meet Tabitha and George in a lively disco bar in town on the day of her birthday. Even though loon pants and flared trousers had not been in fashion in the south of the country for years, the young of Sheffield were oblivious to that fact. "Flash Dance" faded to "Beat It" as the more popular girls pointed their fingers at young men aspiring not to do so. George and Jack found a space for their Theakston's Old Peculier next to full ashtrays smelling of cheap cigarette stubs.

'Isn't there anywhere better than this?' yelled George.

'Noo, lad,' replied Jack in a faux Yorkshire accent. 'This is the north of England remember. And this is considered trendy.'

A large girl pushed her way past Jack, placing her hand on his shoulder as she did so. 'Anyone sittin' 'ere, luvs?' she asked.

'Yes – soon. Sorry,' replied Jack but wondering how long Tabitha would be.

After another two pints each, much glancing at the door, and scowls from the girl who had asked for the seat, Tabitha had still not arrived.

An hour later, the barman shouted, 'Last orders', and then inevitably and promptly at 11 p.m. yelled, 'Get yer beer off... 'Ave yer no 'omes ter go to?' The music stopped and bright lights were switched on to encourage the drunken mob to disperse into the night.

'I'm worried about Tabitha,' said Jack. 'She often used to be late but it wasn't like her to just not show up. And it's her birthday. You know how she liked to be the centre of attention. I'm going to drive to her house to see if she's OK. She gave me her address. It's not far from here.'

George pulled a face at Jack.

'What?' asked Jack.

'You're well over the limit. The police seem to be making extra use of those breathalysers. And you already have a motoring record – remember?'

'Well, we can't just ignore the fact that she hasn't turned up.'

'Not used to being stood up, are you? Look, give me the address. I'll go on the way back to my hotel. You can walk to yours from here. I'll call you to let you know what's happened. Maybe she just forgot.'

*

Back in his hotel room, Jack explained on the phone to Angela what had happened, then asked, 'What are you wearing?'

'Nothing. And I wish you were here,' she purred.

'Well, I asked for that, I suppose, but stop it. I must work. I'll have to leave you to whatever it is you are about to do. Night.'

Jack hung up and tried to refocus his mind back on to his strategy for achieving what his senior colleagues at Arnold Foundries plc thought was impossible.

Brian Oldsworthy, the production director of Barnsley Stampings, had introduced Jack to the senior union representatives whose support would be key to avoiding a strike. Jack would try to obtain their support for a compulsory twenty-five per cent reduction in the workforce at the same time as pushing through a twenty-five per cent pay cut for those remaining. Carey's reminder that the MTU had agreed to neither in their history swirled around his mind as he tried but failed to sleep. He picked up his copy of *The Times* and applied his racing mind to the crossword.

George arrived outside Tabitha's first-floor flat soon after midnight. As he parked his car he noticed that the lights of the flat were on. Taking the stairs two at a time, he reached the front door and knocked gently. No reply. He knocked again and thought he heard a movement from inside but nobody came to the door. Convinced that there was someone inside the flat, he knocked again, harder this time, and called out Tabitha's name. Still no reply. George knelt, pushed open the letterbox and peered into the hall inside. A chair was on its side in the entrance to Tabitha's bedroom, a broken gin bottle lay on the carpet and some underclothes were scattered on the floor. George could just see the edge of the sofa in the sitting room. Draped from the end of the sofa was a hand, motionless and male. George banged hard on the door and tried but failed to force it open.

*

'Which service do you require?' asked the operator.

'Police. And I think ambulance,' replied George, rubbing his forehead and shaking slightly from the cold inside the phone box, which smelled of urine and old cardboard.

Within ten minutes, blue flashing lights appeared around the corner beside the phone box next to the flat, where George was waiting. Two police cars stopped abruptly beside him. Two policemen and a policewoman came up close to George and appeared to sniff his breath. One of the men asked him to point out Tabitha's flat. As they all mounted the stairs, an ambulance arrived.

At the door the police repeated what George had done but having failed to persuade anyone to answer it one of them said, 'Police. Please open the door now otherwise we shall have to force it open.' No response. The man who appeared to be in charge nodded at one of his colleagues who reappeared moments later with a metal battering ram which they used to break open the door.

The man on the sofa appeared to be asleep or otherwise unconscious. On the small table in the middle of the room lay several half-empty bottles of various spirits, a few half-smoked cigarettes and some white powder, sprayed across the tabletop. Next to it lay a rolled-up £10 note. The man's naked body was barely covered by a white towelling dressing gown, several sizes too small and tightly drawn around his rather rotund frame. He looked middle-aged and Middle Eastern. Two paramedics gave him their attention and tried to revive him. As they did so, the female police officer came out of the bedroom. Looking at one of her colleagues, she jerked her head towards the room without speaking.

On the bed George saw the naked and bloody body of Tabitha. She lay on her back with her eyes open and a startled look on her face. Blood seeped from her mouth and nose. She was pale and motionless.

'This one will be DOA,' said the policewoman to the paramedic, who was feeling for a pulse on Tabitha's neck.

'So it seems,' came the subdued reply.

The man on the sofa appeared to have regained semi-consciousness, but could not speak. He was half carried down the stairs to the waiting ambulance.

Two of the policemen then turned to George, who felt faint, and asked him to sit down.

'We want to ask you some questions,' said one.

George looked at him, waiting.

'Please tell us where you were over the last two hours.'

After George told them, in some detail, one asked, 'Do you have a key to this flat?'

George thought this was a strange question, as of course he hadn't. *Why do they think I might have?* he thought.

'When and where did you last see Tabitha alive?' asked another officer.

George replied that he hadn't seen her for a while. They asked several other questions which seemed irrelevant and to which George did not know the answer but which made him nervous.

'You've obviously known Tabitha for some time. What was your relationship?'

'We were friends. Nothing more.'

'Are you sure there was nothing more? Ever?'

'No. One of my old friends was close to her. But not me.'

'Were you jealous of him?'

'No! Why are you asking me this sort of question?'

The two policemen asked George to stay in the sitting room, while they left the flat. The policewoman remained where she was. About ten minutes later, the men returned.

'George Thomas, I am arresting you on suspicion of the murder of Tabitha Davis. I must warn you that anything you say may be used in evidence against you.' He felt a shiver down his spine and handcuffs close tightly behind his back as he was led down the stairs to the waiting police car.

*

The next morning, Jack wondered why he had not heard from George. He had called his hotel but there was no reply from his room. And now he had work to do. He decided to go above the heads of the factory shop stewards to try to gain the support of the local area union representative, Des Norris, in advance. Norris was known to be corruptible and enjoy expensive brandy. He relished his power and access to the top management of local industry. They arranged to meet.

A small man with thinning brown hair kept in place with rather too much gel ambled towards the bar, smoking an untipped Navy Cut cigarette. Ash dropped to the floor as he asked the barman for a pint of mild and looked round as if trying to find somebody. He wore a worn imitation-leather jacket whose pockets were torn from years of hastily removed cigarette packets. The man matched Brian's description of Des Norris and so Jack took a chance and approached him.

'Excuse me, sir, are you Mr Norris, by any chance?'

'Aye, lad. And you must be Jack. Pleased to meet you,' he said, not holding out his hand. 'We'll sit at that corner table in the alcove. I'm known here. Nobody must hear what we are talking about. I assume it is something that I'm not going to like, otherwise you wouldn't be asking to see me.'

'Well, I'm asking for your help. We have a big problem and I understand that you have sufficient influence to be able to help us with the solution. A man of your experience will, I think, be able to understand our predicament. I need an ally with power. You could be that man. Please could I show you this in strictest confidence? I have not shown the local reps.'

Norris nodded as Jack pushed across the table the same spreadsheet that he had given to Carey. As Norris silently studied the figures Jack hoped that he had flattered his ego sufficiently to soften him up.

'Can I get you a brandy, Mr Norris?'

'Now you're talking, lad. I'll have a large Rémy Martin VSOP.'

Please, thought Jack, though not articulating what his mother would have said.

When Jack returned with the brandy, Norris said, 'You seem to have a problem, lad.'

'I thought you would spot it, but I'm not confident that your shop stewards in the factory would be clever enough to do so, which is why I came to you first.'

'Well, they don't have my experience. Anyway, how does this affect my members?'

'You must be very busy. What else have you got on now – that you can talk about, of course?' said Jack, changing the subject until Norris had finished his brandy. 'Another?' asked Jack when he had.

Norris was smoking his third cigarette when Jack returned to his seat with Norris's second double brandy.

'What can I do for you?' asked Norris with a change of tone that gave Jack the confidence to start to explain his plans.

When he had done so, Norris stood and said, 'You won't get any of my members to volunteer to take redundancy and the MTU has never accepted a compulsory situation, let alone wage cuts.' He put the spreadsheet in his inside pocket and strode from the room without another word or looking back.

*

Jack had still not heard from George. On his way to the factory the following day he passed WHSmith to pick up his usual copy of *The Times*. As he approached the news stand a full-page colour photograph of an attractive girl caught his breath. Unable to take in what he thought he had seen, he looked again and then tentatively walked towards the racks of newspapers. Other journals carried the same photograph. *The Times's* headline read *University graduate murdered in her flat*. Underneath the headline was a large picture of Tabitha. With a trembling hand Jack reached for the paper, pulled it from the rack and started to read. A man had been found unconscious in the flat. Another man had been arrested. Feeling unsteady, he sat heavily on a nearby chair.

'Have you paid for that, sir?' asked one of the staff stiffly.

'Umm, no. Not yet. Sorry,' Jack replied, still sitting and handing the shop assistant the paper and some money.

Bewildered, Jack looked for the nearest phone box. He called George's hotel again.

'We haven't seen him for a couple of days,' said an anxious female voice. She spoke without drawing breath. 'I probably shouldn't say but the police were here, asking us to show them into his room. And when we did they poked around in his things. They seemed to be looking for something. We said that he should have checked out and was late paying his bill and one of them laughed and made some quip to his colleague that he had bigger problems than that and that it may be some time before we saw him again. Is he in some sort of trouble?'

After having called Barnsley Stampings to postpone his meeting Jack decided to drive to the police station to find out what had happed to George. And, of course, to Tabitha. He noticed small groups of people pointing at their newspapers. He was irritated by their behaviour and wondered: *What draws people to share the news of unpleasant events with others? Why do passers-by slow down to see an accident, even when they're not able to help? Why are we drawn to read about warfare, then say "how awful" to each other before reading more? And what, anyway, is the attraction of horror films?*

Jack arrived at the main police station in the middle of Sheffield. He was turned away from the front of the building by a woman at the other end of the intercom who briskly informed them that the parking spaces there were reserved for officers. Having left the car around the rear of the building he walked hurriedly through pouring rain, without an umbrella, back to the front entrance. He rang the bell. Nothing. He rang the bell again. Eventually a crackly voice from the intercom asked, 'Have you an appointment?' Jack wondered who would have an appointment to enquire about the possibility of the arrest of one friend and the murder of another.

'Why are you here?' asked the voice. Jack explained and asked if he might come in out of the rain.

'One minute,' said the voice, as the rain seeped its way under Jack's collar.

Five minutes later the voice asked him to report to the duty sergeant, a buzzer sounded and the door edged open to allow a drenched and apprehensive Jack to enquire after his friends.

Jack gave the reason for his visit again to the duty sergeant. He raised his eyebrows and stared for a while at Jack, biting his pencil.

'Just go through that once more, please, sir,' he said.

After he told his story for a third time, the policeman turned to him with an expression which Jack knew meant he did not believe him.

The sergeant said, 'You had better come with me, sir.'

Jack was ushered into a small room painted light blue and smelling of bleach. He assumed that a previous suspect had been sick on the floor. The fluorescent light, brown at one end, flickered as if it was about to fail. He waited.

Shortly, a man and a woman in their forties entered the room and asked Jack to tell his tale again. There was not much to relate. But this time it was recorded. He had been with George in the pub waiting for Tabitha. When Tabitha had not turned up, George had said he was going to look for her. And he had not heard from him since.

He had seen the newspaper reports, and phoned the hotel and was obviously very worried. When he had finished, the man confirmed that George had been arrested on suspicion of murder.

'That's just not possible. I know him. He wouldn't do such a thing,' said Jack. 'I've told you. We are old friends. He went to check if she was OK. That's all.' The police exchanged glances.

'Where did you go after you say Mr Thomas left you?'

Jack's spirits sank. Could it be that the police might think he and George were both involved in Tabitha's death?

After explaining his movements, the policeman left the room.

'Stay here, please, sir,' he said.

Half an hour later, the door of the small room with the still flickering light opened. The two police officers stood in the doorway.

'Thank you very much for coming in, sir. We have no more questions, for now,' said the man. 'We shall continue our inquiries. If we need you, we'll contact you again.'

'But what about George?' asked Jack.

'He will remain in custody.'

As Jack drove away from the police station, he went through in his mind the story he had told the police. Again. Surely, his version of events was the same as George's. But what would happen if it was not?

*

The following morning, Jack drove back to Barnsley Stampings. On the radio news, Mrs Thatcher repeated her mantra that she would never give in to terrorism. The IRA had detonated another car bomb, killing several passers-by. Days lost to strikes were up again. Jack tried to turn his mind away from the face of Tabitha, which had etched itself indelibly into every thought, so that he could focus on overcoming the task of achieving the objective of huge cost savings at the factory. Norris had rejected his plan, as Carey had expected and as Marwick had warned him. What now?

Jack wandered down to the factory superintendent's office. It was occupied by a large man. Indeed, he took up so much of the small office that there was little space left for anything or anyone else. He sat behind a tiny desk and had unfortunate flaky skin which left a large amount of dandruff on the neck and shoulders of his dark blue blazer. His name was Greg Jacobs. Brian had warned Jack that Jacobs was diabetic, which led him to mood swings that could be difficult to handle. Not only was he the factory superintendent but he was also the site's MTU senior shop steward.

'Good morning, Mr Jacobs,' said Jack. "You can call me Mr Jacobs," Greg Jacobs had announced in front of his junior stewards to some muffled laughter when they first met.

'What can I do for you, young man?' he asked now.

Why does everyone up here call me "young man"? thought Jack.

'Well, we have a problem that I need to talk through with you, please.'

'Management are the ones with the problems, not us. And you are paid to solve them,' Jacobs quipped in his usual unhelpful tone. The other two men in the room, in light blue oil-stained overalls, stared at Jack, one with a raised eyebrow.

'I need you onside for this one because without you I shall have trouble doing what we need,' said Jack rather obviously.

Jacobs roared with forced laughter, and so the junior stewards laughed too, some unsure of what they were laughing about. 'Us onside? If I have guessed correctly what you are going to ask there is as much chance of that as your car starting in the morning once we have dealt with it.' They all laughed again.

Jack explained his plan and asked the stewards to keep it confidential for now.

'We'll have no trouble keeping that confidential, young man, as what you have suggested isn't going to happen and the last thing I'll do is worry my members with some management fantasy. I suggest you go back down that motorway and tell Carey from me where he can stick your plan. And if you need me to spell out where that is I shall be pleased to do so, with a drawing if required. I think our meeting is at an end.'

Jack stood to go and said, 'I'm sorry you feel the way you do.'

'Close the door behind you. And remember, the higher you fly, my lad, the harder you are going to fall.'

As Jack closed the door and walked away from Jacobs's office, he could hear more laughter. The Strawbs' song "Part of the Union" played on his mind.

As he passed Brian the production director's office Jack came to a decision.

'Brian,' he said, closing the door firmly behind him and dropping his voice, 'I think I am going to have to talk directly to the men. Both Jacobs and Norris have rejected my plan.'

Brian did not say anything but was clearly not surprised.

Jack continued, 'What time would it be good to call a meeting of the whole factory, do you think?'

'After the end of the shift tomorrow probably. It being Friday they can talk about it to their wives over the weekend. If we have any chance of succeeding the wives will be key. They're usually in charge up here. And they are more likely to see sense than their husbands. Shall I arrange it?'

Jack agreed and returned to his office to prepare some flipcharts that would spell out in simple terms the difficulty the company faced. The solution to the problem would be very hard for the workforce to accept, but it had to be explained so that the solution was obvious.

That night, back in his hotel room, Jack called Angela.

'I think you're mad,' she said when Jack explained his plan. 'You mean you are going to ask the men to accept that twenty-five per cent of them will lose their jobs and the rest have to take a twenty-five per cent pay cut? And this when both the senior factory and area union reps have rejected the idea? Have you told Bill Carey?'

'Yes. He seemed circumspect, but accepted that if I don't go ahead, the company would have to close. And then I would have failed.'

'Jack, don't you think you might be being set up? Can you trust Carey? If you fail to persuade the men to accept your plan, which seems likely, he will have to sack you. He will blame your inexperience when he explains what went wrong to the board and to his precious suits in the City. Or a bunch of teenage scribblers, as I believe they are known. Are you sure he won't say you acted without his authority? It isn't your fault that the company is losing so much money. But it will be your fault if you precipitate a strike. Let the people who caused the problem sort it out. Please tell Carey that you don't think the plan will work and then come home, here, to me.'

'Tempting as your last suggestion may be, I am going to give it a go. After all, what have I got to lose? They said it was an impossible task and so Carey may not sack me if I fail. But if I succeed, what then? I will have single-handedly saved the company and the group results for the year. Without this the board will be faced with putting out a profit warning. The shares will tumble and Carey's success to date will be at an end. If I succeed, he will owe me. So,' Jack added in a more soothing tone, 'goodnight. Sleep well.' He hung up before Angela could reply.

That night, Jack could not sleep. He paced the room rehearsing his presentation to the factory and when he stopped thinking about that for a moment, the image of Tabitha and her violent death returned to haunt him.

*

'Jack, Sheffield Police is on the line for you,' said his secretary.

'Please say that I am about to address the whole factory and take a message.'

'I've tried that but they say it's urgent and insist on speaking to you now.'

'Oh all right, put him through.'

After a click, the police officer came on the line and said, 'Mr Mayhew, Detective Superintendent Parsons here. We would like you to come to the station immediately, please. We have some further questions we need to ask you.'

'I'm afraid I have a very important meeting in fifteen minutes. I can't possibly come to see you now. Can we please meet tomorrow sometime?'

There was a brief pause. 'I'm afraid not, sir. My invitation is more in the nature of an instruction and so I advise you to make your way here at once.'

'Are you arresting me?' asked Jack, shaking slightly. There was a pause.

'Will I need to, sir?' came the reply.

'No. I'm on my way,' said Jack, bewildered and apprehensive.

Jack put down the phone, asked Brian's secretary to rearrange the meeting for next Friday and made his way in his car to the police station. When he arrived, he noticed George through the window of an adjacent office.

The police officer who interviewed Jack a few days before took him into a side room. He simply asked whether he recognised the man in the photo put in front of him, without saying who it was. Jack said he did not recognise him and asked, 'Is that the man found unconscious in the flat?'

'What man? Tell me what you know about a man in the flat.' Before Jack could answer, the telephone on the desk rang. DSupt Parsons listened to the voice on the other end before replacing the receiver. He looked at Jack and then out of the window, putting his fingers together and tapping them against each other whilst holding his index finger to his lips.

Eventually he said, 'Thank you for coming in, sir. If we need you again, we shall be in touch.'

George was sitting slumped on a low wall outside the police station when Jack arrived. He looked tired and pale. 'Thank God,' said Jack, putting an arm around his friend's shoulder.

'What happened?' asked Jack.

'The unconscious man is no longer unconscious. The police have questioned him for an hour in his hospital bed. I think that's why I've been released. My guess is that they think the man in the flat killed Tabitha. But we shall see.'

CHAPTER 14

Clement Slimbridge had not been popular at school. After all, an ambition to train as an accountant was not considered cool to the "lads" who controlled the social environment. It would have helped had he been good at sport, or "games" as the more old-fashioned staff called it. But Slimbridge was generally uncoordinated. Being skinny and having acne did not help him get accepted. He was picked on by the strong and popular, and the weaker ones joined in, in an attempt to curry favour with those who counted. The often-repeated cruel joke was: "Where's Slimbridge, the one with the lymph?", "Do you mean limp?", "No, he walks with a lisp."

Later in his school career, Slimbridge became more confident. He was at least intelligent and this gave him some ability to circumvent or challenge his tormentors. Eventually they gave up. But the emotional legacy of his school days left him with a nature that some called snide. And he was ambitious to show those more charismatic and popular than himself that he was at least as smart as them. To start with he devised schemes designed to deprive his contemporaries of their pocket money. At primary school he would offer to buy chewing gum and cigarettes for those who were not encouraged by their parents to indulge and charge them a stiff premium, often not telling the truth about the cost of his supplies. At secondary school he would borrow money from his contemporaries and promise them a high return. This worked while he could borrow more money from others and used that to repay the first borrowers with handsome interest. Neither he nor his naive customers knew a Ponzi scheme like that was illegal; he didn't care either. Naturally enough, the scheme had a limited life and its collapse left all Slimbridge's "investors" with heavy losses.

Only one of his scams had caught the attention of the police, but there were no consequences. Now, several years later, Slimbridge leaned back in his mock-leather chair; it tilted grudgingly and he put his feet up on the desk in front of him and gazed out of the window at the crowded Birmingham street below. He wore a mid-brown suit, clean and pressed. A dull polyester tie from an ordinary college in the Midlands was tight around his neck, with a small knot. Light brown plain socks. Brown lace-up plastic shoes. Cigarette ash from a "B and H", as he called them, fell on his jacket, which he brushed, irritated, to the floor. His wet lips soaked and discoloured the filter. In the corner of his office were two old metal filing cabinets of the type used for three decades. One of the drawers refused to close properly and revealed buff, overfilled paper files. On top of one of the filing cabinets stood an over-watered rubber plant, the leaves turning yellow at the edges. One had dropped into its pot. A small humidifier on his desk made a slight whispering noise as the fan inside it puffed feeble clouds of steam over the desk. 'Found this in a shop near our villa in Almería,' he would say proudly. 'Helps with my asthma.' The "villa" was a small flat with no air conditioning above a kebab shop at the wrong end of town.

A buzzer in the phone on his desk sounded. 'Yes, June,' he said to his secretary. Then, 'Come in.'

June pushed open the door of the office with her shoulder. She carried a pile of files in a green wire tray, struggling to keep them on top of each other. She had broad hips and a bottom too large in relation to her chest. The lower half of her wobbled and moved in the opposite direction to her top half as she staggered towards the desk and put the tray down heavily on the edge. Probably in her early fifties, and with neat, unimaginative hair, she gave a sigh and then said, 'There you are, Clem. That's the information on all those companies you asked James to investigate. Happy reading. I'm off.'

Slimbridge looked at the clock on the wall, which had stuck at ten minutes past two, its second hand moving one second in each direction, and then at his watch. Five to seven.

'Leaving early again, are we?' he said with a lopsided smile.

'Very funny,' came the reply as June left the office without looking back at him.

Slimbridge pulled the wire tray towards him and lifted the first file off the top. A neat white label announced the name "Jordan Steel Fastenings Ltd". He looked at the front page, being a report mainly consisting of figures, which James Beasley, his unqualified finance director, had compiled for him. He picked his nose and placed the file on the floor.

The second file he looked at was labelled "Tipton Foundry Ltd. A subsidiary of Arnold Foundries plc".

*

Jack stood next to a small, low crate, trying to hide his nervousness. It did not need to be high because when he stood on it to address the men he would be tall enough to look over their heads. As they ambled towards him they talked to each other in lowered voices, exchanging views about what Jack would say. The usual cacophony of high and low-pitched clunks ceased as all the machines were switched off. Silence. The smell of warm oil lingered in the air. Near the back of the assembled crowd stood Greg Jacobs. He appeared to be chewing gum and stuck his tongue into the side of his cheek as he winked at the other two union reps next to him. They chuckled dutifully.

As Jack stood on the crate, he looked into the eyes of some of the men and began his by now well-rehearsed lines.

'Good afternoon, chaps. I don't intend to keep you long. I know at least one of you will want time to visit the bookies before you return to your wives for the weekend.'

Two people laughed.

'None of what I have to say to you is good news, and I am very sorry to have to say it. It will affect you and your families and I wish this were not the case. But there will be much worse news if I do not say it.'

There was a murmur as the men exchanged glances.

'As you know, the company recently lost its largest customer, accounting for thirty-five per cent of the company's sales. We lost the business because one of our competitors offered a much lower price to our customer. I have here in my hand a letter from them confirming the reason which I shall pass around in case anyone wants to read it. These sales have not yet been replaced and so it must be obvious to all of you that we have to take some action to cut costs.'

There was a further murmur, with the words "Redundancies" and "I told you so" reaching Jack's ears. Someone near the back muttered loudly, 'Over my dead body.'

'Yes, I'm afraid there will need to be redundancies. But that will not be enough. Take a look at this set of figures.'

Jack turned over the top sheet of a large flipchart.

'This is an abbreviated set of our last year's accounts. You can see that we made a small profit with the business we recently lost. But take that off and see what happens.'

Jack put a line through the sales figures, knocked off thirty-five per cent of the sales and wrote the new figure next to it. He then reduced the materials figure by the same proportion, put a line through the profit figure and replaced it with a large loss.

'We don't think that we can reduce the workforce by more than twenty-five per cent and still keep the factory open. So, bad news as it is, assume we make twenty-five per cent of the total workforce redundant, including office staff. This is what happens.'

Jack adjusted the figures accordingly, stood back

and paused while he let his audience take in the figure representing another large loss.

'Here's the problem.' Jack moved over to a second flip chart and lifted the top sheet to reveal another set of figures.

'These happen to be the accounts of our biggest competitor, Aztec Stampings. We fight them for almost every job. You'll see that they are about the same size as us. But you will note here that they made much more money. Can anybody see why that is?'

A few men nodded their heads, although Jack was not convinced that enough of the men understood.

'Let me help. This is the amount of wages we pay per pound of sales. And this is what they pay. As a percentage of sales this is what it looks like.'

Jack wrote the figure forty-eight per cent next to Barnsley's wage cost and thirty-nine per cent next to Aztec's.

'Can anybody see the problem?' asked Jack. One or two people looked at each other.

'Here it is rather more clearly. Our average wage cost per hour is three pounds forty pence. Theirs is two pounds sixty.'

As Jack wrote those figures on each board, some men shuffled their feet, one shouted 'Rubbish' and others shook their heads and looked at the floor.

Jack paused, looked around the factory and then at Greg Jacobs. He shook his head and pursed his lips. Jack sensed Jacobs was going to speak and so said, 'Gentlemen, I think you can all see what our problem is. If we do not take this action, harsh as it is, we shall all be out of a job as the company will have to close. My co-directors have already agreed to take a twenty-five per cent pay cut and, sadly, one of them, Mr Bailey, has already left us.' There were some raised eyebrows in front of him. 'I shall be addressing the office staff separately later. But for now, I'd like to see the three union reps in my office right away to try to agree what needs to be done.'

'And after that meeting,' shouted Jacobs, 'which will be very short, I will see everyone on the car park. We are not going to accept what Mayhew is obviously going to suggest. The MTU has never accepted compulsory redundancies in their history, and it is not going to start now. Don't worry, chaps, your union will defend you,' he finished, his voice raised and his clenched fist pumping the air.

Some men cheered and looked angrily at Jack. A few looked frightened. One or two nodded and looked as if they understood.

Jacobs refused to take a seat in Jack's temporary office. He thumped the table with his fist.

'We don't believe any of your figures. They were worked out with a management calculator which you can stick up your arse. You will not make any of my men redundant and you will not take a single penny off their wages. If this company goes down I shall make sure that I bring the management down with it. Have you experienced an all-out strike before? You'll have one on your hands unless you immediately withdraw your plans. Remember the pub bombings? It isn't just the IRA you need to worry about. If I were you I'd make sure that you look under your car each evening as a few of us are pretty angry. With you. And it is personal.'

The words "it is personal" resonated in Jack's ears as he pushed a sheet of paper over the desk towards Jacobs.

'This first list is of the names of people in the factory who regrettably we are going to have to make redundant. Some departments will close completely. Others will be slimmed down. And here is the second list of the remaining men and their new wage rates, twenty-five per cent lower. If the wage cut is not accepted, we shall have to close the factory and make *everyone* redundant.'

Jacobs, red in the face with rage, said to his union colleagues, 'Right, let's talk to our members on the car park, where I am sure they will vote for a strike.' As he turned to leave the room Jack thought he noticed a slight pause in Jacobs's stride as he noticed the name of G. Jacobs on the first list.

*

As Jack paced up and down in his office, he considered whether to remind Carey that there might be a strike. But simultaneously with his meeting with Jacobs, he had asked Brian, the production director, to pin on the factory noticeboards the list of those being made redundant, and the new pay rates for those remaining. So now that he had published the names of those losing their jobs, it would be clear to those who were not on the list that they were safe. Jack decided not to phone Carey. After all, he had Carey's authority to proceed with the plan. Hadn't he? And what if Carey changed his mind and instructed Jack to cancel it? Jack would then have failed, and his credibility and perhaps career at Arnold Foundries plc would be at an end.

Jack had decided to watch the vote from an office overlooking the car park. As the men assembled, the grey Sheffield afternoon asserted itself and a slight drizzle began to fall on them. Some huddled into groups, speaking softly and pointing at each other and the grimy noticeboard under cover near the factory entrance. Some men walked over to the board. Some of those looked crestfallen but others seemed more cheerful. Jacobs stood on a box at one end of the car park, flanked by three of his union colleagues.

As the last man joined the group in front of him, the pace at which Jacobs chewed his gum increased, his cheeks flushed red, his fists clenched and then he spoke. His speech was short but impassioned and ended with the words:

'So, comrades, your union as always is here to protect you. We shall not let this company slash your hard-earned wages while management line their pockets. Nor shall we let them put you on the dole. Let's send the young man packing back down the motorway and vote against his disgusting proposals, and then for strike action.' Some men cheered. 'So, first, put up your hands to vote against the management proposals.'

Jack's heart leaped and eyes widened as he tried to take in the scene. The vote looked evenly divided. Jacobs appeared for a moment anxious before he instructed, 'Those against the management's proposals to make you redundant and for a cut in pay stay here. The rest go to that side of the car park.'

The men looked at each other awkwardly. Initially very few moved. Then, one by one, some of them pushed by their colleagues, some mouthing at them, others jostling, eventually a total of what looked like half of the men stood on one side of the car park whilst the others remained where they were. Jack bit his lip. His co-directors, who stood alongside, looked anxiously at him.

'Geoff, you count this side and Bert, you count the other side,' said Jacobs, chewing furiously.

After the count was taken, Geoff and Bert whispered in Jacobs's ear. He smiled.

'I'm pleased to announce that the motion to reject the management's ridiculous proposals is carried by fifty-six to fifty-five. So now, we shall vote on strike action—'

'What about the votes of you four?' shouted a voice from the back.

Jacobs looked at his three colleagues and smiled. They would all vote against the management's proposals.

'Fair enough,' he said, and indicated towards the group in front of him who were those who would support him. But as he walked towards them, the other three union reps walked in the other direction, towards those in favour of the redundancies. Looking through the office window, and unseen by those in the car park, Jack smiled.

Jacobs looked alarmed and desperate. He was on the losing side. Not only that but he would himself lose his job. 'We can't let management get away with this. I urge you to vote now for strike action. Those in favour, raise your hands.'

As Jacobs raised his and looked around for support, one of the union reps who had voted for the redundancies shouted, 'If we strike, management may not pay us any redundancy money at all, because we will have broken our contracts and effectively dismissed ourselves.'

Jacobs, holding his arm aloft, looked around at the men. Three people raised their hands. As the rain began to fall more heavily, Jacobs stepped down from his box, put on his coat and without looking round trudged out of the car park and on to the street.

*

Jack felt both relief and elation as he walked down the corridor back towards his office. But he also felt sympathy for those who had lost their jobs. Some had families. Others had mortgages that would go unpaid. Jobs were hard to find. Some would never work again. As he forced himself back into the belief that the actions he had taken were necessary to protect the livelihoods of the balance of the workforce, he noticed Des Norris coming out of another office. As Norris closed the door behind him, and checked there was nobody looking, he winked at Jack.

Hiding his surprise, Jack said, 'Good afternoon, Mr Norris. I wondered whether I might see you here. Can I have a word?'

Alone in Jack's office, Jack was the first to speak. 'I didn't think that you were going to allow that to happen.'

Norris lit a cigarette, gave Jack a long stare and then smiled. 'I was just seeing what you were made of. I had to let the local reps approach me first, didn't I? And so when they did, I could pretend to be surprised at your plan; but I had already thought the matter through. My job is to protect my members, and by not forcing a vote that would have led to the closure of your factory, that is what I have done. I knew you had no choice. And, of course, it was clever of you to put only Jacobs amongst the union reps on the list of redundancies and to prime Bert to remind those who might strike of their legal position on redundancies.'

Jack took Norris by the hand, shook it warmly and said with a smile, 'Thank you, Mr Norris. I thought you were shrewd, and now I know you are. Thank you for doing the right thing.'

Norris took a large drag on his half-smoked cigarette, stubbed it out in the dirty ashtray on Jack's desk and reached into his inside pocket. 'But your problems are not over, young man. Here is a list of all those you have made redundant. The union is sponsoring all thirty-seven of them to take your firm to an industrial tribunal. We shall be seeking financial redress for unfair dismissal. I think that is the least we can do for them... don't you?'

As Norris turned and left his office, the colour drained from Jack's cheeks. If he lost the tribunal cases, the firm would have to close.

*

Clement Slimbridge and his unqualified accountant, James Beasley, sat in Carey's secretary's office waiting for their appointment. Carey, as usual, was running late. A middle-aged man dressed smartly in a dark blue suit appeared at the doorway to the office and asked if Slimbridge knew where Carey's secretary was.

The sound of the muffled laughter of a man and a woman leaked under the closed door.

'I think she is in there,' said Slimbridge to the visitor, who rolled his eyes slightly and left.

Mrs Braithwaite had received a generous "retirement" package and had been replaced as Carey's secretary by Samantha Barker. She was referred to privately and unkindly by some in the company as "Barker-a-bit-of-a-dog". She was blonde, of course, pretty, medium height, ample-chested and, crucially for Carey, rather younger than himself. She was twenty-eight. And it seemed that she fulfilled one of Carey's intimate needs for a "permanent under-secretary".

Samantha emerged from Carey's office, straightening her tight red dress, and looked surprised to see the room was not empty. Blushing slightly, she said, 'Good afternoon, gentlemen, may I ask who you are?'

Slimbridge told her and explained that the receptionist had showed them into her office when she received no reply on the telephone for half an hour and that Carey was forty minutes late for their meeting.

Samantha bristled slightly, adjusted her hair nervously and took them into the adjacent boardroom. After five minutes, Bill Carey appeared.

'I do apologise, gentlemen. Something came up. "A little local difficulty", as my chairman calls such things. Anyway, all timings around here are approximate. My colleagues gave me a clock for my office that just has one hand. The numbers read oneish, twoish and so on.'

Slimbridge forced a laugh, rather too enthusiastically.

'Anyway, tell me about your interest in our subsidiary, Tipton Foundry.'

As Slimbridge and his accountant worked their way through their lengthy list of questions, Carey looked impatiently at his watch. He was polite, yet distracted. As he drew the prospective purchaser's attention to the disposal timetable, Samantha appeared at the door and said, 'Mr Carey, Jack Mayhew is on the phone. He says it is important and you would want to be interrupted.'

Carey made his apologies to Slimbridge, leaped to his feet, made quickly for his office and picked up the phone. 'Yes, Jack. What news?'

Less than a minute later, Samantha noticed him punch the air and put down the phone with a triumphant smile on his face.

'Tell Angus Marwick to drop what he is doing and come with me to Sheffield, and with a cheque for £5,000 made out to Jack Mayhew. We are taking our young flyer out for a long and expensive meal.'

*

Arrangements were made for those losing their jobs to collect their redundancy cheques the next day, even though it was a Saturday. Jack explained to Angela that he would stay in Sheffield that night so that he could be present. It was not their fault that they had lost their jobs, he said. He had learned that the workforces of the Midlands and north of England were fundamentally honest and hard-working. The caricatures painted by Monty Python and others in his school days were meant to be a joke, Angela reminded him. Jack had tried not to appear patronising; he now knew that the flat caps, different modes of speech and ferreting of his schoolboy memories masked sincerity, humour and a determination to make the best of their often difficult circumstances. Although Jack could not lighten the blow for them, he could at least look them in the eye, thank them for their work and wish them luck.

'I'm proud of you. That's the Jack I love,' said Angela. 'Not just for your achievement but for having the sensitivity and being man enough to face those who have had their livelihoods curtailed by you. Most people in your position would simply leave that job to others.'

One of the last to come to the office to pick up their money was a young man in his late twenties. He was a junior union representative. In his right hand he held the hand of a small girl, perhaps five years old. In his left arm he held a baby.

'Hello, Tom,' said Jack, looking at the children and guessing Tom was their father. As he gave a slight smile he wondered how long Tom would be able to feed and clothe them before his money ran out. The little girl looked sad, as if she knew why her father was there. She wore what Jack assumed was her best dress. Pink. To see where Daddy works. Worked. She looked up at Jack with large round innocent eyes.

'Jessie, say hello to Mr Mayhew,' Tom said.

'Hello, Mr Mayhew,' said a timid and faint voice. 'Why has Daddy got nowhere to go to work any more?'

As Jack bit his lower lip, tried to keep his composure and think of an answer to give a five-year-old girl, Tom came to his rescue. Holding out his hand, he said, 'Mr Mayhew, I'd like to thank you for the way you have handled this. It can't have been easy for you. I'm sure you will do very well in your career.'

As Jack took Tom's outstretched hand and shook it gently, he looked him in the eye. All he could manage to say before Tom turned and left the office with his small children, was: 'Thank you. I hope you will all be OK.'

After they had left, Jack turned away and looked out of the rain-lashed window at the grey sky, the lump in his throat replaced by a tear in the corner of his eye.

*

Bill Carey was often late into the office and late for meetings. But he nonetheless worked long hours and frequently into the night. Sometimes he could not be contacted. Even his closest secretary appeared not to know his whereabouts. Or did she know, but would simply not tell anyone? Either way, it was unusual for the chief executive of a public company to go missing. And rather than asking a secretary to dial someone's number and put them through to him, as was customary, he would regularly use the private phone on his desk. Jack had assumed that this was because his conversation might be share sensitive and he wanted to be sure nobody could listen in. But Jack wondered if there was another reason.

'What do you think of him?' asked Carey, as Slimbridge left the office after a second meeting to discuss Tipton Foundry. That too had started late.

'So long as he delivers the promised money, I don't suppose I mind,' replied Jack. 'But don't you think there's something shifty about him? I've had my fingers burned before, as you know. And so I guess my instincts have been sharpened by experience. But it's your call.'

Carey pursed his lips and nodded, gazing at a pile of documents in front of him. 'As everyone has gone home, I'll shred this lot on the way out. We'll have dinner and discuss our next moves.'

The two men talked amiably while Carey fed each sheet of paper into the shredder. As the last piece ground in, the machine caught Carey's tie and pulled it into the shredder. As his neck was dragged down towards the rotating knives, Jack hit the large red stop button. Carey stood upright and laughed as he noticed that most of his tie had disappeared, leaving only the knot and a mangled piece of thin red material against his neck.

'Thanks for stopping it, Jack,' he said as he held up the remains of his tie with a grin. 'You missed an opportunity, though. I thought you would have had your hand firmly on top of my head, pushing it down into the shredder.'

Jack laughed. 'No, I need you to pull me along. I'm holding on to your coat-tails.'

'Only for now,' added Carey, looking sideways at Jack. 'Before long you'll be pushing a knife between my shoulder blades.'

Jack was puzzled by the remark. Was Carey somehow suggesting that Jack was after his job? And that he would do anything to get it? Was he testing Jack's loyalty?

They ate dinner at one of Carey's favourite Italian restaurants in a backwater near Oldbury. 'Dee feesh is as beeg as a whale,' said Julio, the owner and chef. Carey invited both the barely adult waitresses to join him and Jack at a nightclub in Birmingham after they had finished their shift. Giggling, they declined. Although not an overly handsome man, Carey was tall, charismatic and could be charming. He could also be aggressive and unpredictable, although these characteristics he tended to reserve for colleagues. He liked to keep them on edge; uncertain and insecure. He expected hard work and loyalty and yet he had been known to dismiss senior colleagues without notice and for reasons that did not seem apparent to others with whom he and they worked closely. It had been noted that at least one senior colleague had been fired simply because Carey had taken a dislike to him. Or so it appeared. He had been one of the company's most effective operators. Did Carey feel threatened? Jack wondered.

'Slimbridge is going to take Tipton Foundry, and he has asked for an option on the balance of the foundry division, or shares in the plc in lieu, whichever he chooses,' said Carey as they finished the red wine.

'Are you going to give it to him?' asked Jack. 'He doesn't seem to be the type of person we would want close to our existing operations, especially since it's the largest part of our business. And he would no doubt ensure that he has a right to monitor the division's progress during the period of the option.'

'Yes. It is a two-year option that he is paying a silly amount of money for. It is only exercisable after the first year. For some reason he's asked for the exercise price to be linked to the share price of the whole group. He obviously feels that price is heading south and so he can pick up the division cheap. But as you know, I have other ideas. I intend the share price to double over the next two years. I have made it known to the City that the foundry division is non-core, which they like. And so that's going to be a lot more expensive for Slimbridge.'

'What about the option to take shares in the group instead? Wouldn't that put us under threat?' asked Jack.

'Why would he want those? At the current price he could only convert to about ten per cent of the group. What good would that be to him? And then, under the rules, he would have to make a bid for the whole group. He's not going to be able to do that, is he? Anyway,' said Carey as he signed the bill, 'let's go into town and pick up some ladies, shall we?'

Carey was married and with a son. But Jack knew that this did not deter him from having more than simply a roving eye for other women. On the way into Birmingham, he asked Jack if he was faithful to Angela. Jack said that he was, but thought to himself that if he were not, he certainly would not tell Carey. To do so would be to give his boss powerful leverage over his loyalty. 'Oh, really? You can tell me. And I'm sure you can be persuaded,' said Carey.

'Please get a couple of girls for us,' he said to the miniskirted hostess as they sat at a small table near the stage. Jack felt uncomfortable, but tried to look relaxed. He did not know what to say to girls for hire, except to ask them why they did it.

'Champagne for the ladies, please, and what do you want, Jack?' asked Carey above the noise of the music.

'I'm driving, Bill, so nothing, thanks.'

'I think I'll be staying in town,' said Carey, winking at Jack behind the back of the girl sitting on his lap. 'Aren't you going to do the same?'

Jack shook his head as the girl next to him looked disappointed and ran her fingers through his hair. The one on the stage finished her strip with a final knickerless flourish and the music changed.

'This is me,' said the girl sitting with Jack as she stood, climbed the stage steps and grasped the brass pole with both hands. Sensing the moment, Jack made his apologies to Carey and his female companion, and left.

Back at their flat in Harborne, where Angela and Jack had moved to be closer to Jack's job, he described Carey's behaviour to Angela. She gave him a long look. 'Is he trying to set you up or trap you? I wondered about that when he asked you to go and sort out the place in Sheffield. Is he paranoid?'

'Perhaps all of those things,' replied Jack as he pulled her warm body close to him.

CHAPTER 15

Jack and Angela lay on the grassy bank beside the river at his mother's house. Languid water like mercury flowed effortlessly between tall reeds and then over shorter ones on which black-winged mayflies played. Larger blue-tinged dragonflies hovered. Two small ducklings, like a drawing from a children's book, sought the protection of the reeds near the riverbank, pushing their way in noiselessly. Silver discs of light danced on the water, which rippled gently in the breeze. The sound of tranquillity. On the opposite bank, two large cows peered at the scene in front of them, their long eyelashes blinking in the sun. The smell of cut grass drifted in the breeze. And did those feet in ancient time. Bucolic England.

Jack had his shirt unbuttoned and his strong yet lithe arms were folded behind his head. He gazed at the pale blue sky. Angela quietly admired his torso, without allowing Jack to notice. Now in his early thirties, his body remained honed. He still had the classic shape of the ancient Greek ideal of an athlete. The muscles of his neck were sleek and those of his upper body firm and rounded yet of refined proportion. He had broad shoulders on a chest that tapered down to his waist. Small, fair hairs, though darker than those of his head, lay in a thin line below his navel, disappearing under his well-used brown belt as though showing the way. Angela looked away, smiled at her thoughts and pushed her sunglasses back up her nose. She wore a mid-length dress, smart enough to comply with what she thought would be suitable for the girlfriend of his mother's dear son. As they were out of sight, she had pulled it up to the top of her long thighs to catch the sun. Her neat breasts were covered by the dress and unusually by a bra she thought she should wear for the occasion. As Jack put his hand on her ankle, she tossed her dark hair, looked across at the cows and said quietly:

'What was it you wanted to tell me?'

'Remember what happened to the restaurant? Steve and the fire and so on?' Angela nodded, smiled and put a sympathetic hand on Jack's leg.

'Well, George called me the other day. Firstly, he told me that the trial of the man the police have charged with Tabitha's murder is next week. At last. Secondly, he told me that he has discovered that the police have failed to pin anything on Steven and that having been discharged from his bankruptcy he now has a restaurant of his own. It's on the Arthur's site. Looks very much like it did before and even has a cryptic name like Phoenix Arizona or something. You know, Phoenix rising from the ashes. Cheeky bugger. Anyway, I'm going to get even with him. But I don't want Steven to meet quite the same end as Benedict Osbourne...'

Angela squeezed Jack's leg and said, 'Darling, why don't you let that go? Things are going well for you at work, you've been promoted, given another company to run and, well, what do you hope to gain?'

'I shall gain the satisfaction of revenge. A dish best served cold. Why should he get away with it? He caused me great pain.' Jack explained the outline details of his plan to Angela. Then he said, 'Before you say anything about that, I've also thought of a way of making things up to my staff – the ones I mistreated – at the same time.'

'You didn't mistreat them. It wasn't your fault they lost their jobs.'

'No, Angela. I mistreated most of them in another way too. I'm not proud of it. In fact, I am ashamed of my behaviour.'

'In what way did you mistreat them?'

With evident regret, Jack told Angela for the first time of the relationships he and George had had with the staff at the restaurant.

'Not great,' said Angela when he had finished. 'But you always were a naughty boy. That's part of what women like about you. Anyway, you didn't rape any of them, did you? They were all complicit – except for the fact that they didn't know until later that they were one of several. Anyway, knowing you as I do, they probably quite enjoyed it.' Angela gave Jack a playful slap.

'Well, don't you think I abused my position as their boss as well?'

Angela thought for a moment and then said, 'I don't suppose you threatened them with the sack or that they thought they might lose their jobs if they did not fall for your obvious charms. Women like powerful men, remember. And you were very young, so I forgive you. And I wasn't around... Anyway, I think there is a more deep-seated reason for your behaviour, even now.'

'What's that?'

'You were sent to boarding school when you were only eight years old. You were a sensitive little boy who needed the love and close proximity of his mother. So you were bound to feel an acute sense of separation from her. Perhaps more than that. Perhaps you felt rejected by her. You wouldn't have understood that this was not something your mother would have wanted. You wouldn't have understood why she behaved the way she did and so took her actions to be rejection. And so you still harbour – even now – a fear of rejection by women, especially those you like, or are attracted to. I have noticed how you respond even to a smile from a woman. You want their affection and not their rejection. So you...'

Angela looked up at Jack. His shoulders shuddered as he buried his head in his hands and let out anguished sobs, buried deeply since childhood.

Angela took Jack in her arms and rocked him like a baby, stroking his hair. When his sobbing ceased, she continued to hold him close to her. The warm air of the riverbank mingled with her sweet, reassuring breath as she lifted Jack's chin towards hers and kissed him tenderly on his lips. With her next kiss Jack sat upright and knelt over her, kissing her as urgently as he had ever done. The lovers heard Jack's mother's car disappear up the drive and away from the house. With his hands gently on Angela's shoulders, Jack eased her flat onto the long grass.

The lapping of the water nearby accompanied their love-making as Angela welcomed Jack's desire to lay claim to the security of the woman he loved.

*

Angela and Jack watched the activity at Phoenix Arizona from the bar opposite. George was right. The decor was very similar to that of Arthur's. Pastel tones. Ceiling fans. Large green palms. Some expensive cars were parked nearby out of which heavily peroxided, overdressed and no doubt over-perfumed ladies wriggled their way. Adjusting their dresses, they coupled arms with their men, for balance rather than affection. Not many tables appeared to be empty. *Not bad for a Wednesday lunchtime*, thought Jack.

As Angela sucked on the straw of her Harvey Wallbanger, Jack poured another Budweiser into his tall, cool glass. "Nothing's Gonna Stop Us Now" played –rather too loudly – although Jack was pleased by the possible irony. Someone nearby was smoking an expensive cigar. He scribbled in his small black notebook, a Filofax that had been a gift from Sandy Brockhouse, the group chairman, when Jack was appointed to the board. 'Congratulations,' he had said as he handed the gift to Jack. 'You are one of the youngest main board directors of a fully listed company in the country. I am expecting great things. As Bill said at the AGM, the only thing against you is your age, but that is not your fault and it will also take care of itself.'

'What are you doing?' asked Angela.

'I'm making a note of who Steve's main suppliers are. I won't be able to note all of them but from today and previous visits, I already have quite a few, including who he buys booze from. That will be his most significant creditor.'

'Why do you need those?'

'I explained the other day, when we were by the river. But you seemed distracted and so perhaps you don't remember,' teased Jack.

'You were, you mean,' Angela replied, swatting his arm.

On the way back, Jack made some calls from his newly acquired car phone.

'You just love that, don't you, you big businessman, you,' quipped Angela.

'I find it really useful actually, though I read that in the next ten years, two-thirds of the population will have a completely mobile phone. I don't see that, do you? I mean, you've got one in your car and one at home. Who on earth would want to walk around with one?

'Do you remember the old joke about Lew Grade and Bernard Delfont?' continued Jack. 'It's not so funny now more of us have car phones, but in the sixties, only the very richest people had them. Grade and Delfont were great TV moguls and rivals. Grade's in his car one day and decides to wind up Delfont, so he calls him at his office.

'"What's that noise in the background?" asks Delfont.

'"Oh, it's a bus next to me. I am calling you from my car."

'Delfont says nothing but resolves to acquire a phone for his car immediately, so as not to be outdone. The following week, Delfont proudly calls Grade in his car from his own vehicle. During the conversation, Delfont hears another telephone ring and says, "Lew, I thought you were in your car. What's that ringing?"

"'Sorry, Bernard, I have someone calling on the other line. I'll have to pick up the other phone. Bye." Back then two phones in one car would have been unheard of!'

Angela laughed. 'That was funny in the sixties, but I suppose we'll all have two phones sooner or later,' she said.

One of the calls Jack made was to Simple Loans Ltd, run by a bright, ambitious Jewish friend of George's, affectionately known as Sleaze. They arranged to meet the following week.

*

Isaac Simple must have enjoyed Shakespeare. That he called his factoring and loans company after himself reminded Jack of Simple, the servant in *The Merry Wives of Windsor*. But he appeared anything but simple. A clever Jew in the mould of Shylock seemed more fitting. George referred to his tight, thick black locks as "permahair". Not a tall man, but strong-looking with a firm handshake, he fixed Jack with a steely gaze from dark eyes.

'What interest do you have in this restaurant?' he asked Jack.

'None,' he replied. 'Let's just say there is an opportunity for you to make some money.'

'That usually appeals,' said Simple, looking sincere. 'So what's the plan?'

227

'All I need you to do, for now, is to offer a substantial but irresistibly cheap loan to the owner, secured on the lease of the building. If he takes it he will have a lump sum as a result, which I guess he will spend on a Ferrari within three weeks. If you make him an offer he can't refuse, and you keep completely confidential the fact that I have even met you, I will make up the difference between your normal margin and what you will make on the deal. And as an act of good faith, I'm prepared to give you this.'

Jack pushed a brown envelope over the desk to Simple. He opened it and counted the contents.

'A grand,' said Simple with a raised eyebrow. 'You must badly want me to do this. Can I ask you why? And what is in it for you?'

'I'll tell you when you can show me that you've done the deal with Steven Gregson. And then there'll be more money in it for you.'

'I like the sound of it. I'll let you know.'

*

'When's the industrial tribunal?' asked Carey. 'I don't want it to damage our share price before our takeover of Rockson Engineering plc has gone unconditional. It's fully underwritten but I don't want those banks to be left holding the baby.'

Jack noted Carey no longer called the company by the code name Weasel, as they all had done to keep the takeover secret. 'It's not for a couple of months,' replied Jack, looking over his coffee cup. 'Our solicitors have briefed the best counsel available and they are cautiously optimistic.'

'They always are,' replied Carey. 'A barrister friend of mine once told me that you can never be more than seventy per cent sure of winning any case in court, and as I say myself, if something can go wrong it will. So you had better make sure all the angles are covered. While you are doing that, take a look at this. When we've finally got our mits on the business, I will need you to go over to the USA and shut Arron Steel Inc., this company we are about to pick up with Rockson. It is haemorrhaging cash. If we shut it swiftly and stop the losses, we can write off the costs of closure against the acquisition provision and our shares will rise.'

'They seem to rise whatever we do at the moment, whether we buy, sell, close or announce plans to develop a business. The market seems to be crazy right now. Do you think it could be riding for a fall?' asked Jack.

'Wash your mouth out,' replied Carey with a laugh. 'I've just cut you in for some more share options so let's hope not.'

Angus Marwick appeared at the office door. 'Bill, sorry to interrupt. Mr Slimbridge and his team are finally ready to complete. It was a while ago we agreed this in principle so I just want to make sure you're still happy with the terms of the option for him to buy the balance of the division and in particular that being related to the group's share price. The way the deal is geared, they would pay handsomely if the share price increases but could pick it up for very little if the price drops. For example, if the share price were to halve, which we know it won't, but if it did, they could buy most of the group for a fraction of its worth and make us vulnerable to a bid. And so would the alternative you have offered him of buying shares at a fixed price. I know he is paying for the option but are you comfortable with it all?'

'Angus, is the share price going to tank? No? In which case, get on with it,' replied Carey.

As Marwick left the office, Carey winked at Jack, shook his head and said quietly, 'Bloody finance directors. They're always so cautious and miserable.'

Jack simply smiled, but did wonder himself whether the risk was worth taking. *Still, it's not my deal this time*, he thought.

'Mr Carey, it is time you left for your meeting in London,' said Samantha, his secretary, with a slightly sheepish grin.

'OK, I'll be right there. Could you please tell Julie that I am leaving now?'

Jack watched through the office window as he unlocked his car and put his overnight bag in the boot. As he did so both Julie, his new assistant, and Samantha appeared with what seemed to be their own overnight bags, which Carey added to his in the boot. All three of them then left in Carey's car, the girls talking animatedly as they turned onto the road in the direction of the motorway.

Jack wondered why Bill needed to take two secretaries with overnight bags to a meeting in London. But having witnessed his behaviour in the nightclub, he could guess.

*

At the preliminary hearing of the magistrates' court, the man George had discovered in Tabitha's flat had pleaded not guilty to her murder. The magistrates had not granted bail and so the man had been in jail for the months before the trial in the Crown Court commenced.

The Crown Court was packed. Over to the left of them, George and Jack could see Tabitha's white-faced parents, whom they had met at her funeral. That had been a desperately sad occasion. As Angela had remarked, no parent wants to bury one of their children, let alone one who appeared to have been murdered. Tabitha's father had told George that they did not know who the man was and the police would not tell them anything at all about the circumstances of Tabitha's death, or about the man in question. Indeed, the police were keen to find out from them more about where she worked and what she did for a living. That she was an estate agent in Sheffield was all her parents knew. She must be doing well, they thought, as she always seemed to have plenty of money. They said she had many friends, some of them wealthy, and travelled abroad a lot. They did not know whether she travelled alone or with those friends. So her parents had had to wait until this moment to find out the truth of what had happened.

Mustapha Ibrahim pleaded not guilty to murder and the prosecuting barrister then opened by describing the scene the police had discovered in the flat. His claim was that Tabitha had been strangled by Ibrahim using a cord around her neck. There was evidence of cocaine and alcohol in both main rooms of the flat. There was blood on the walls and a dressing-gown cord lying near to the bed where Tabitha had been found. The bruises on her neck, of which large pictures were passed to the jury, were consistent with the view of the pathologist that strangulation was the cause of death. Tabitha's mother caught sight of one of the pictures and started to cry softly into her husband's shoulder.

Ibrahim's defending counsel argued that this was a clear case of manslaughter as a result of a sex game that had gone wrong. Tabitha's parents looked at each other in anguish as the details of the game were described by the barrister. There was something toe-curling about a man in a gown and short wig describing the detail of a sexual perversion to a middle-aged female judge, thought Jack.

The prosecution's first witness was a girl who looked about twenty-eight. She had long, artificially blonde hair, wore too much make-up, an expensive-looking but rather brash jacket and a short skirt.

'Please tell the court your name and occupation,' said the barrister.

'My name is Roxanne Cuthbertson, and I work in a bar.'

'How well did you know Tabitha Smith?'

'Oh, quite well. We used to go out together at night.'

'Miss Cuthbertson, I believe you have another name, do you not?'

The witness paused and looked at the judge, who raised her eyebrows.

'Miss Cuthbertson?' said the barrister.

'Well, yes. Sometimes I use the name Roxy Anderson.'

'And why do you do that?'

'Because I don't always want people knowing my real name.'

'Miss Cuthbertson, please tell the court why you do not always want people to know your real name?'

'Because I do another job sometimes.'

'And what might that be, Miss Cuthbertson?'

She looked at the judge again and the barrister said, 'Well? Remember you are on oath and you are obliged to tell the truth. What is that truth?'

'I am a…'

'Please speak up, Miss Cuthbertson. We cannot hear you.'

'I am a call girl.'

'No further questions,' said the prosecution barrister as he sat down, pulling his gown around himself.

*

After lunch, the case continued. That Tabitha had been friendly with a call girl had surprised George but as Jack observed, there was no reason to suppose that Tabitha knew that she was one. After all, Roxanne used two names. *And how well does anybody know anybody else?* Jack wondered.

It was now the turn of the defence to ask her the questions.

'How friendly were you and Tabitha?' asked the defending barrister.

'As I said earlier, we used to go out together.'

'Did you work together?'

'Yes, she sometimes worked in the bar with me.'

'Did you work together in your other… job?'

'What do you mean?'

'I think you know what I mean. Did you work together as prostitutes?'

'How dare you?' muttered Tabitha's father rather loudly, before the judge warned him not to say anything. Tabitha's mother looked blankly at Roxanne.

'Well, Miss Cuthbertson?' prompted the barrister.

'Yes, we did sometimes.'

There was a gasp around the court. Tabitha's mother looked as though she was going to faint. Her father put his arm around her.

'And did you know the accused?'

'No. But I know Tabitha had seen him a few times. He paid her good money, you see.'

'And how much is "good money"?'

'Two, sometimes £3,000 a night.'

Tabitha's mother wailed and sobbed into the sleeve of her husband's jacket while he held her tight and looked as though he too was going to cry. The judge decided to adjourn proceedings whilst those dozen or so friends and relatives in the court who had been shocked by what they had learned tried to compose themselves.

Jack and George left the building. Jack, who did not smoke, asked George for a cigarette. He was shaking. Neither of them spoke. Then Jack sat heavily on the stone wall outside the court, put his head in his hands and murmured, 'This is all my fault.'

'What do you mean?' asked George, putting a hand on his friend's back.

'It's my fault that she became a prostitute. I taught her.'

'That's ridiculous, Jack. How can that be?'

'We treated them all badly. They might just as well have been hookers. They slept with us because we employed them. We rewarded them with a job instead of paying them for sex. They probably wouldn't have done it otherwise. It's all my fault.'

'Jack, it isn't. I seem to remember they enjoyed it.'

'How do you really know? They might have been pretending. And anyway, even if they did, that does not make what we did right. It's my fault. If she hadn't become a hooker, she wouldn't have been murdered. How can I ever make amends? It's too late for her and her poor parents.'

'Jack, it's hard to say you are overreacting. We're all in shock. But I think to blame yourself is a bit much.'

'No, George, this is my fault. I can't go back in there or look her parents in the eye. Please let me know what happens to that man. I feel sick. I've got to go.'

Jack pulled on his coat and started to walk away from George. He then stopped, turned to face his friend and said, 'Sorry. Too many things have gone wrong. I'll see you soon,' and then trudged, hunched, towards the station.

CHAPTER 16

Jack glanced at Angela as she came out of the shower. Even though she was a few years older than him she looked the same age. Water dribbled off her long dark hair and traced a fine line down her back and around the cheeks of one buttock as perfectly as a drawing by Matisse. When she had dried herself she resembled a painting by Degas. When she caressed body lotion into her long legs Jack could smell the sweet scent from where he sat at the other side of the room. As he was about to offer her his assistance, the telephone rang.

'I've completed the transaction to give £100,000 loan to Steven Gregson. It is secured on the lease but also on the stock and debtors. So effectively it is secured on the whole business. And I cut my margin by three percentage points to persuade him to go ahead, so you owe me the difference, each year,' said Simple.

'Excellent,' said Jack on the other end of the phone. 'Now I'd like to buy the loan off you. I will give you £110,000 for it. So you will have made an immediate ten grand for your trouble.'

'Why would you want to do that?' asked Simple.

'Because with the loan comes the security. And that is what I'm interested in. And remember, Steve Gregson must not know about this change in the arrangement.'

'OK, you have a deal. I still don't know why you would want to do this, but we can complete the paperwork over the next week. I'll do my best to ensure the arrangement is impossible to circumvent. By the way, do you know the definition of circumvent? It's the opening in the front of my boxer shorts.'

Jack laughed and thought he liked people who could make jokes about their own religion. 'See you then, Isaac, and thanks.'

As Jack put down the phone, he winked at Angela, who was now dressing, and clenched his fist in triumph. He could not think of a better way to spend some of the money he was due to make on his share options as a result of the share price increase. He had one more job to do to cap off a good week.

'Angela, I have got tickets for *Cats* for tomorrow night and I've booked dinner at Langans after.'

'Wow. How did you manage that? It's been a sell-out for months.'

'I called the box office. They said there were no tickets for tomorrow night. I said there must be and could they please look again. They said no, there were no tickets, so I said what would you do if the Queen and Prince Philip wanted to come? They said well, in that case two tickets would be found for them. So I said that I had news for them, the royals were not coming and so could I please have theirs.'

'You are such a star, Mr Mayhew. And I love you,' said Angela, giving Jack a hug and a kiss.

Jack grinned. It was going to be a perfect end to the week.

Jack had asked for a quiet table in the corner of the busy restaurant. Now was not the time to bump into Michael Cain, he thought. Crisp white linen tablecloths, plain large yet thin wine glasses. Oysters and champagne, which Jack was pleased Angela had ordered. Then seafood, with which they drank Puligny Montrachet and afterwards with their beef a bottle of Château Grand Puy Lacoste.

'Darling, you are pushing the boat out. Quite a celebration. You must be pleased with your latest deal,' said Angela, smiling and taking Jack's hand, which rested on the tablecloth.

'Yes. But I'm celebrating something much more important. Or at least I'm hoping to.'

'What's that?'

Jack put his hand on top of hers, squeezed it and said, 'Angela, would you do me the honour of becoming Mrs Mayhew?'

Angela paused, looked Jack in the eye and then said, 'You don't even need to ask. Of course I will. I was your matron once; I might as well be your wife now. Not much difference, really.'

They both laughed, their heads touching each other until a waiter said, 'Will there be anything else, sir?'

*

After the takeover of Rockson Engineering plc was declared unconditional, the share price of the enlarged company increased twenty per cent in a single day. At the press conference, Jack outlined the profit-improvement strategy for the combined enterprise, which largely consisted of merging factories and closing others. Most of the questions were directed at Jack, who wasn't sure whether that was because his area of responsibility was the most challenging, or because he was by far the youngest on the board. The pretty journalist from the *Financial Times* asked the most questions and collared him afterwards over coffee. She asked if they could include him in a feature called forty under forty. The article was to highlight forty of the most promising young business people in the country. Jack was flattered, but felt tense at the suggestion. What would Bill Carey think? He had already made more than one reference to the fact that he thought Jack was after his job.

'Another plc chairman said to me recently that bosses of public companies who feel paranoid are not. Everyone *is* out to get them,' Bill had said. Bill was now calling himself William. Jack figured that now Carey had taken over the chairmanship from Sandy Brockhouse, he thought this gave him more gravitas, not that he ever said so. Jack declined the offer by the *FT*, and the journalist's tempting and slightly flirtatious invitation to lunch, but added, 'Perhaps one day.'

As Jack was no longer in possession of inside information on the company, he was no longer in purdah and so was free to exercise his share options. He had been well rewarded for his successes, particularly in turning around Barnsley Stampings. He had been promised more if he was successful in dealing with Arron Steel Inc. So he exercised all his share options and sold the lot. He had made just short of half a million pounds: the first substantial money he had made in his life. He then asked Angela to telephone the bank and find out how much was in their deposit account. She called him back immediately with shrieks of delight.

In the event, Jack's trip to Houston to make arrangements for the closure of Arron Steel would have to wait until after the tribunal case against the company had been heard and settled. The case was listed for the following month. He had to be there. If he lost, Jack knew that Carey would fire him. "Success is shared, failure is personal" was one of Carey's favourite mantras.

*

'Court rise,' said the official as the three tribunal members filed into the room. Jack immediately spotted which one was the union man. He wore his badge proudly on the wrong brown and curling lapel.

'Sir, as you know, I represent thirty-seven applicants who have a justifiable claim against the company for unfair dismissal,' said the barrister for the applicants. Paid for by the union, noted Jack.

He made a strong-sounding case. Not only was there no redundancy situation but the notice of redundancy had been incorrectly filed, in breach of the statutory time limit for redundancies to be made. And the selection criteria and process had not been agreed. Furthermore, the criteria had not been consistently applied, and so the redundancies were automatically unfair.

Counsel for the company asked for an adjournment so as to check the details of the allegations being put to the tribunal. 'If any one of these allegations is correct, we will have lost,' said his barrister. Jack went white. 'But I think they are wrong on all counts. I don't need this adjournment. I'm just making them think they have us on the ropes. Don't worry. You did a good job. You'll be fine.'

You will be fine, thought Jack, *as you get paid either way.*

The company's barrister was in a flamboyant and confident mood. He dealt with each of the union's points swiftly and comprehensively. And he made the tribunal laugh. *Not a bad thing*, thought Jack.

The tribunal adjourned to consider their verdict for what seemed like an age. They then filed back into the room and the chairman spoke.

'We have carefully considered the submissions of both parties and thank them both for their clarity. We find that there was a clear case for redundancies to be made. We find that the redundancy notice was filed in a timely manner. We find that the criteria for selection for redundancy was fair. We would like to remind the claimants that it is entirely appropriate for management to devise whatever selection criteria they wish, within the law. Finally, however—'

A fire alarm sounded in the corridor outside and an official entered the room and asked everyone to leave. Once they were all in the car park, Jack approached the chairman of the tribunal and asked what he was going to say.

'I'm afraid I cannot tell you,' he said, somewhat sternly.

Jack's confidence faded. Surely he would give Jack some hint if he was not going to lose the case. The official finally announced that they could return to the rooms whence they came.

'I apologise for that,' said the chairman. 'It seems to have been a false alarm. To continue and conclude, we find unanimously that the criteria for selection for redundancy were applied fairly and so in conclusion there has been no unfair dismissal. We therefore dismiss the application and award costs against the applicants.'

Jack tried to look dignified. Triumphalism was not called for, at least not in public. When the union and the tribunal had left the room however, Jack's barrister shook Jack warmly by the hand and said, 'Never in doubt.' Jack thanked him, sat back on his chair and breathed a welcome sigh of relief.

*

One of the covenants on the loan that Steven Gregson had taken out in the name of Phoenix Arizona was that if any two consecutive monthly interest payments were more than a week late, the loan was repayable on demand. So far, the payments had been received on time. Given Steven's profligacy, Jack felt he would not have to wait long. He was wrong about the Ferrari. The new car sitting at the front of the restaurant each day was a black Lamborghini: property, no doubt, of Phoenix Arizona.

Jack still found the name of the restaurant irksome. Steven was casting himself in the role of saviour. Even though arson had not been proved, the police still had their suspicions and so the file remained open. Steven had employed some of Jack's old staff, including Mona's daughter, Sian. Jack had heard that Mona was unemployed and had found life both financially and emotionally difficult since the break-up of her last relationship. Now happily married to Angela, Jack felt unable to engage with Mona emotionally. Indeed, he imagined Mona would still not see him. Jack had also heard that Steven was badmouthing Jack, blaming him for the failure of the business and the unemployment of the staff. Jack longed to get even.

George called Isaac Simple Porky or Isaac O'Bagel to his face which invariably made Isaac smile or award George with a playful thump. Although a serious lender, Isaac didn't take himself too seriously. He had opened an account for his business at Phoenix Arizona. His colleagues invariably drank champagne and left large bills on the account. At the time of making the loan to Steven, Isaac had told Jack that he intended to do this, to make good use of the credit facility so as to have additional leverage on Steven and to keep a close eye on the restaurant itself. Even though Isaac had now divested himself of the loan, he continued to make substantial use of the account.

Indeed, Steven had taken Isaac and some of his colleagues to Cheltenham races. Whilst not as important as Gold Cup week, the summer races were none the less eagerly anticipated in the area. The course was exposed and despite being summer, it was windy as usual. But on this occasion the sun shone. And as always there was an abundance of large hats on female heads large and small. It had rained and so the going was soft. The going being soft also meant that the same large-hatted ladies, who wore high stilettos, sank into the turf. Ladies tottered, some fell, others lost shoes in the mud. Slight-chinned young men with thinning hair in mock-tweed brown jackets and matching brogues were heard more than once to say, with a guffaw, 'Another faller at the first, what?'

Isaac had warned Jack that he would be at the races with Steven, but as Steven had hired a box with some of his new-found cash, it would be easy for Jack to keep out of his way. Steven would keep to the tote and so this left Jack and Angela free to move about the stewards' enclosure without risking a meeting that Jack wished to avoid. Or so he thought.

Whilst at the rail near the finishing post, through his binoculars Jack spotted Steven place bets with several bookmakers. Having done so, he left the open area and headed back towards the boxes. This pattern repeated itself before each race, with Steven's gait looking noticeably less secure each time. And not once did Jack notice Steven return to any of the bookies to collect any winnings.

The following day, Isaac confirmed that Steven had been lavish with his entertaining. He had visited the Tote prior to the first race but he had not returned there subsequently, claiming that he could get better odds with the bookmakers next to the course. Steven had initially boasted about the large size of his bets, but had later become quiet on the subject, becoming more vocal generally as he drank his way through the wine provided in the box. Isaac concluded that Steven had lost heavily on the day. *Only a matter of time*, thought Jack.

A month later, Steven missed the first interest payment by over a week. Jack called Isaac to tell him and to encourage him not to settle his restaurant bill. Jack had already registered a new company and trading name: Montecristo's. Dumas's revenge novel seemed to him to provide the perfect name. He created 101 shares in the company and carefully wrote the names of the new shareholders on each share certificate. One person had just over fifty per cent of the share capital. Jack asked a local signwriter to make a sign with "Montecristo's" in large red letters. When he asked Jack what the sign was for, Jack merely replied that it was for a new restaurant he was opening. The site was to be a surprise.

The following month, Steve paid the second consecutive interest payment late. On the letterhead of his new company, Jack wrote the letter to Steven that he had wanted to write for several years, and put it in his pocket.

*

When the jumbo jet landed at Houston Airport, there was a slight jolt as the undercarriage touched the warm runway. A faint smell of burning rubber reached Jack's senses as some of the smoke from the tyres was sucked into the cabin by the air conditioning. Jack had been told by Bill Carey to travel business class, as he would need to be fresh for his first meeting with the management of Arron Steel Inc.

During the flight, one of the air hostesses had seemed to pay special attention to him, even asking him where he was staying in town. The oil price was sub-twenty dollars a barrel, which meant that in Houston oil dollars were scarce and engineering companies related to the sector were in trouble. This was the reason for Jack's visit. The Intercontinental Hotel was offering rooms at a third of the usual price, bringing it into the price range for British Airways' hostesses.

'Well, I am staying there too, Mr Mayhew,' she said as she leaned across him to give him his breakfast. 'Perhaps we will see each other.'

She smiled at Jack with blue eyes and a perfect mouth. Her perfume was strong, as he had noticed earlier, and Jack wondered whether she had applied it each time she was about to enter the cabin to serve him.

Angela's smiling face drifted though his mind, clouded by the effects of a long trip at altitude. *Perhaps in days gone by we might*, thought Jack. But no longer. Not since Angela. And Angela was now his wife. In her he had found a beautiful and sympathetic woman who understood him. She understood his ambition. She understood his insecurity and what drove him. She understood his fallibility.

Jack was picked up by the managing director of Arron Steel, Don Jameson. In his broad Texan drawl, he exuded immediate although perhaps insincere warmth. He wasted no time in laying claim to his Irish ancestry, reminding Jack that his name was of course Irish. Jack wondered why all Americans wished to have Irish blood. Jameson was a typical oil man. Everything was big. Everything was doable. The oil price would rise, demand would pick up and his new bosses across the pond would no longer have to send large amounts of cash to him to prop up the business. All would be well.

On arriving at the factory, Jameson took Jack immediately to the stockyard. There he met Douggie Watershed. Douggie wore a large brown Stetson hat and cowboy boots. No spurs, thought Jack, although they would not have looked out of place and neither would a horse tethered to the railings. Jack had never experienced such humidity. And the temperature in the shade was ninety-five degrees. Fahrenheit, of course. The Americans would never convert to Celsius. There was no shade and so Jack, being dressed in his thick blue woollen pinstriped suit, quickly ran with sweat. He had missed the fact that a cool autumn in London would nonetheless equate to a hot and humid day in Texas.

Douggie kept Jack standing in the heat whilst he slowly explained that the rusting stock in front of him was actually oil-field gantry equipment of great value, as demonstrated in the balance sheet of the accounts. Jack thought the stock was probably worthless.

With his energy depleted by the sun torture treatment (Jack thought this was a deliberate tactic), he and the directors then assembled to discuss the fate of the business. Of course, Jack had not disclosed to the rather aggressive border police the fact that he had been sent to close it. When asked by them the purpose of his visit, he had been economical with the truth. Just "on business" was enough. Carey had warned him – tongue in cheek – that if he were honest that he was in the USA to close a company and therefore make good American citizens redundant, he would be put on to the next plane home, no doubt after an unpleasant few hours at the President's pleasure.

Perhaps Jameson had some idea of the reason for Jack's visit for, after having again exaggerated the chances of recovery of the operation, he said, 'But if you are unhappy with your investment for any reason, we would be happy to take it off your hands – for a dollar.'

The balance sheet included $2 million of debt, the stock was worthless and the company was haemorrhaging cash at the rate of $500,000 a year. At a dollar, the company was overvalued.

Jack thought for a few seconds and then said, 'Well, we need to be certain that you can settle the bank debt of two million dollars. If you can convince us of that, you may have a deal. Don, you have a week to come up with the evidence that this can happen.'

'No problem, sir,' said Don in his broad Texan drawl and smiling confidently.

Late that evening, Jack was taken to Rick's Bar. A well-endowed girl wearing a black basque and holding a small tray showed them to their table and asked them what they would like to drink. The large flashing sign outside the bar had promised something called table dancing; Jack had been thinking of Alpine après-ski, where he had danced on the tables with his university friends all in their ski boots. Now he was puzzled: the table was so small he wondered how anybody was supposed to dance on it. And he couldn't see any ski boots.

After the drinks arrived, Douggie, with a lecherous grin on his face, pushed a $5 bill down the front of the waitress's basque. Someone else pushed one inside the back of her knickers. The waitress then removed her basque and started to dance at their table, her young and firm breasts moving in perfect synchronicity with the rest of her body and the music. *So this is table dancing,* concluded Jack, as his mind slid to thoughts of Angela. He resolved to leave as soon as it would be polite to do so.

Jack could not get away until the early hours of the morning but once back in his hotel room he telephoned Angela. As he chatted through the events of the day he could sense that Angela wanted to speak about something perhaps more important.

'What, darling? Are you listening to me?' he asked.

'Of course, Jack,' she said with a snigger.

'What then?'

'I've got something to tell you. Some news.'

'Well, go on. I'm on the edge of my seat.'

'I'm going to have our child… You are going to be a daddy… I'm pregnant.'

Jack almost dropped the receiver. He found it difficult to express his true delight down the phone and wished he could take Angela in his arms and tell her properly how thrilled he was.

After they had spoken excitedly for twenty minutes, Jack said goodnight to Angela and went to bed. He fell asleep feeling as contented as he had ever been.

*

A week later Don produced a letter from the Wells Fargo Bank which contained their offer to refinance the $2 million debt which would allow Jack to sell the business for a dollar.

This would remove the need for all closure costs, stop the annual losses of half a million dollars a year and put $2 million into the bank of Arnold Foundries plc. Jack called Bill Carey, and told him the news.

'Unbelievable. Fantastic!' Carey chuckled. 'When will you complete, or close as they call it over there?'

'A couple of weeks, maybe. It's a simple deal. No warranties.'

'Great. Call Aquila PR and get them to draft the press release. The shares are £2.30 today. If they don't go north of £2.50 when this is announced I'd be surprised. Well done, Jack. Let me know when you complete and then come home. Oh, and you can keep the dollar consideration for yourself.' Carey laughed at his own joke and hung up.

*

The lawyers for the deal were on the top floor of a tall downtown office block of the type not yet evident in the UK. A giant wall of glass reflected the bright Texan sun. As Jack waited for a lift, he noticed that the women coming out of them all looked like extras appearing in the TV series *Dallas*. Big hair. Padded shoulders. Maximum make-up. He smiled to himself as one of them encouraged him to "have a nice day".

His lawyer was called Jo DiMarino, a short Italian Jewish-looking man in his thirties with dark close-cropped curly hair that appeared to be a solid, unmoving mass. He reminded Jack of Isaac Simple. *Why do clever young Jews all have the same hair?* wondered Jack. Jo wore strong cologne.

'Jack, we are ready to close the deal now. So I hope you have your lucky pen with you!' he said.

'How's your day been so far?' enquired the *Dallas* extra as she showed Jack into the boardroom. 'I just love your accent, sir,' she added flirtatiously, smiling with her head on one side.

'Well, thanks,' replied Jack. 'But I don't have an accent.'

The girl looked puzzled and asked if he knew Charles and Di and "do you have dollars over there?".

Jack assumed that she was one of the majority of US citizens who did not possess a passport and thought that the UK was such a small island that everyone knew everyone else.

Having signed the deal, exchanged contracts and completed with the purchasers, Jack left a message with Carey's secretary to tell him that "the eagle had landed". He looked over the press release announcing the deal once more and then stood over the fax machine whilst it was sent to the UK for announcement when the markets opened after the weekend on the morning of 19 October 1987.

As Jack settled into his seat on the aeroplane that Sunday afternoon, he read that storms were brewing in the Atlantic but that they were not expected to reach the UK. And, of course, he would be flying over them.

When he arrived at Heathrow mid-morning the following day, he phoned the stock market reporting service to obtain the share price as soon as he could. It was bound to have put on at least twenty pence from two pounds thirty. Jack would receive the grateful thanks of the entire board and their shareholders, and perhaps a bonus which he would put on one side for his first-born child. The recorded system gave him the share price. One pound fifteen pence. *Surely some mistake*, thought Jack, sweating and nervous as he dialled the number again. One pound fifteen pence, confirmed the message. The share price had halved on the news of Jack's work in Texas. *Please let that not be true*, he thought. He would surely be fired.

Jack searched feverishly for a newspaper. The front page of *The Times* carried photographs of cars on one side, trees collapsed across roads and news of rail chaos. A hurricane had unexpectedly hit the UK. The weather forecaster Michael Fish was on the receiving end of comments ranging from jokes to mild abuse for falsely assuring British television viewers that the storm would not hit the mainland. He was plainly wrong. The financial pages did not carry news of Jack's deal as the press release had been embargoed until after that edition had been printed. So Jack hurriedly rummaged for the *Evening Standard*'s first edition. *Stock market meltdown* was the headline.

Jack knew that his sale of Arron Steel Inc was important to Arnold Foundries plc, but did not expect that it would shake the whole stock market. It soon became apparent that virtually all stocks had endured a catastrophic fall in their value, some more than the fifty per cent suffered by Arnold Foundries. With considerable relief Jack realised that the reason for the sharp fall in the value of their share price was not his deal. The newspaper did carry a small announcement severely edited from the press release he had faxed to Aquila PR but the financial pages were dominated by the crash and the possible consequences for public companies as a whole and the economy in general. Jack decided he needed to go into the office rather than home, to join Carey and his colleagues and assess the impact of the crash. But as Jack approached his car to drive to Birmingham, he remembered with a jolt and a sick feeling in his stomach the option over Arnold Foundries plc shares that Carey had agreed with Clement Slimbridge.

*

On arriving at the office, Jack was informed stiffly by one of Carey's now three secretaries that he was unavailable. He was locked in a meeting with his non-executive director, who had arrived to assess the impact on the company of the collapse in the share price. In particular, Jack thought, they would want to consider how they could protect themselves against the effects of the possibility of Slimbridge exercising his option over the shares. Jack calculated that the reduction on the price was so severe that the option would enable Slimbridge to purchase twenty-five per cent of the group for a knock-down price. If he did that, he would have a strong platform from which to bid for control of the whole group.

Jack heard shouting from inside the boardroom. A red-faced colleague, who looked as though he was in tears, left the room. Carey's secretaries scurried about adjusting their hair and skirts, trying to look purposeful.

Success is shared, failure is personal, thought Jack as he left the office. *And if Carey is not available, I have something else to do.*

As he settled into his car, Jack felt for an envelope in the inside pocket of his jacket. He pulled it out and read what was written on the envelope in his own hand. "Steven Gregson, Phoenix Arizona, 12 Broad Street, Bath." *Now is the time to pay a visit*, thought Jack.

*

Jack parked his car at the end of the street and walked up towards what had been his restaurant. He felt the cold wind more sharply than he would have done had it not been for the contrast with the sticky, humid heat of Texas. The cold wind of failure was about to be replaced by the warm glow of revenge. He had caught the sun, lightening his already blond hair and making his skin seem more tanned than that of his fellow countrymen. He did not notice the admiring glances of two women in their thirties as he approached the door of the restaurant.

Not much had changed since he had owned the restaurant when it was called Arthur's. He had already noted the decor when he had sat in the bar opposite with Angela. But the general ambience was similar, too. The music was contemporary and the waiting staff all young and female – except for Steve, the owner. *The current owner*, thought Jack. *For now.* A waitress, young and seductively dressed, as in his day, began to lead him to a table in the middle of the room. There was no sign of Steve, but nonetheless Jack asked to sit at a small table at the back of the room, where he could watch for Steve's arrival with one eye on his crossword.

After half an hour, when Jack was on his second glass of burgundy and had finished his duck liver pâté, Jack noticed a black Lamborghini draw up and park at the front. Steve got out – white shirt, dark hair, black jeans – and appeared at the restaurant. He worked his way around, looking pleased with himself, glad-handing the customers in what was by then a nearly full restaurant. As George would have said, he oozed several million volts of synthetic charm. He had not spotted Jack and did not do so until he was in front of his small table. When he did eventually notice Jack, he looked startled and turned away. Jack stood and said, 'Mr Gregson, I have a letter for you.' Jack handed Steve the letter he had written before he left for the USA. Steve took it, raised an eyebrow, looked at Jack and put it in his pocket.

'I advise you to read it now, Steve, as it affects your immediate future.'

Steve hesitated, perhaps smelling a rat.

'Open the letter,' said Jack, fixing him with a resolute stare.

Steve turned and moved to an alcove at the back of the restaurant where there was no table, opened the envelope and started to read. As he did so, he sat heavily on the nearest chair. He read the letter again. Jack observed him closely with a mounting feeling of satisfaction.

Dear Steven,

On 1 August this year, a company controlled by me purchased your company's debt owed to Simple Loans Ltd.

Interest and repayments on that loan are due monthly on the first of each month.

We note that these payments were more than seven days late in the month of August. You will be aware that this is an event of default and that in these circumstances we may request repayment of the principal and interest on demand. We refer you to clause 12 (i) of the agreement.

We note further that in the month of September, the payments were again late. You will be aware that in the circumstances of this repeated default we may request immediate repayment of the principal and interest in addition to exercising our rights under the security provided by your company. We refer you to clause 12 (ii) of the agreement.

As a result of these defaults, the lease, stock and all other assets of your company now pass into our ownership with immediate effect. Because the value of the assets will not cover your indebtedness, we hereby give you notice that we shall pursue you personally for the difference. Our actions will include petition for your bankruptcy, should that be necessary.

Yours sincerely,
Jack Mayhew
Montecristo's Ltd

When Steve had read the letter a second time he looked over at Jack, pale but with an angry and defiant expression. Jack returned his gaze, but with a rather different look on his face. It was one of passive aggression. Both men remained motionless for a few seconds. Then Jack stood, and walked slowly towards Steve, who stood to meet Jack face to face. When they were in touching distance of each other, Steve raised his arm as if he were about to hit Jack. Jack grabbed his wrist firmly and said, 'I don't advise you to do that. You wouldn't want to add a charge of assault to your inevitable bankruptcy, would you?'

Before Steve could answer, Jack added, 'Steve, this is now my restaurant. And it will not surprise you to learn that I don't need you. You are fired. Please, give me the keys to the premises and your car, collect your personal possessions and leave immediately. Oh, and I know who tampered with the brakes on my car.'

Without replying, Steve turned to the nearest two waitresses and said, 'Tell all the staff to stop work and meet me now in the wine bar opposite. Mr Mayhew is trying to take over the restaurant.'

The girls, who were juggling trays of plates, looked at each other nervously. Jack, who had heard what Steve had said to them, walked up to them, smiling reassuringly, and said quietly, 'No – don't do that. This is now my restaurant. Steve has left my employment and you can all stay.' Jack paused and added words the girls could only take at face value. 'You are safe with me.'

The girls exchanged glances again, this time smiling. They grinned sheepishly at Jack and disappeared into the kitchen with their trays as Steve threw his car and restaurant keys onto the floor and disappeared from the premises, and Jack hoped into oblivion.

TWO DOWN, thought Jack.

*

Jack remained at the restaurant for the rest of that evening, and was later joined by Angela. By the time she arrived, Jack had written the names of eleven women on eleven different envelopes into which he had placed a share certificate bearing the corresponding name. The names were Fiona, Sandy, Sian, Vicky, Beryl, Laura, Steph, Sophie and Jane: the girls whom Jack and George had trifled with several years ago. Jack sighed as he addressed Tabitha's envelope to her parents. The eleventh envelope, which contained a share certificate for just over fifty per cent of the share capital in Montecristo's restaurant, was made out to Mona. With her share certificate Jack included a note which read, *I did untold damage. I'm sorry. It is not enough, but I hope this will go some way to compensating you, your daughter, Sian, and the other girls. With love, Jack.*

One of the current staff was Sophie, who had worked for Jack and was now the deputy manager. At the end of the shift, she accepted Jack's offer of becoming manager in place of Steve with surprise and obvious delight. This was only surpassed when she opened the envelope addressed to her containing her share certificate.

'But why?' she asked.

'Let's just say that I owe you,' Jack replied.

He asked Sophie if she could deliver the other share certificates to those named, but she only knew where half of them lived.

'Do you know where Mona lives?' he asked, unsure that she would still be at the address he associated with both intense pleasure and acute pain.

'Yes, she hasn't moved in a long time.'

'Would you please deliver her envelope to her and ask if she could send the others to the intended recipients?'

Sophie agreed happily and after a celebratory glass of champagne, Jack drove Angela home. Pregnancy suited her. She was flushed, alluring and radiated a contentment unique to her sex and condition.

'What about the Lamborghini?' she asked.

'It's Mona's.'

'That was a great thing you have done for those girls, especially Mona. I'm proud of you,' she said, reaching a warm hand over to Jack's knee.

'They deserve it. I had to do it. It wasn't just about Steve, although I do feel better now we are somehow square. I can't easily forgive him, though.'

'I know,' she replied, 'but I guess you could say you are now even stevens.'

CHAPTER 17

The following summer

> *Glories, like glow-worms, afar off shine bright,*
> *But looked to near, have neither heat nor light.*
>
> John Webster

Jack's reputation in the City was now assured. Since his success at Barnsley Stampings, Arron Steel and at the industrial tribunal, he had enjoyed the winter and following spring months consolidating his reputation amongst his colleagues. He sensed some jealously amongst the older ones, but his position on the board, at the moment at least, seemed impregnable. And Carey seemed more relaxed now that the share price had recovered some of its losses since the crash. They were still vulnerable to a bid from Slimbridge or others, but less so.

The annual company cricket match was always eagerly awaited, but not simply in anticipation of the cricket. Here was an opportunity to get even. With the boss who gave you a bad appraisal. The colleague who could teach

Machiavelli a thing or two about internal politics. Here was the possibility of hitting a boundary towards the typing pool in the hope of being noticed. The prospect of catching the chairman LBW. Here was the chance to let the sun shine on others. So much more than a cricket match.

The Black Country is close enough to the chocolate box, languid villages of east Shropshire to bus head-office staff out for the day. Some hopeful young executives had suggested a five-day test. But of course, to the ambitious and gravelly-mannered Carey, one day was plenty.

Two old coaches arrived at the village green at Hopton Wafers belching exhaust fumes with an enthusiasm that the drivers joked could convert this otherwise quaint village into an outpost of the Black Country. Out of the coaches skipped secretaries wearing their best attire but claiming it to be one of many outfits. Junior male office staff tried to look relaxed. Long floral skirts pulled from the back of wardrobes where they had waited since the late seventies for another outing were pressed into service by some of the older ladies attending their first match. The younger ones inevitably took advantage of a mufti day by ensuring their taste for the shortest of skirts remained as fashionable as they had been twenty years earlier. Their mothers would have worn the same, and probably did. Bosoms were not as camouflaged as they were at the office and hair flowed more freely.

A small marquee had been erected the day before by foundrymen, excited to have a day off. Next to this were assembled an odd assortment of coloured deckchairs, dusty directors' chairs from the back of garages and an old hammock, strung between two small and bending apple trees. Two of the ladies mixed Pimm's, uncertain of how much lemonade should be added, whilst swatting away eager wasps. Crates of bottles of Brew XI ale – "for the men of the Midlands" as the advertisement claimed – were stacked next to a table of pint glasses. On an adjacent table were bottles of Berry Brothers and Rudd's Good Ordinary Claret and white wine in tubs of ice next to Paris goblet wine glasses. Three men attended to two pigs that had been skewered and roasted slowly for several hours. A table groaning with white bread rolls, or baps as the locals called them, stood as though in anticipation of an invasion of the starving.

Two Jaguar cars purred onto the grass and positioned themselves under the shade of a large oak tree. Four directors alighted in smartly pressed and suspiciously new cricket whites. Bill – now William – Carey arrived in his black Jag with his wife, Sarah, and nine-year-old son, John. Carey insisted his was the only black car in the group. Distinctive, menacing and determined. Sarah, a slim blonde, was dressed in red. She looked strained and Carey looked a little sullen as if there had been "words in the car" as Jack's mother used to say. Carey forced a smile as he greeted his colleagues and Sarah marched John off towards the marquee, no doubt to investigate the possibility of Coca-Cola. The sun shone brightly and with very little breeze there appeared to be a conspiracy to ensure that the fielders would flag in the heat.

As Jack and Angela arrived, a man in a neighbouring car played "I Don't Like Cricket, I Love It (Dreadlock Holiday)". *My, how we laughed*, thought Jack, grinning at the self-confident, beer-bellied man. Jack spread out a rug in the shade of a lime tree. He had thought that Angela might want to lie down, now that she was eight months pregnant. But she patiently reminded him that she would be more comfortable sitting upright and on a chair. Jack scurried away to find one. A bee settled on her shoe. The smell of cut grass and strawberries mingled with faint wisps of smoke from the pig roast.

'I had better go and greet the team,' said Jack, who had been elected captain of one of them, against his wish. Bill Carey, inevitably, insisted on being captain of the other team. The church bell softly struck twelve.

Lunch was approached with enthusiasm and increasing levels of laughter. *Why do men in groups appear to force their laughs? Can everything be so funny?* thought Jack. As the Brew XI made its increasingly agreeable way through the men of the Midlands, the ladies, giggling on outspread rugs, had little need of flirtation. The senior management, emboldened by Good Ordinary Claret, pressed their relationships with their secretaries as best as they were able under the watchful eyes of their wives. More than one man was dragged gently away.

'Perhaps we had better play cricket, before matters get out of hand,' said Carey with a wink at Jack. Having won the toss, Jack elected to bat. He reasoned that much of Carey's team would be snoozing in the outfield and so boundaries would come more easily. First in were Jim and Sam, both large security men, broad and with huge hands. Sam had dark hair, swept back over a broad forehead. Jack was reminded of Alan Bates in *Far from the Madding Crowd*. Their batting was as agricultural as Jack had hoped and so the pair hit enough boundaries to rack the score up over fifty before Sam was caught for thirty-eight. Jack was next in. He winked at Angela as he strode purposefully to the crease. She smiled. Jack loved pregnant women, but he could not have known how much he would love his own.

Jack played with a rather more refined style than Jim, having been coached in the public-school manner. He was content to remain in, in the Geoffrey Boycott role, while Jim pushed the score towards a hundred. Sensing that others would like a bat, Jack lashed out at a loose ball and was caught on the boundary for a respectable twenty-six. At tea, Jack declared, giving Carey's team a couple of hours to overtake their total of 118 for 6 wickets.

After tea, wickets fell quickly, mainly to Sam's fast bowling, so that Carey's team were 63 for 6. Next man in was Carey himself. He looked flushed. *Is it the heat, the wine or the fear of losing?* thought Jack. He brought Sam on to bowl again, having rested him after taking four early wickets. As if with renewed energy, Sam bowled aggressively at Carey. Had he something else to prove? Was he getting even? Carey pushed a ball towards the boundary and on his second run seemed out of breath. After the next over, when no runs had been scored, Sam again bowled ferociously at Carey. After another run, Jack noticed Carey grab at his chest. He was now very red in the face. On the next run Carey seemed to be more out of breath. As Sam thundered down the field towards the crease again, Carey dropped his bat, clutched at his chest with both hands and collapsed to the ground. He seemed to be in great pain.

The fielders gathered around while he gasped for breath and Sarah ran over to him with a look of alarm.

Someone yelled, 'Call an ambulance,' but Jack was already on the phone in his car to do so. When it arrived, Carey appeared to be unconscious. His small son, John, crying and pale, was led away by two of the older secretaries whilst Sarah knelt over her husband as he was lifted onto a stretcher. She and John then joined him in the back of the ambulance as its blue lights flashed their alarming way to Kidderminster Hospital.

The match was of course abandoned and Jack agreed with the umpires that a draw was the only appropriate result. The joyful mood having been broken, both spectators and players drifted quietly away from the ground, unsure of what to say to one another.

*

The following morning, Clement Slimbridge was driving his Rover 3500 up the M6 towards one of his manufacturing businesses near Manchester. Traffic was heavy. The dry spell of the previous two weeks had ended and summer rain lashed at his smeared windscreen. Must get some new wiper blades, he thought, as he struggled to look through the blur. He pulled into the service station near Stoke-on-Trent to refuel and grab a cup of coffee. He needed to be fully alert for what promised to be a difficult meeting at Hyde Steels, which was proving more challenging to turn around than he had thought. But turnarounds always seemed to be more difficult than he had anticipated. As he rejoined the motorway, the newsreader on the *Today* programme was coming to the end of the headlines.

'Finally, the death of William Carey, the chairman of Midlands mini-conglomerate Arnold Foundries plc has been announced. He died of a heart attack yesterday afternoon whilst playing in the annual company cricket match. He was forty-three. And now the weather…'

Slimbridge did not hear the rest. He gripped the wheel of his car, came off at the next exit and headed back down the motorway towards his office in Birmingham. *This might be my chance*, he thought. Picking up his car phone, he called James Beasley.

'James, Bill Carey has died. Call my broker and sell 100,000 shares in Arnold Foundries stock.'

There was a pause. 'But that's about four per cent of the entire issued share capital. You don't own anything like that number.'

'I know. But I will do by the time we have to settle.'

'Isn't that fraud?'

'Not if I can settle when I have to. By then the price will have crashed, which is what we want. And if my option shares haven't materialised, I will buy them cheap to sell, so we'll be fine.'

'I don't feel comfortable doing that, Clem. You may not be able to settle and then we'll both face jail. I'm afraid you'll have to call the broker yourself. Sorry.'

Slimbridge put down the phone. 'Loser,' he muttered.

*

Jack was preoccupied with the reactions to Bill's death and in particular the consequences for the business and himself. So he felt yet more uneasy when Tabitha's father, Jim, asked to see him. Jack could guess that Jim had not yet come to terms with the circumstances of her death, or of her double life. How could he? Jack still felt guilt that there had been some connection with the way he had treated her and her brutal end, despite George's attempts to assure him there was no association. And even though he had confessed his promiscuous past to Angela (whose own history was not exactly one of model behaviour), her soothing words had failed to banish his belief that he was somehow responsible.

Jim seemed keen to meet at Montecristo's. After all, it now belonged partly to him. Jack wondered whether a father suffering shocking grief might want to relive vicariously his daughter's happier times.

Jim seemed worn. He had aged in the months that had passed since the trial. Nonetheless, he managed to smile at Jack with a greeting that seemed warm.

After coffee had arrived, and they had exchanged the usual pleasantries, Jim said, 'We can't accept your kind gift of shares in this restaurant. We haven't done anything to deserve them. And Tabitha would have wanted you to keep them. You meant a lot to her.'

Jack swallowed his coffee and gazed into his cup before looking up. Jim wore a look of sadness that Jack found hard to face.

'Jim, I want you to have them. Thank you for telling me that I meant a lot to her. But I didn't treat her or some of the other staff that well. She probably didn't tell you.'

Jack regretted his choice of words. There was evidently a lot she had not told her family, or friends.

'Jack, it wasn't your fault that the restaurant burnt down and so it wasn't your fault that she lost her job.'

'It's not just that. I'm afraid I didn't treat her well. As her employer. As a young woman should be treated. With respect.'

'I'm sure you did. She was fond of you.'

Jack was unable to allow the conversation to dig up the past any further. So he made an excuse about another engagement and stood to leave, wrapping both his hands around Jim's, which held the share certificate. As he left the restaurant he was still troubled by the memory of his treatment of Tabitha and the other young women, but he hoped he had left such behaviour behind him. He also hoped that L. P. Hartley's words at the opening of *The Go-Between* would eventually allow him to subdue the persistent feeling that he was in some way responsible for Tabitha's death. *The past is a foreign country: they do things differently there.*

*

'You need to announce a new chairman without delay,' said Michael Bland, the urbane managing director of Macfarlane's, the merchant bank that had advised both Sandy Brockhouse and Bill Carey throughout their time at Arnold Foundries. 'The shares have not recovered since the crash and they fell another eight per cent on the news of Bill's death. And now you have had a big seller this morning who we can't identify and so they have fallen another six per cent. You don't need me to remind you that this makes you vulnerable to a bid, and not only from Clement Slimbridge. Now might be the time to split the role of chairman and chief executive. The City increasingly don't like one person combining both roles.'

Angus Marwick and the company's only remaining non-executive director, Johnny Roland, looked at each other and nodded. Jack sat alone at the other end of the table, whilst the only other director, David Parsons, gazed out of the window. David was approaching retirement and wanted to ensure that his plans for winters playing golf in the Algarve were not interrupted. *Someone else*, he thought, *not me*.

Marwick and Roland left the room and walked into Carey's vacant office past two secretaries who were hugging each other and crying. Marwick had long ago guessed that they were both closer to Carey than they ought to have been. Whether Carey's wife had also guessed crossed his mind. Or did she know?

'We don't have many choices, do we?' said a pinstriped Roland to Marwick in a resigned tone. 'We don't have the people to split the job. You have often said as finance director that you don't feel that you have the leadership qualities to be a chief executive and David plainly wants to retire. My days as a chief executive are over, I really don't want to be chairman and so that only leaves young Jack.' Roland raised an eyebrow.

Marwick smiled almost patronisingly and said, as persuasively as he could, 'He is only thirty-four. He is too young to be chief executive and certainly too young to be the chairman of a public company. He would probably be the youngest in the country. And with our share price so low it would be unlikely that putting him in either role would result in anything other than an even lower share price. And then a bid would surely follow. Whoever we put in the job would be taking a poisoned chalice; but if we appoint Jack, we would probably all lose our jobs as a result of a takeover. And so I can't support appointing him.'

Roland walked slowly around Carey's old desk and looked out of the window before asking, with his back to Marwick, 'Who else do you suggest?'

'It would have to be David. Or, dare I say, yourself, Johnny?'

'Well, you know how I feel… David wants to retire, you don't want the job and you think Jack is too young. And we have no other choices. I will go and talk to our only option and see whether he can be persuaded.'

Roland left the office and went to find the man whom he would try to persuade to take the combined job of chairman and chief executive of Arnold Foundries plc.

*

June was sitting with her feet up on the lowest open drawer of her old metal desk and filing her nails. Her ancient typewriter stood idle and a pile of grimy buff folders lay haphazardly on her desk. The office clock was still stuck at ten past two. James Beasley was trying to edge the large crust of a ham and tomato sandwich between both corners of his wide mouth. Part of the tomato lost its grip on the bread and landed on the accounts on the desk in front of him just as Slimbridge entered his office.

'June, get hold of Francis Lamb at Morgan's Bank straight away, please. James, what about the news?' Beasley gestured to his full mouth, grunted and shook his head by way of reply.

'Bill Carey has died. There is no one credible to take his place so the shares have fallen still further. So I want to talk to Francis about exercising our option over the foundry division of Arnold and use that as a platform for a bid for the whole group. Do you think that is doable?'

Beasley could not answer without spitting out a small piece of ham to join the tomato on the paper in front of him. 'It might be. Let's see what Francis says,' he replied, seemingly unconvinced he knew the answer himself.

A buzz sounded on the telephone on Slimbridge's desk. 'Mr Lamb for you, Clem,' said June over the phone.

'Francis, good morning. I've got you on speaker phone and James Beasley is with me.' Slimbridge added, 'My finance director,' as if Lamb might need reminding.

'Good morning, Clement. I can guess why you are calling. I have heard the news and already asked one of my team to run the rule over the numbers. With the share price as depressed as it is, 90p currently, you would be able to take twenty-eight per cent of the equity under the foundry division share alternative option already granted to you. With such a high percentage we would be obliged under the rules to make a full bid. But I imagine that is what you have in mind.'

Slimbridge nodded. 'Yes. And they have not yet announced a successor. They've only got the boy, Jack What's-his-name, and a couple of chaps at the end of their careers. It's a soft target. So if we move quickly, it should be a shoe-in.' Slimbridge smiled at his use of two appropriate clichés.

Lamb did not reply immediately, as if making some calculations at his end of the phone. Slimbridge had had the feeling for some time that he was not to Lamb's taste. He and Beasley had trawled around the City looking for support for months after they found Alvechurch Industrials, their listed cash shell into which they intended to inject their businesses. Morgan's were keen to develop their operations in the Midlands and Lamb was their new man charged with achieving it. He was affable and Slimbridge had been told that he would do anything for a fee. This would be a large one. At length, Lamb said, 'Your own share price should respond well to the news of your cheap acquisition of Arnold shares, at least initially, and that will make a full bid easier, especially with a share-for-share bid of this type. I would advise against a cash alternative, at this stage.' Lamb felt that the underwriting would be difficult but did not want to dent Slimbridge's confidence, however misplaced. 'So I will prepare the necessary board resolutions. As you know, with a bid for a public company you don't have the opportunity of much due diligence. But at least you know about the foundry division.'

Slimbridge rubbed his hands together, lit a B and H, polished his brown plastic shoes on the back of his calves and paced up and down his small office as if prematurely preparing his victory speech.

*

Johnny Roland sat opposite the only remaining candidate for the job of running Arnold Foundries plc, trying to hide his nervousness behind a confident and avuncular smile. If he could not persuade him to take the job and then agree terms acceptable to both parties by the end of the day, the share price would go into free fall. Worse still, for Roland, he would find himself forced to take the job himself, albeit in an interim capacity. He did not have the will or the energy to fight the inevitable takeover battle but if the man the other side of the desk turned him down, he would have no alternative.

'It's a massive risk to me personally,' said the man. 'And I'm not sure that I want to expose myself to the risk of failure at this level at this stage of my career. Aside from anything else, it would not be fair on my wife.'

'We will have to make it worthwhile to you, and take into account the risk you would be taking. If a bid comes our way, which we both acknowledge it may, we will need to have put you in a position with a high level of personal financial protection.'

'Such as…?'

'We will put you on the same salary that Bill Carey was on immediately and cut you into a million shares under option at the current low price. So if the price recovers to where it was before the crash you will make yourself a profit of almost one and a half million pounds. And we will stitch into your contract a three-year termination provision to protect you if you lose your job as a result of a takeover. You could retire on that lot'

'I know time is of the essence. Let me call my wife and see what she says. Thank you, Johnny.'

'One more thing. I do not want to be chairman. And so we would be asking if you would become both chairman and chief executive, effectively executive chairman. I know that is becoming unfashionable and the City therefore aren't keen, but that is what we are offering you.'

The press release announcing the new executive chairman was timed to coincide with the opening of the stock market the following day. The shares did not move. The headline in the business section of the early edition of the *London Evening Standard* read: *Jack Mayhew appointed the country's youngest chairman of a fully listed company.*

CHAPTER 18

'I had no idea you were so ambitious, darling,' said Jack's mother, Catherine. 'What drives you, do you think?'

Jack smiled, shrugged his shoulders and breathed in the nutty aroma of his coffee.

'I think I can answer that,' said Angela, rubbing her now very pregnant middle and puffing a little. 'After yesterday's false alarm, today could be the day,' she added. 'At least my case is packed.'

'What was your answer?' prompted Jack. He and his mother both looked at her with raised eyebrows and heads tilted in the same direction: a family trait.

'He's basically insecure.'

'Do you really think so? He comes from a very loving family,' said Catherine, perhaps a little offended. Her son was surely perfect. Or at least only she could admit to any weakness.

Angela shuffled awkwardly, but blamed a twinge. 'Well, he was sent off to boarding school far too young, don't you think?' Catherine didn't immediately reply, remembering her discussion with his father on the same subject thirty years earlier and her own unhappiness as she left him at the top of the school drive, both of them crying.

Then she said, 'His father said it would make a man of him, and it seems to have worked.'

'But at what cost?' ventured Angela. 'And of course, his family have been mainly high achievers and so he has had pressure on him to match up to their success.'

'Well, he has certainly done that. Head of house, Oxford and now I read that he is the youngest chairman of a public company in the country, which Jack, modest as always, didn't even tell his own mother. So we have done something right,' added Catherine, taking a mother's credit for a son's success.

'Are you aware, Catherine, how much he needs validation and approval, particularly from you, and from his father when he was alive? He loves the good press he gets but if there is anything slightly critical of him or the business, he takes it rather badly.'

'Angela darling, aren't we all like that? One thing I can promise you is that lump inside you will want to please you and Jack just as much as you say Jack wanted to do the same. It's human nature… Jack, you are rather quiet. Are you OK?'

'Yes… but I was miserable at my prep school. To start with. You knew I was. We shan't be sending the lump inside Angela's tummy to boarding school before he is thirteen and if it is a girl, probably not at all. I don't remember a happy girl at boarding school while I was at Worchester.'

'Until you broke into their dormitory, that is… And I remember a certain under-matron who rather enjoyed your company,' quipped Angela and laughed, before gripping her stomach and saying, 'Jack, I think it is on its way. Can you get me back to hospital now, please?'

Jack drove too quickly along the wet roads to the Queen Elizabeth Hospital. The traffic was heavy as Birmingham drivers ignored advice from the Met Office to stay at home due to hurricane-force winds and floods. The wind and rain lashed at the car, and the traffic ground to a halt, but neither Jack nor Angela admitted to their mutual anxiety that Angela might have to give birth on the back seat.

The traffic then eased and with some relief they parked at the entrance of the maternity ward and Jack guided Angela to the door, holding her arm with one hand and her small blue suitcase with the other. Once in bed, the midwife told Jack that Angela was only four centimetres dilated and encouraged him to go home and let his expectant wife rest. He emphasised that both he and Angela wanted him to be present at the birth of their child and the midwife reassured him that they would phone home when the birth was imminent, which it wasn't yet.

Unable to rest at home, and reassured that the birth of his child would not take place that night, Jack drove to the office to continue to shore up his company's defences against the possibility of a takeover bid.

*

'They've made the boy executive chairman! Hallelujah!' exclaimed Slimbridge as he dialled Francis Lamb's direct number.

'Francis Lamb,' said a voice, as smooth as oil on silk.

'I want to exercise now, Francis,' said Slimbridge, picking his nose. 'Their shares won't rise now they have appointed a school-leaver as chairman. How ridiculous. He's wet behind the ears.'

'I wouldn't underestimate him, Clement. I have been watching his progress. He has been a key figure in the successful turnaround of Arnold Foundries. And I would wait a day or two. The share price is down a penny this morning.'

'What if someone else jumps in? There must be many vultures circling.'

'If they know about your option in which you will pick up twenty-eight per cent of the shares, they won't. And if they don't know they would soon find that their bid will cost them much more than yours. Let's wait a couple of days and then go. I'll have all the documents ready by then.'

June placed a greasy bacon sandwich on his desk, still in its paper bag, and announced that she was going into town to see the doctor. *Don't forget the slimming pills*, thought Slimbridge, as she struggled through the office door.

*

As a substitute for supper, Jack's secretary presented pizza smartly on china plates. Whilst they munched, Jack and Angus Marwick combed through the option agreement that Bill Carey had given Slimbridge, against their advice, in one more attempt to find a loophole. The senior partner of Youngman's solicitors in town, "Bunions" as Jack called them, had failed to find a way out of the contract. But he would say that, wouldn't he? Jack remarked. Because they had drafted it. A lawyer would not admit to a document that was not watertight.

As the office clock left by Bill Carey passed nine o'clock, the phone rang. 'Good evening, Mr Mayhew, it's the QE in Birmingham here. We have been trying to get hold of you for a while. There was no answer from your home number and so Mrs Mayhew asked that we try this number. Your wife is in the final stages of labour and she would like you to come to the hospital as soon as possible.'

Jack grabbed a slice of pizza and his coat and rushed to the car park. Both he and Angela had been determined that Jack would not miss the birth of his first child. He had joked that Angela would have to be there but that he would try his very best to be with her. He felt his breathing quicken as he drove sharply out of the car park, narrowly missing the gatepost. He had not felt it appropriate to take over Carey's black Jaguar, opting to keep his existing car. The Birmingham traffic moved slowly through the wet as Jack struggled to get a clear view of the road, dimly lit by the lamps in a dreary yellow. An elderly lady, pushing a shopping basket on wheels, hobbled slowly across the zebra crossing in front of Jack's car. He fought his impatience and forced a smile at her as she waved her thanks to him. Jack wondered if her husband had been present at the births of any of her children. The blue flashing light of an ambulance forced Jack to the side of the road. He considered following in its wake, breaking the speed limit in the process. But whilst he would happily pay the speeding fine in order to see the birth of his first child, he did not want to court an argument with the police should he be pulled over. A policeman urging a man to "Follow me, sir" when told why he was rushing only happened in the movies, he thought.

There were no parking spaces near the maternity ward and so Jack parked in a general space several hundred yards from where he wanted to be. A man in a wheelchair blocked his path as he tried to run towards the maternity unit. He apologised, pushing past and adding as cheerily as he could that his wife was about to have their baby. 'Don't miss it,' said the man, smiling and encouraging Jack to run on.

A couple about Jack's age emerged through the double doors of the maternity block with the father holding what Jack assumed to be a newborn child. He moved slowly as if frightened to drop it. His wife was fussing over the baby's clothing. 'Congratulations,' said Jack, holding open one of the doors for them, but not wanting to wait.

The public lift to the third floor, where Angela was no doubt struggling to give birth and anxiously asking when her husband was arriving, was out of order. So Jack used the stairs, taking two at a time. He noticed that he was not as fit as he had been, and paused for breath on the second floor.

When he burst through the door of ward thirty-two, and looked towards the bed in which Angela had been, it was empty. He turned to the nearest nurse and asked feverishly, 'Where is my wife, Angela Mayhew?'

'In the delivery room, over there,' she replied with a gentle smile.

As he approached the door, which bore a sign saying "No Entry", he heard the cry of a newborn child. The door opened and the midwife appeared. She smiled at him and said, 'Congratulations, Mr Mayhew. You have a baby boy.'

Through the door he could see an exhausted Angela. From her bed she smiled and reached for him with a limp, naked arm. As she did so a nurse presented him with a small bundle. His anxiety about missing the birth, his disappointment that he was not at his wife's side and that his business had interfered with this precious moment evaporated instantly as he set eyes on his son for the first time.

'Oh my god,' he muttered eventually, as he bit his lip and tears overwhelmed him.

*

When Alvechurch Industrials' bid for Arnold Foundries plc was announced, the shares in the target leaped by forty per cent, in anticipation of a counter or increased offer.

'Slimbridge will pay more if pushed,' said Bland, urbane and reassuring as usual. 'So of course, we must reject his initial offer and see what happens. My people are already well on with the defence document. Your plans for increasing earnings per share, Jack, were very helpful and, if I may say so, well thought out. Even though Alvechurch will end up with the foundry division either way, you have demonstrated that the future for the balance of the group without it is much more positive. And then of course, there is the poison pill... But, nonetheless, I'm bound to advise you that I've already heard from some of your main institutional shareholders that they are minded to accept the higher offer, if and when it comes.'

Jack had realised since Bill's death that his tenure at the helm of Arnold Foundries might be short-lived. Even though his share options and severance terms together were now worth around three-quarters of a million pounds he was determined to see off Slimbridge and remain as executive chairman.

*

'What's a poison pill?' asked Angela over supper, when their baby son, Tim, had finally stopped crying.

Jack looked tired and strained. He paused, looked up from his plate of pasta, took a deep breath and said, 'It is something that will leave a nasty taste in the mouths of our aggressors should they be successful in taking over our company. You must not discuss it with anybody.'

'Of course I won't. I won't understand it anyway, clever clogs. What are you going to do?'

'We are going to contract to buy another business, code-named Ferret, but that can only happen if and when a bid for our company is accepted by a majority of our shareholders and goes unconditional – that is to say completes.'

'What is the problem with that?'

'We'll pay top dollar for Ferret with borrowed money secured against the value of the shares. So if the shares fall following the takeover, which they often do as the reality of what the aggressor has taken on becomes clear, then they will find the bank knocking at the door for their money back.'

'Mmm. Sounds pretty poisonous to me. Remind me not to cross you, Tarzan,' said Angela, kissing Jack on the forehead before she climbed the stairs once more to comfort the baby, who was now crying again.

CHAPTER 19

Having dropped Angela at the end of the short gravel path to the austere Victorian church, Jack parked with two wheels of his car up on the pavement a hundred yards away. A cold wind appeared to be heralding an early autumn as it whipped some crisp brown leaves from the ground into the air and spun them around in increasingly tight circles until they dropped to the earth again. One caught in Jack's black coat, which he crushed between finger and thumb before casting it aside and pulling the coat tight around his body.

A large crowd of what seemed to Jack like several hundred people tried hard not to jostle each other on their way to the church. It was as if each potential member of the congregation was struggling to tread a sensitive path between a desire to find a seat in the church and the solemnity of the occasion. George had come to the funeral to support Angela as Jack would have other duties. He had intercepted Angela and helped her to a pew near, but not too near, the front.

Most people had opted to wear black, there not

having been any other direction on the matter from those organising the service. There were some brightly coloured ties, purple shirts and even some hats. On his way up the path, Jack spotted a journalist from the local paper. Whether he was there to collect business news from one of the many senior figures attending from Arnold Foundries plc or to cover the service, Jack was unsure. But either way, Jack was not prepared for an interview and so avoided eye contact with the man.

By the time Jack joined Angela in their pew, the church was overflowing. Strangers nodded politely to each other, unsure of how far forward to sit. Family greeted each other with hugs and the hushed voices appropriate to the environment. Jack liked this solemnity. Although not sure of his religious convictions, he was certain that conversation should be avoided and if essential should be whispered. There could be no quiet contemplation if the population of Birmingham engaged in vociferous debate on the referee's decision at the last Albion versus Villa derby.

The organ ceased playing what Jack had thought was some gentle Bach. There was a silence. Then to a loud and recorded rendition of the well-known chorus from Carmina Burana, six male colleagues of Jack's bore the coffin down the aisle to its resting place at the altar rail at the front of the church. *Typical Bill Carey*, thought Jack. He had planned his own funeral.

*

Jack received rather too many compliments for his reading, he thought. In contrast, the friend of Bill's who gave the eulogy seemed rather ignored. At the wake he stood awkwardly on his own in a corner of the room, clutching a warm soft drink. Others drank noisily around him. It had struck Jack that Bill had had few friends. Indeed, Bill had said as much a couple of years earlier, dragging heavily on a cigarette after losing to a rival in a bid for another public company.

More remarkable to Jack and other observers was the sight of what appeared to be an additional grieving family following the coffin. Bill's wife, Sarah, was a slender blonde. She walked with her arm around their son, John, who, whilst grimacing to hold back his tears, tried to be manly now that his dad was not there to support his mother. But behind them walked a dark-haired woman of similar age to Sarah and another boy in similar distress. The two women had exchanged sideways glances with each other yet did not appear to be close. But now, after the service, they were engaged in conversation over a second glass of wine. They were smiling and there was a hint of conspiratorial laughter, heads together as if enjoying a private joke. Some shared secret about Bill, perhaps. The two boys, who seemed about three years apart in age, eyed each other sadly and with an uncertainty that Jack found puzzling. He decided he should speak with Sarah, to offer his condolences and help over the coming months. And he would perhaps introduce himself to her female companion. Angela was rocking Tim gently in her arms and talking to George.

'I'm so sorry, Sarah. What a dreadful shock for you both.' Sarah gave a half-smile and raised one eyebrow. 'I mean for you and John.' Sarah nodded without saying anything but appeared to relax a little. She did not introduce her companion and so Jack introduced himself. He had hoped that Kate, as her name turned out to be, would tell him how she knew Bill and then he could deduce why she was following the coffin alongside Sarah. But no such information was forthcoming. At the best of times it had been hazardous to ask such a question about Bill, but now might be even more awkward. They chatted amiably for a while, Jack telling both women how much Bill had done for his career. He risked a joke saying that perhaps he had gone too far this time. He was relieved when both women laughed. *Thank goodness for red wine*, he thought.

'Bill thought very highly of you,' said Sarah. 'In fact, he often said that you would take over from him one way or another. I don't think he planned it to be this way, though. But of course, you knew he was ill, didn't you?'

'Ummm, no, I didn't. What was the problem?'

Sarah confirmed what Jack now realised should have been obvious in the light of Bill's early death. 'He didn't tell many people. He thought it would have been seen as a sign of weakness. That's probably why he didn't tell you. He would have been frightened that you might take advantage of it,' she said, half laughing.

Jack didn't think Sarah was joking and added, 'You know he did seem generally paranoid and convinced that someone, particularly me, would knife him in the back, as he put it. But such a thing never crossed my mind. I wouldn't do that to anyone, even metaphorically, at least not to someone who had done so much for me.'

Jack felt it was time to move on and so, still not knowing anything significant about Sarah's companion and her son, he left to join Angela.

'Darling, do you know who that is?' she asked Jack as he gazed lovingly into his son's eyes.

'No, I don't. She didn't mention a connection to Bill and neither did his wife. They seemed to know each other, though, and Kate – that's her name – seemed close to him. All very odd.'

'George, come here and tell Jack what you just told me,' said Angela to George in a loud stage whisper.

George sidled up to Jack as if he was about to tell him a secret. 'One of Bill's close friends just told me something interesting. Do you not know who the lady talking to Sarah is? And the little boy?'

'No, I don't, George. But you have the air of someone about to let me in on something riveting so please go on. The suspense is killing me.' Jack looked over to the two women and two boys, standing isolated from the rest of the wake.

'Well, until today, nobody knew except Sarah and obviously Kate herself. She is Bill's other wife. Although they weren't legally married, he was living with both of them as man and wife. The other boy is his son. Bill was leading a double life.'

*

Jack and Angus Marwick squeezed into the black cab with Michael Bland after their fifth presentation to shareholders.

'How did it go?' he asked.

'Not well, I think,' replied Jack, looking at Angus, who nodded gravely. 'All five have indicated that they are likely to accept Alvechurch's higher offer. One was quite blunt that the deal we did to give such a high platform to them through the option agreement was rash at best. And although they lay the blame at Bill's door they also feel that we are partly responsible for not standing up to him. One added that he did not wish to speak ill of the dead, but...'

'Those five account for over twenty per cent of your institutional shareholder base. You have two more to see. With those plus the option shares that will be held by Alvechurch it will be all over. I'm sorry.'

There was a silence in the cab as they pulled up in front of E and G Holdings, the fund manager of which was one of Jack's most loyal supporters.

'Good luck, gentlemen,' said Bland as Jack and Angus splashed into a large puddle in front of the office building.

Jack looked down at his wet trouser leg. 'Looks like it's one of those days,' he said, unsmiling.

Eric Mathews, the senior fund manager, who represented Jack's last realistic hope of support, greeted them at the top of the lift.

'Can I have a word with you alone, please, Jack?' he said.

Jack followed Mathews into a small office, leaving Angus awkwardly in the reception area. Jack pulled a face at Angus as the door closed behind him.

'Jack, I wanted to see you on your own because I want to confide in you. We know that you raised doubts about the option given to Slimbridge at the time. Bill told us. So we also know that your warning was ignored. We have had doubts about Angus, and the other directors have frankly been Bill's puppets. In our view, and that of other large shareholders with whom we have spoken, you are the best thing about Arnold Foundries. We like your survival plan but we have to look after our own investors and so we have no real choice but to accept the offer now on the table. I'm sorry, Jack. At least you are young and able enough to bounce back.'

'So I guess you don't want to hear our presentation then?' asked Jack meekly.

Mathews simply smiled, offered his hand and said, 'Helen will show you out.'

Although Jack knew the game was up, he went through the motions with the final shareholder of the day. He seemed willing to back Jack at first but having spoken to the other shareholders he went cool on him.

Jack and Angus sat in a rather grim cafe at the wrong end of Old Street discussing fickle and fair-weather friends and waiting for Michael Bland to pick them up. Michael had promised lunch at his club, whatever the result, but Jack was not hungry.

*

On 3 December, Alvechurch's offer for Arnold Foundries plc was declared unconditional. Jack sat at the kitchen table looking out of the window whilst Angela busied herself feeding Tim. Porridge dribbled down the baby's chin. The wind blew against the long branches of a horse chestnut outside the window, bringing down large brown leaves as it did so. The Victorian window rattled slightly in its sash casing.

'How do you feel, darling?' she asked, carefully, pouring Jack some more strong coffee.

'Rather numb, now that it is all over, I suppose. I'm not looking forward to my meeting with Clement Slimbridge. He has a manner that will make it hard for me not to feel humiliated.'

'Jack, you did your best. And remember you were put in an impossible position. The chalice you were passed was certainly poisoned. You knew that. And look on the bright side. How much are your share options worth?'

'Well, those and my severance, if the bugger pays me all I am due, are worth three-quarters of a million pounds. Not bad, I suppose.'

'Enough for you to buy the yacht you have always promised yourself?'

'More than enough. Let's go to the Oyster base next week, shall we? They're in Southampton.'

As Jack stood and walked towards his coat, Angela took him by the hand, wrapped herself around him and said, 'That little boy who sneaked into my room at school has come a long way, hasn't he? I'm very proud of him. Superstar.'

Jack kissed her forehead, prised himself away from her, kissed the top of his son's head and left the house. As he drove to his office for the last time, he wondered for how long he would be unemployed.

*

When Jack arrived at his office, he saw three unfamiliar cars. One, a three-year-old light blue Rover 3500, was parked in the space marked "Chairman". Jack did not approve of personal parking spots and neither did Bill.

'If you are that important you had better arrive before everyone else,' Bill would say. And so when Jack became chairman only recently, he did not park in his space. Jack thought he could guess who had done so.

The foundry chimney towering above Jack's head continued to belch yellow-brown smoke, unaware of the impending change in management. The smell caught the back of his nose, acrid and rich. The receptionist smiled at Jack when he entered the reception area of his office. When Jack smiled back and asked her how she was, she burst into tears.

'Everybody says you will lose your job, Mr Mayhew. It's so awful. We shall all miss you.' She felt for her large blue suede handbag and burrowed to the bottom for a handkerchief. Jack offered his. The receptionist snivelled, shook her head and found her own.

'I'm sure you will all be all right,' said Jack, placing his hand on her arm before he mounted the stairs towards his office for the last time.

There were more tears from two of the three secretaries whom Jack had retained following Bill's demise. One of them, Samantha, said, 'There are five men in the boardroom. They said they were waiting for you and we were to send you in as soon as you arrived. One of them has already been into your office and looked through some of your drawers, and taken down your picture of Angela and Tim from your desk. When I asked what he was doing in your office he said that it wasn't yours any more, but it was his. Is that true, Jack? He didn't seem very nice.'

'Well, technically yes. But I think they could have

been a little more gracious, don't you? Don't tell them I am here just yet. I'll go into the boardroom in a moment.'

Jack walked into his office. An unfamiliar coat was draped over one of the chairs. His photographs of Angela and Tim were stacked up on another chair. The ashtray had been used and there was a smell of cigarette smoke in the air. An empty packet of Benson and Hedges tipped cigarettes lay tightly screwed up in the bottom of his wastepaper basket. A cheap and battered black briefcase stood at the side of his desk, one of the drawers of which was open. Jack quietly pushed the door closed, sat lightly in a chair next to the desk and gazed out of the window. Men in overalls stood in groups at the foundry gate. The clank of moulds being knocked out took Jack back to his first interview with Bill and Angus. '*I think you are a flyer,*' said the ghost of Bill gently in his ear. '*Aw roit, Fred,*' said the foundryman. '*The higher you fly, my lad, the harder you are going to fall,*' threatened Jacobs, the union rep. '*Sid, young man, call me Sid,*' said Bailey. '*No problem, sir,*' drawled Texan Don. '*Have a nice day,*' said the Dallas extra. The factory siren sounded and Samantha gently opened the office door, drawing Jack back from his reverie.

'They are asking where you are, Jack,' she said softly.

'Tell them I am coming now.' As Jack made his way between his office and the boardroom and he straightened his tie, the ghost of Bill whispered, '*Success is shared, failure is personal.*'

Jack opened the door of the boardroom to find it occupied by five men. Two were familiar: Clement Slimbridge and James Beasley. Slimbridge was dressed as usual in his worn brown suit and matching scuffed brown plastic shoes. The knot of his Terylene tie was small and greasy. He looked sweaty. The three unfamiliar men, dressed smartly, stood as Jack entered the room. Beasley made to do so but noticed that Slimbridge stayed sitting and seemed to think better of it. Jack remained standing, not having been offered a seat.

One of the smartly dressed men introduced himself as James Sanderson, Arnold Foundries' new solicitor, and moved towards Jack with something in his hand. He said, 'The new board, appointed by the company's shareholders, has just met.' He shuffled somewhat uneasily on his feet in front of Jack. He looked over towards Slimbridge, who returned his glance but did not look at Jack.

'I have been instructed by the board to give you this. It is a copy of the board minute recording your dismissal and confirmation of your severance.' Sanderson paused, looking slightly apprehensive. 'I have been asked to accompany you to what was your office whilst you clear your desk and then accompany you off the premises.'

Jack looked at the other two men, who he assumed were new directors, and then at Beasley, who initially looked at him but then turned away. Slimbridge looked firmly at the boardroom table.

A box had been provided for Jack to pack up his things. When he had done so, the solicitor said, 'Please confirm that you have not taken any company property.' Jack said he had not. 'Then all that remains is for you to give me the keys to your car.' Jack tried not to look fed up. The lawyer seemed to be searching for words, then muttered, 'Sorry. We have ordered a taxi to take you home.'

Samantha had been one of Bill's many girlfriends. She had not yet got over his death. But when she put the rest of Jack's possessions next to the box that he had carried down the stairs to the waiting taxi, she gave him a tight hug and kissed him on the cheek. As Jack sat in the back of the taxi he turned to wave. Samantha had covered her face with her hands and was sobbing.

The taxi arrived at Jack's house in heavy rain. Angela opened the front door and looked bewildered and alarmed. Seeing that Jack had more to bring in than he could manage on his own, she helped her unemployed husband to the door with his box and other possessions, in silence. As Jack took the front door in his hand to close it behind him, the taxi driver said, 'That will be £12.50, please, sir.' *The final humiliation*, thought Jack. *They wouldn't even pay for my taxi.*

Angela took her beaten husband into her arms and cradled him for as long as he would allow. He sighed deeply but quickly broke away. She had rarely seen him cry and he did not do so now.

Then, whilst Angela made strong coffee, he sat looking at the unopened envelope he had been given by Sanderson. He glanced at an inscription above the Aga which read "A good man cannot be harmed". Socrates.

'How did it go? Not well, I guess,' Angela enquired. Jack did not answer, but forced a smile.

'It's over now,' he said, reaching for the letter. After he had read it, he pulled a face and tossed it towards Angela.

'Surprise, surprise. They aren't going to pay my severance. I'm going to have to make them. So it isn't over.'

...THREE.

*

'Do you think you should still buy this?' asked Angela as they pulled into the car park at the headquarters of Oyster Yachts.

'Yes. I've still made a decent sum of money from my share options, which by the way I exercised and sold immediately I left. As you know, it has been a dream for me to own one of these and, well, I shall need something to do whilst I plot my return to Arnold Foundries plc.'

Angela paused, took a deep breath and said, 'Darling, why don't you just let it go and do something else?' She put her hand on Jack's knee, looked over at him and said softly, 'Revenge isn't that attractive, you know.'

Jack thought for a moment and then said, 'This isn't really about revenge. This is about doing the right thing for the shareholders – and getting my severance paid. I could sue, but I would rather take back control of the company and get paid that way. That poison pill will threaten to bankrupt the business, so Slimbridge will fail. But I know how to fix it. And... so... I need to return to save the business and ensure the shareholders retain some value in their shares. I owe them that.'

'Are you sure that's what it is about? You were vengeful towards Benedict Osbourne and Steve Gregson. But did the act of getting even itself really make you feel any better?'

'Well, it was a step towards it.' Jack paused and then added, 'All the great Christian and Buddhist teachings say the same thing, don't they? If I choose to forgive them, I will be able to let it go. I think that's what is in your mind, isn't it?'

'Yes. So why not forgive Slimbridge and move on? Turn the other cheek. "Forgive them for they know not what they do" and so on.'

'Perhaps I shall,' said Jack pensively. 'But only after I have got even.'

CHAPTER 20

Six months later

Bright foam sprang from the bows of the boat as Angela peered over the side. She gazed at the water, dark blue, then azure, then brilliant silver and blue the colour of bluebells. Jack had ensured that the hull of the Oyster was also blue – dark blue – this being Angela's only nautical requirement. She nonetheless appreciated the high gloss mahogany fittings, sturdy and substantial. Jack had specified electric winches and so the boat was manageable by a crew of just the two of them.

Angela could smell the sea. Jack insisted that her body was still youthful enough to wear small bikinis especially now that she had stopped feeding Tim. Pushing her long hair away from her eyes, she clutched her gin and tonic more tightly as the boat heeled over slightly in the quickening breeze. She glanced over at Jack at the wheel, who waved and grinned, his naked torso responding to the pull of the rudder as the boat tried to move to windward. He had caught the Greek sun and it suited him. His blond hair, blowing in the wind, appeared bleached and accentuated his blue eyes. Strong legs extended beneath his dark blue swimming trunks, flexed against the tilt of the boat. Angela wondered if she had ever seen him happier.

She had tried again to dissuade him from attempting to return to Arnold Foundries, but she knew it was an impossible task. She had argued that he had already achieved enough in his career and had everything he needed. A healthy son, a lovely house, a yacht and plenty of money; to say nothing of a loving wife. And she reminded him again that vengeance was seldom attractive and of a zoological study which suggested that all the animals studied demonstrated a capacity for forgiveness. Even hyenas can forgive.

'Though not cats,' Jack had countered, 'but you know I'm not keen on those…' and added, 'I'm with the Dalai Lama. I can't quote him exactly but he said it is important to draw a distinction between forgiveness and simply allowing others' wrongdoing. We try to address the wrongdoing to encourage the person not to commit those acts again, not only for his own sake but also to protect others. I like to think I can address wrongdoing, be it my own or that of others, and then forgive. Does that sound pompous?'

Angela did not reply, but rolled her eyes and smiled.

Jack reached for his large mobile phone and waved at Angela to take over the helm.

'Put it on autohelm,' she shouted above the wind.

Jack shrugged, engaged the autohelm and sat heavily on the leeward side of the boat, his feet up on the table in the middle. With a can of beer in one hand he spoke earnestly into the phone and then listened with a look of concentration. Angela shrieked and pointed over the starboard side of the boat as two dolphins leaped and disappeared before reappearing the other side.

Jack put down the phone, moved up the boat closer to Angela and said, 'That was Michael Bland. The board of Arnold have put out a profit warning due to "problems with the new acquisition agreed by the previous management".'

Angela looked puzzled.

'A profit warning means they are not going to make as much money as the City think they are. They hate that. And problems with the new acquisition – that's the poison pill at work. I lost the line as the signal is not yet good enough offshore. So I need to head back. And then I think we'll have to return to the UK. I'm sorry.'

'Don't apologise, darling. It's been a lovely three days. Anyway, I would be very happy to relieve the nanny two days early. I'm frightened that Tim will have changed, or that he won't recognise me…'

Jack winked at her and swung the yacht through 180 degrees, letting out the mainsail as he did so. The boat stopped heeling over and headed swiftly back towards Skiathos, bucking slightly in the following waves.

*

Jack and Angela sat in a quiet corner of the airport. She gazed out of the window with a wistful look.

'What's troubling you, darling?' said Jack.

Angela sighed, looked at the floor and muttered, 'Don't let your ambition drive you too far.'

'What do you mean?' said Jack.

'I mean that your insecurity has fuelled your ambition, as it does many men. But you have achieved so much. And you are no longer so insecure. Are you?'

Jack stared at his crossword and then chanced a glance at Angela.

'I'm worried that your ambition may be about to do you no favours.'

Jack did not reply. Instead, he jabbed his pen frustratedly at his crossword. 'What do you make of this? I've been stuck on it for days. Three down, narrow river crossing, ten letters.'

After a moment's thought Angela replied, 'I have no idea. But if I know you, you won't rest until you've solved it.'

Jack grinned at her and pushed the newspaper into his bag as their flight was called.

*

'Some shareholders have already contacted me and asked what you are doing,' said Bland, leaning back in his elegant leather chair in the bank's boardroom, surrounded by expensive contemporary art. 'I managed to get out of them that they might support your return, if you can produce a credible plan. They told me enough to make me think that they regretted supporting Slimbridge, but of course most of them will be too proud to admit that.' Bland paused and then asked, 'Have you got a team together?'

'Well, I've identified a new finance director and I think that will be enough. The last thing Arnold will need is a load of new overheads. I shall take no salary until the rescue is complete, but others will need paying.'

'I assume you have not invited any of the old guard.'

'No. As you said at the time, the shareholders partly blame them for the present difficulties. So, no.'

'And your plan?'

'It's based on the previous one. It is going to be tough though to keep the banks onside now that the business is swimming with debt. There will probably have to be some forced sales but then we shall risk breaching our covenants, give the banks an excuse to call in their debt and force the directors to appoint receivers.'

Bland thought, looked at his pen, and then said, 'You have to be careful that you are not identified as the reason for the Ferret acquisition going wrong. After all, it was you who put it in place as a poison pill. It *is* poisoning the new management but you need to be sure that it is not going to kill you.'

Jack looked out of the window and then back at Bland. 'Our PR people will have to package our announcement so that the market is in no doubt that the problem has been Slimbridge's handling of the existing businesses and his slow integration of the new one. If he had been quicker about that then he would not still be carrying the extra costs. And that has led to the profits warning which in turn has caused the collapse in their share price which has meant that the bank may call in their loans, those being secured on the value of the shares. And that is why the company is on the brink of bankruptcy.'

Michael Bland smiled. 'Very good. Almost plausible. But as another plc chairman once said to me, "You just have to be careful that you do not believe your own bullshit".'

*

Jack sat in the middle of the long table flanked by his new finance director, Gregory Macintyre, and Michael Bland. The company's solicitors and PR agents Aquila sat on the front row in front of the press.

Gregory Macintyre spoke from a prepared statement in a soothing Edinburgh accent. He was a little older than Jack, with greying hair, and very experienced in corporate recovery. He had been a partner of one of the major accountancy firms and Jack and his advisers thought of him as an internal receiver.

'Arnold Foundries plc are pleased to announce that they have received the support of fifty-three per cent of the votes of the ordinary shareholders to replace the existing management. No offer will be, or needs to be made, for the company. Jack Mayhew will shortly be appointed executive chairman—'

'For the second time,' someone whispered loudly, causing a quiet titter around him.

'—and I am to become finance director. Non-executive directors will be appointed in due course.' *If we can persuade anyone to take the job in a bust company,* thought Jack. 'Are there any questions?'

Since he didn't really want any questions, Jack was about to declare the meeting closed when Sarah

Broadhurst from the *Financial Times* spoke up. 'Can I ask, Chairman, what has gone wrong at the company and, more importantly, what are you going to do to fix it?'

Jack stood and glanced down at his pre-prepared answer. He and his team had suspected this question would come.

'Sarah, thank you for your question. Unfortunately, the current management have not managed the existing businesses well, they have been slow to integrate the new acquisition and so are carrying excess costs. This has led to a profit warning which has provoked a collapse in the share price. Because the banks have lent against the value of the shares, they now have the opportunity to call in their loans. The job of my team is to stop that happening and to restore shareholder value.' Before the journalist could ask Jack to remind the press who it was that contracted to buy the new business and arranged the loans secured against the value of the shares, Jack said, 'And now, if there are no more questions, I declare the meeting closed.'

Michael Bland and the team from Aquila the PR agency smiled at each other. *Just be sure you don't believe your own bullshit*, they thought. Although none of them was quite sure whether it was bullshit or not.

*

Jack drove towards his old office in a suitably low-key car: a four-year-old Jaguar XJ6 in an obsolete model. A new car would look extravagant and send out the wrong message to those who were supporting him to rescue the company. He needed to signal a time of austerity. First-class rail and air travel would be cancelled. Anything that did not pay the bills tomorrow would be cancelled today. Because Slimbridge's team had neglected to chase customer debts for fear of losing their business, Jack's team would issue numerous demands for payment with court proceedings to follow. Creditors would be pushed to the limit. There would be factory closures and forced sales of underperforming businesses at distressed prices. Anything that could be sold at a substantial premium over net asset value would also be sold, as the resulting cash injection would more than compensate for the loss of asset value supporting the bank loans.

Jack smiled as he recalled a line from *Measure for Measure*: *Dressed in a little brief authority.* He was going to ensure that Slimbridge's authority would be both little and brief. Jack intended his to endure. The sun peeped out from behind a thick white cloud as he parked his car in a space other than that reserved for the chairman. That of course was taken by Slimbridge. Jack was pleased that Slimbridge was there. What Jack was about to do would have given him far less satisfaction had it been carried out by remote control.

'Welcome back, Mr Mayhew,' said a man crossing the road in front of the office and waving at Jack. Jack thanked him and smiled, although who the man was, he did not know. Jack was tanned from the few days on his yacht in the Aegean and wore a new sharp charcoal-grey suit, a white shirt and a conservative tie. He wanted to look confident but not flash. The livelihoods of several thousand families now rested on his shoulders. He pushed open the swing door to the office reception. The receptionist was the same woman as on the day he had left. 'Welcome back, Mr Mayhew,' she said. 'Are we glad to see you.' It was not a question. She looked as though she was going to throw her arms around him.

'Thank you, Sheila. It is nice to see you.' Not waiting to be asked, he said, 'I'll go straight up.'

At the top of the stairs Jack was greeted by his old secretary, Samantha. She also looked pleased to see him but seemed a little too nervous to express her feelings. After all, she still worked for Slimbridge, although he had brought his secretary, June, with him. She pointed to the closed door of Jack's old office as if to indicate that Clement Slimbridge was inside. Jack could smell cigarette smoke. He hesitated for a moment outside the office, as if uncertain. *Show some respect*, he thought to himself, not wanting to conduct what was about to happen in the same way as others had to him. He knocked on the door.

'Come in,' said Slimbridge. Jack opened the door and stood looking at Slimbridge without speaking. He did not seem surprised to see Jack, but unlike the last time they met, he stood and looked Jack in the eye.

Angela had reminded her husband to be dignified. Jack had wanted to simply snap, 'You're fired.' But instead he said, 'Good morning, Mr Slimbridge. I'm sorry that it has come to this' – he was not – 'but you know that it is my duty to ask for your resignation. Our solicitors will be in touch with yours later today to agree your severance terms. It is our intention to honour your contract in full. I will leave you now to pack up your things and say your goodbyes.' Jack took a step towards Slimbridge, who was still standing behind his desk, and offered his hand. Slimbridge took it. 'Goodbye, Mr Slimbridge,' Jack said.

Jack turned and left what was to be his office again. He smiled, winked at his secretary and said, 'I'll see you later. I want to give Mr Slimbridge some space. Be nice to him, but try to encourage him to leave by lunchtime. I shall be back after that.'

Jack walked down the stairs and back towards his car, smiling as the penny dropped. Narrow river crossing. Ten letters. S l i m b r i d g e.

THREE DOWN, he thought as his smile broadened.

CHAPTER 21

The following month

There are two things above all that make people love and care for something: the thought that it is all yours, and the thought that it is the only one you have.

Aristotle

'If you don't mind we'll drive down to Mylor harbour separately. After the weekend I'll need to go straight to London to see some of the shareholders. Shall I take Tim or will you? And do you want to take Jane?' asked Jack as he packed his sailing clothes.

'I'll take Tim,' replied Angela, emerging from the bathroom and rubbing her wet hair. 'You'll be on your phone the whole time anyway. Sometimes I feel like throwing that thing into the sea. But I suppose you could use the time while you are driving to work and then promise me you will switch it off. And don't worry about Jane. I know you've tempted the nanny to a weekend at sea but I'd like to spend the time just with us. I've hardy seen you the last few weeks.' Angela glanced at Jack with a concerned look on her face. 'Will you be all right driving on your own? You look very tired. You need a rest.'

Jack did not reply, but nodded and tried to smile. He had arranged to have the boat brought back to the UK so that he could use it more regularly now that Arnold Foundries was taking more of his time. But nonetheless he had hardly used it since returning to the chairmanship of the company. And he indeed had not seen much of his wife or young son. He had resolved to be more present whilst Tim was growing up but the demands of rescuing the business prevented him from doing so. He missed the time that he had spent alone with Angela and Tim. Since committing to the shareholders to try to restore some value in Arnold's shares, both his time and his emotional energy seemed to have been sapped to the point that he felt separated from his wife and son. Even when they were together, he was distracted and frequently too tired to give either of them the attention he wanted. Yet his love for Angela seemed to have deepened since she had given him his son. His mother had warned him that he would be forever changed when he became a father. He was. And since his mother had died shortly after Tim's birth, he felt an increased sense of responsibility. He had been very close to his mother, and missed her. He was determined that as soon as the rescue was complete, he would leave the company and devote his time to Angela and Tim. He yearned for those days.

The sun shone brightly over the Cornish coast. A light breeze greeted the Mayhew family as they arrived at the small, attractive marina. A fresh smell of English seaweed greeted them as they scrambled onto the boat, Jack clutching Tim tightly in his strong arms. The boat bobbed gently in the breeze and the restful sound of water lapping against the dark blue hull lulled the small family into a restful mood as Jack pottered about readying the boat to slip its mooring at the quayside. Angela held Tim, who was now starting to walk, whilst Jack fired up the engine and loosened the ropes holding the boat to the jetty. He let the bow line slip to allow the light wind to nudge the front of the yacht away from the jetty. As the boat turned away, he let the stern line slip and gathered it in. The Oyster's engine throbbed gently and emitted a low growl as Jack increased the revs and pointed the yacht towards the opening between the ends of the harbour walls. A calm sea beckoned.

Once clear of the harbour, Jack brought the yacht head to wind and then pressed the switch to unfurl the mainsail and then the large genoa. The boat bucked slightly as the sails filled and Jack cut off the engine. It shook a little as the propeller stopped. The only sound was then the wind in the sails and a slight splash from the bow as the yacht cut through the water. Jack set the autohelm and sat next to Angela. Taking his son in one arm and Angela in the other, he looked up the mast, grinning broadly.

'That's the most relaxed I've seen you in a month,' said Angela, squeezing Jack's thigh and kissing him on the cheek. Tim wriggled, keen to be free to explore his new surroundings. Jack placed him gently into the safety of the well of the deck in front of him, sure in the knowledge that he was not yet mobile enough to clamber up and disappear over the side of the boat. Jack looked deep into the eyes of his wife, put his hand on her cheek and gently turned her face towards him.

'I'm sorry I've been a bit distant. When this rescue phase is over, I shall leave the company and devote myself to you and Tim.' He paused. 'Have I told you recently that I love you?'

'No, you haven't… but I know.' She kissed his lips with the kind of kiss familiar to young lovers. 'I'll wait. But don't be too long. I miss you.'

Jack stuck his leg out in front of Tim to prevent him from falling down the steps leading to the galley as he moved to retrieve his toy car. Tim looked up at his father and shrieked and giggled, slapping him on the leg in mild protest at being restrained. *He should be clipped on*, thought Angela.

'He needs his time with you,' she said, chuckling at her son and pulling him up onto her lap.

Lunch on board involved some light pink rosé from Provence and some fat crab sandwiches that they had bought on the quayside. Jack looked up from his glass to the full sails and then at his beautiful wife and son.

'It doesn't get much better than this, does it?' he said.

Angela just shook her head and tossed her hair in the breeze.

When they reached the car park, Jack kissed his wife and son, bade them farewell and jumped into his recently acquired Aston Martin. Angela put all their gear in the boot of the Jaguar, strapped Tim in his baby seat in the front next to her and waved at Jack, letting him pull out ahead of her.

As they reached the winding road to head north, Jack glanced at Angela in his rear-view mirror. He hoped that she could see him smiling. She waved her fingers at him whilst firmly gripping the steering wheel. As they arrived at a relatively straight section, both Jack and Angela accelerated. A lorry approached them on the other side of the road which appeared to be going too fast. As it passed Jack it swerved.

The noise of the lorry smashing into the front side of the Jaguar drew Jack's attention back to his mirror. He watched, as if in slow motion, as the lorry careered into the Jaguar, pushing it into a tree next to a ditch beside the road. The driver's side of the Jaguar was crushed by the lorry to the horrific sound of screeching rubber, a loud bang, tearing metal and smashing glass. The two vehicles came to rest in the ditch, the lorry's engine buried in the Jaguar driver's seat and a branch of the tree wedged through the broken passenger window.

Several cars stopped, the occupants running to the scene. There was a brief silence. Steam rose from the lorry's radiator. The driver of the lorry lay slumped over his steering wheel. The caved-in driver's door of the Jaguar had crushed Angela, whose bloody face stared lifeless at the sky. A branch of the tree lay embedded in one of Tim's temples, which had collapsed far into his skull.

Desperate and frantic, Jack tugged at the passenger side door to get to his son. Unable to move it, he hurried to the other side where Angela's body sat pinned to her seat by the bonnet of the lorry. Prevented by the crumpled metal from getting close to her, he slumped with an anguished wail onto the grass verge, overwhelmed by despair.

Jack sat alone, having driven home in a daze from the hospital where his wife and child had been taken. They had been pronounced dead at the scene of the crash. Their laughter appeared to echo with the wind outside, mournful, harsh and taunting. Each memory of their voices, Tim's toys on the floor, Angela's hat on the kitchen table, edged Jack deeper into a trough of despondency.

Unable to eat and wary of the depressive effect of alcohol, Jack stood watching the steam from the kettle. It became the steam from the radiator of the lorry. Sirens. Blue flashing lights. Kind words. Anxious glances. An arm around his shoulder guiding him away from the ambulance in which lay the mutilated bodies of his wife and son and into the back of a police car. Jack had sat, vacant and staring at the ambulance in front of him as it pushed its hopeless way through the traffic.

He looked at his briefcase and wondered how he would be able to concentrate sufficiently to deal with the responsibilities which lay ahead. They seemed mountainous yet insignificant by contrast with the sharpness of his anguish.

Jack stared at the floor, consumed by the agony of lost voices.

*

George sat next to Jack at the funeral. White-faced and with a blank expression, Jack stared at the coffin of his wife and of his son lying pathetically on top. He mouthed the hymns and sat gazing at the floor during George's eulogy. Looking directly at Jack, George quoted Gerard Manley Hopkins:

'No worst, there is none. Pitched past pitch of grief,
More pangs will, schooled at forepangs, wilder wring.'

And then Psalm 22: "*I am poured out like water, and all my bones are out of joint.*"

At the wake, Jack greeted as many of the large number of mourners as he could. He felt as if in a trance, simultaneously numb and sharply bereft. Friends would speak to him yet he felt as though he were at the bottom of a swimming pool, looking up at them. He left as soon as he felt able, alone.

CHAPTER 22

A week later

Jack's colleagues had noticed that he was not able to concentrate on the demanding set of business decisions before him. His usual ability to separate work from matters at home, which he had led others to emulate, deserted him. He could not look at the picture on his desk of Angela and Tim without his grief overcoming him; and yet neither could he bring himself to remove it.

Several shareholders had rung him to send their condolences, but Jack had suspected that they had other reasons to speak to him. Their man already had a demanding job. They knew that his work would be compromised by the distractions of grief.

The previous day Jack had taken Gregory Macintyre with him to meet the bank. They presented their rescue plans, which they had sent to the bank the week the new board had been appointed. It was plain from that meeting that the three generally humourless men representing the bank had doubts that the plan was achievable without them being required to loosen their covenants beyond the point at which they were going to be comfortable.

'These assets sales will bring down the debt,' the sour-faced man from the bank's intensive care department in London had intoned, 'but we doubt that you will achieve the prices you suggest. And the discount to asset value that is more likely to be achieved will further erode our security.'

'But we intend to sell the businesses that will command a premium first so that your security will be strengthened in the process,' Jack had replied, struggling to retain his usual persuasive tone. The three bankers looked at each other in silence, searching each other's faces for clues as to their opinion.

'I notice your creditors have grown hugely. I know this is part of your strategy, but are you in possession of any writs?' asked the local director hesitantly. He had lost credibility with his bosses in London, which was why the bank's intensive care unit was now in charge.

Jack shuffled his feet and so Macintyre said, 'Yes, we do have some, but we have spoken to them all and explained that we cannot pay yet and that if they bring down the company they are unlikely to get anything, as they stand behind the bank.'

'Who are already underwater,' added one of the men from intensive care. 'And winding-up orders?'

'No.'

'Not yet,' observed the banker.

Jack felt that the meeting was slipping away from them, when the second man from intensive care, wearing a sober grey suit said, 'Gentlemen, we want to help you. But we must insist that this plan is delivered in the way you have laid out.

As you know, we need weekly reporting of cash balances, beyond simply what appears on the statements, for each business. And please keep us informed daily of anything that you feel is likely to blow you off course. Equally, please tell us of anything that improves the position beyond your plan. One thing we all know is that when you close loss-making businesses cash flows in. We shall need every pound of that cash.' The senior man, in the grey suit, looked around the table. The other two men nodded.

'So thank you both for coming in to see us,' said the senior man, before adding, 'Mr Mayhew, we are very sorry to hear of your terrible loss. It must make your already tough job even more difficult.' Jack tried to smile.

'Susan will show you out,' said the banker, shaking Jack's hand.

Outside the bank, Macintyre turned to Jack and looked him in the eye. He paused before saying, 'Why don't you take some time off, Jack? You have set the plan in motion; redundancies are happening and I can handle the asset sales. You really need a rest. We can keep in touch by phone now that we all have mobiles.' He then added, 'I know you are fond of Shakespeare. Remember *Julius Caesar*? *Ambition's debt is paid.*'

Jack looked away and after a moment said, 'I'll think about it. Thanks for the offer. I know you can handle it for a while. I don't know how long we've got, though. It only needs someone to issue a winding-up order or to obtain judgement on one of those writs so as to enable them to recover even just their VAT and we are finished. I don't want to leave you holding the baby.' Jack winced at his analogy.

Once back in the office, Jack called though the open door to Samantha. 'Sam, please could you arrange to get the boat moved down to Amalfi. Now that it is autumn, I don't think I shall be using it in the UK. I prefer the sun.'

Samantha knew that the other reason was that he would never want to visit Mylor again.

*

The first substantial asset disposal was completed three weeks later. More demands for payment had been received but some of these could now be satisfied from the proceeds of the disposal. There were others who would have to wait, including one very large one whom Jack feared.

'We've got some breathing space now, Jack,' said Macintyre, coming into Jack's office. 'Why don't you take that break I suggested now? We can cope for a week or so, I'm sure. You told me you have had your boat moved to Italy. We can talk whenever we want between there and here.'

'Gregory, any minute now, any one of our creditors could bring us down. I owe it to our shareholders to stay put. I won't leave a sinking ship.'

'Jack, the board feel that you should take a break. Come back soon. We can cope in the meantime.'

'Oh. It's like that, is it?'

'You know it's for your own good too, Jack. There is only so much that a man can take.'

'OK,' said Jack with a sigh. 'Thanks. I'll leave in the morning.'

CHAPTER 23

Jack's mobile lit up and vibrated against his glass of negroni.

'Hello.'

'Jack, I've been trying to reach you all day. Has your phone been off?'

'Yes, sorry – I'm on holiday, remember? What's up?'

Jack's secretary, Samantha, normally so calm, was agitated. 'I don't know how to put this gently, but some bailiffs turned up last night as I was leaving. They slapped tickets on everything and took some files. They told me to leave and locked the place up. They would only let me take my own personal stuff. Anything they thought was yours they took. I'm so sorry… Jack? Jack?'

Jack switched off his mobile and threw it into the sea. The Amalfi coastline shimmered in the warm night air. The faint sound of music and laughter from nearby bars mingled with the gentle lapping of water against the hull of the yacht. Jack started the engine and pressed the button on the windlass to raise the anchor. The motor hummed powerfully as the anchor warp disappeared smoothly into the bow of the boat. As the anchor broke the surface of the deep blue water, it glistened in the moonlight.

Jack set the autohelm to 270 degrees and the boat speed to five knots. He knew that it would not hit land until the next day. The 53-foot Oyster slid gently away from the shore, coaxing its only passenger into the Mediterranean night. Jack stood motionless on the edge of the stern until the lights of Amalfi had disappeared from view. Then, without taking a breath, he allowed his legs to crumple beneath him and collapsed into the sea.

*

Whether we fall by ambition, blood or lust, Like diamonds we are cut with our own dust... Success is shared, failure is personal... Glories, like glow-worms, afar off shine bright, But looked to near, have neither heat nor light... Intercourse never did any good, and it's lucky if it does no harm... All's fair in love and war... Everything that fills up tragedies, everything that overturns cities and kingdoms, is the struggle of wives and mistresses... There are two things above all that make people love and care for something: the thought that it is all yours, and the thought that it is the only one you have... Wise men are harmless: for they do no harm either to themselves or to others... Ambition's debt is paid... A good man cannot be harmed.

It is said that a man's life flashes past him as he drowns. Jack's mother's face appeared to him as if internal to his own. *Failure is not falling over. Failure is not getting up again... This too shall pass...*

Gasping for air, Jack forced his head above the surface

of the water, vaguely conscious of Italian voices shouting excitedly. Then a strong brown hand took a firm hold of his upper arm.

ACKNOWLEDGMENTS

I am indebted to several people who have in their own ways helped me greatly in my task. Firstly, my wife Lucinda, who has given me much encouragement, support and sound advice. Secondly, her now deceased great-uncle Don Morrison, a retired bookseller and publisher of note, also encouraged me and made valuable criticism. Thirdly, my editor Richenda Todd has helped me to shape the book into something more readable than earlier versions.

I wish also to thank Sheila Wood, Ben Gow, Amanda Giles and Gary Bell for their wise words, and my publisher, The Book Guild, whose team have breathed life into my work. Finally, my thanks to all those who have provided nourishment for those spaces where fact and fiction meet. You know who you are.